Lost Sanity

For Brenda
My #1 Fan

Lost Sanity

Brad Kelln

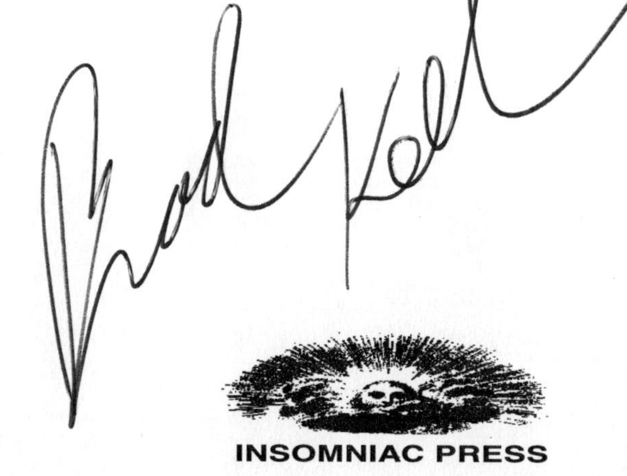

INSOMNIAC PRESS

Edited by Catherine Jenkins
Copy edited by Steven Beattie
Designed by Mike O'Connor

National Library of Canada Cataloguing in Publication Data

Kelln, Brad, 1970-
Lost Sanity: a mystery

ISBN 1-894663-07-1

I. Title.

PS8571.E5864L6 2001 C813'.6 C2001-902149-6
PR9199.4.K44L6 2001

The publisher and the author gratefully acknowledge the support of the Canada Council, the Ontario Arts Council and the Department of Canadian Heritage through the Book Publishing Industry Development Program.

Printed and bound in Canada

Insomniac Press, 192 Spadina Avenue, Suite 403,
Toronto, Ontario, Canada, M5T 2C2
www.insomniacpress.com

No characteristic morphological changes in the brains of patients with schizophrenia have been demonstrated; no specific laboratory findings signal its presence; no consistent premorbid history, course, or outcome can be ascertained; and no single cause is known.

—*Comprehensive Textbook of Psychology*, vol. I

one

85th day since the first rape (friday)

Detective Mitchell Wa took a laboured breath as he walked down the trauma wing of the Atlantic Coast Hospital. He carefully scanned the colourful plastic-coated numbers that were set beside each door. The hallway smelled of disinfectant and stress. Hospital staff in green scrubs, nurses in white uniforms, nervous visitors, and shaken, unsteady patients moved through the corridors.

Wa's steps slowed and he tilted his head to a closed fist and coughed twice. It was a dry cough that scratched the back of his throat before releasing. He shook his head and continued to stride down the hall.

Wa was a twelve-year veteran of the Metro Police Force. The last eight years were spent in the Major Crimes Division where he worked in homicide. He no longer worked homicide.

At thirty-nine, Wa was trim and fit. Silver-rimmed glasses accentuated dark hair and dark eyes. The prescription was weak but he preferred to wear the glasses rather than carry them in a pocket. His slight stature was rarely noticed because of his authoritative command of police procedure and investigative technique. Fellow detectives and officers respected Wa and often deferred to his expertise.

Before he saw the room number he was looking for, he noticed a uniformed police officer leaning back against the wall in an uncomfortable plastic chair. He came to a stop in front of the officer, who quickly dropped the legs of the chair back onto the linoleum and stood.

"Detective Wa," the officer said quickly.

Wa nodded and lifted a hand to his mouth, stifling another dry cough. "Any traffic?"

"Not a person. All clear."

"I'll be a few minutes. I don't want anybody interrupting us."

"Yes sir," the officer replied, as Wa pushed open the hospital door and entered the room.

The hospital room was painted in pale pastel shades. The science of ergonomics left its mark on many public institutions by encouraging interior decorations that induce health. Pale pastels encourage relaxation and healing, or so the research concluded.

The rest of the room was standard hospital issue: an oversized chair in the corner, the adjustable bed, monitors complete with blinking lights on the wall, a door leading to a private bathroom near the main entrance.

Wa moved farther into the room and stood near the bed. He looked down at the occupant. Although the room was only dimly lit, he could see the woman's blonde hair strewn around her pillow. A thin hospital sheet was pulled up to her neck and only a vague outline of her body was visible beneath. The most striking feature, however, was her pale blue eyes that stared straight towards the ceiling. She had not stirred at Wa's intrusion. Except for the eyes, she might have been sound asleep.

As Wa stood there, he wondered if she was going to be able to talk. He needed to speak with her immediately. There was too much at stake to let crucial details slip away in her memory. As he contemplated his course of action, she spoke in a quiet and patient tone:

"Can I help you?"

Wa was taken by surprise at the careful and controlled voice. He composed himself quickly.

"I'm very sorry to disturb you ma'am. I'm Detective Mitchell Wa of the Metro Police Sexual Crimes division. I really need to talk to you about what happened."

Her eyes did not move. She continued staring at the ceiling. She didn't adjust her body to acknowledge Wa's presence.

"Why?"

Wa shifted uncomfortably. "I need to ask you a few questions, check your memory in case there is anything, any clue that could—"

"I mean," she interrupted, "why now?"

He hesitated again before responding, "I'd like to...I mean, it's best to get the details when they might be fresh in a person's—"

"Why are you here so early in the morning? It's only eight o'clock—visiting hours don't start until ten. Why are you here now?"

Wa hated this. He had only worked sex crimes for a few months but he knew it wasn't his calling. Homicide had been easier. He didn't like talking to victims.

"I guess because I don't like to disturb people during visiting hours. In this case, I thought you might have visitors, family or what have you, and I didn't want to take away from their time."

"Thank you." She turned her head in a slow motion that made it look as though it were simply shifting of its own accord, and looked at Wa. "Why don't you sit down, Detective."

He looked briefly at the chair in the corner and then moved toward it. He sat on the edge of the seat and rested his arms on his knees

"What do you want to ask me?" Theresa said.

Wa's preliminary reports hadn't been wrong. Theresa McDouglas was a strong, independent woman. At twenty-four she had finished one university degree and was pursuing graduate studies in history. She lived alone in a small apartment near the university and had a large circle of friends, mostly other students. She wasn't dating anyone at present, but it wasn't for a lack of offers. Friends and family described Theresa as an assertive woman who got what she wanted, and right now she wanted her education. She had decided that no man was going to interfere with her studies.

After flipping open his notebook and pretending to scan the blank page, he addressed Theresa.

"Could you lead me through the night of the incident?"

"When you say 'incident' do you mean the rape?"

"Yes."

"Could you not call it that? 'Incident' makes it sound political or something. It was a rape."

"I'm sorry." He paused to pull in a breath, which instantly brought on a cough. He attempted to stifle it with his hand but was unsuccessful.

"Excuse me," he said. "Could you tell me what happened on the night of the rape?"

"I was at home. I was working on a paper about the organization of Ancient Greek financial systems when someone knocked on my door."

"Do you know what time it was?"

"It was 8:30. There was the knock on the door and I—"

"I'm sorry to interrupt, but I need to get certain bits of information as we go." He waited briefly for an acknowledgment and then continued. "How can you be certain about the time?"

"I was going to take a break at nine to watch *The Simpsons*. I had just looked at the clock and realized I had half an hour to plug away."

"Okay, thanks. Continue."

She took in a long breath and blew it out. "I went to the door and said something like, 'Who is it?' and then opened the door and the guy rushed in and—"

"I'm sorry," Wa interrupted. "What did he say when you asked who it was?"

"I don't remember."

"You don't remember? Do you know why you opened the door?"

"I don't know. He must have said something that made me want to open the door."

"You have no idea what he might have said?"

"No. I don't remember him saying anything."

"Is it possible you asked who it was and he didn't respond?"

"I don't know."

Wa made a note on his pad and told her to continue.

"Well, he came bursting in and grabbed me. He threw me to the floor and flipped me onto my front. He got down over top..."

She stopped and Wa noticed that her eyes were finally closed. He knew she was fighting back tears.

"He got on top of me so I was basically pinned to the floor. I started to freak out and I was swearing and screaming and yelling. He grabbed my hair and I stopped. I think he took me into the bedroom and—"

"I'm sorry to stop you again. I missed something there. What happened when he grabbed you by the hair?"

"I don't know."

"You mean you don't remember? Did he punch you in the head or bang your head against the floor?"

"No. I don't know what happened."

"I don't follow you."

"He grabbed me by the hair and I think he said something. I remember something cold that left a mark inside my ear."

"A mark?"

"Yeah," she paused to search her mind. "Like if you've ever cleaned inside your ear with rubbing alcohol or whatever. That cold stain that's left and then sort of dries and goes away. It was like that. It really left me disoriented, like I'd been spinning round and round in a circle."

"What did that to you? His voice?"

"I guess."

"Could he have put a drug in your ear? Something that made you dizzy and then fall unconscious? Couldn't that be why you stopped yelling?"

"I didn't fall *unconscious*." She exaggerated Wa's inflection on the word "unconscious."

"Well, what did he say? What happened?"

"I saw...," she began, then stopped as if she had reconsidered. "Nothing...I don't know. I don't remember him saying anything. I just remember the feeling and then I don't remember struggling anymore."

Wa rubbed his forehead as he tried to understand what he was being told.

"Okay," he finally said. "Go on. What else can you tell me?"

"Well, he sort of dragged me into the bedroom. I think he was pulling me by a leg."

"Were you bound in some way?"

"No."

Mitchell looked away from his notebook in surprise. "How did he restrain you?"

"I don't know. I guess he held me down."

He waited for her to elaborate.

She glared at him. "I don't know, okay?"

He nodded.

Theresa turned away from him and closed her eyes. She lay motionless on the bed and her bottom lip trembled slightly.

"So I guess that's when I got raped. Right there on my bed. Okay?" A single tear found its way out of her left eye and rolled down her cheek.

Wa waited a moment before speaking softly. "Can you give me a description of the guy?"

Silence.

"Not really," she finally offered.

"Even something basic like how tall he was, or the colour of his hair?"

"Not really."

"Were you blindfolded during the attack?" Wa asked, trying not to sound patronizing.

"No."

"Were you face down on the bed so that you couldn't see him?"

"No."

Wa waited.

"He was tall or tallish. Maybe a couple of inches taller than me."

"Good," he encouraged. "And how tall are you?"

"I'm five foot seven," she said and paused before continuing. "And he was wearing black—like a black shirt and maybe black jeans. I'm not really sure."

She paused again.

"I think his hair was dark and his eyes...were probably dark too."

Wa stopped writing and looked up at Theresa. The motion of his head tilting back put pressure on his throat and he coughed again.

"I'm sorry Miss McDouglas," he said quietly, not wanting to be confrontational. "But I'm having trouble understanding why you don't have a better description of this guy. Was it dark in the room?"

"Yes."

"So dark you couldn't see him?"

"No."

"Did you keep your eyes closed?"

He waited briefly for an answer before he continued.

"Whatever it is, it's okay. I just need to get your story so I can help you. So I can help other women. I want to catch this guy."

Theresa opened her eyes. Her bottom lip trembled and she stared at Wa with a look of panic. "I can't...," she hissed as tears ran down her cheeks.

"Can't what?" Wa urged, leaning forward. He was desperate to put together some of the pieces of this story.

"I don't...want...to say," she managed to blurt out between sobs.

"Please," Wa whispered. "It may help the case."

Her eyes suddenly changed and blazed at him. "It won't help your fucking case!"

Wa sat back, startled by her sudden change of demeanour.

She sniffed loudly and continued to stare at Wa. "How can my dead baby help your case?"

Wa was confused. "I'm sorry. I don't think I understa—"

"No," she interrupted. "Why should you understand? I don't even understand. But my dead baby has nothing to do with this case. Nothing to do with that rapist."

Wa didn't know whether he should nod in agreement or shake his head.

"So why did I see my ten-year-old son standing there in the room?" her eyes glowed fiercely. "Why was the baby I murdered standing there, naked, soaked in blood, watching me with dead eyes the whole time? Why?" She stared at the ceiling. "That's why I couldn't fight the guy off. That's why I don't remember what he looked like. All I can remember is that child...standing there...dead. The baby I killed ten years ago!"

"What?" Wa said with obvious confusion.

"Don't make me talk about this!" she screamed as she sat straight up in the bed. "I killed my baby! I killed him!" And then she began keening in a loud, high-pitched wail that alternated between screams of pain and forced laughter.

two

85th day (friday)

"That's it for today. Next class we'll look at interview techniques and how psychology has influenced police procedure in that area."

Dr. Michael Wenton closed the lid of his laptop computer and reached down to unplug it from the podium. He stood in a lecture hall that seated two hundred students. The class was only half full because most students at the university didn't meet the extensive prerequisites he insisted on for attendance. He didn't want just any undergraduate in his Applied Forensic Psychology course. He preferred motivated students who'd already amassed a basic knowledge of psychology. Even though the course was taught as a fourth year, or Honours level, course, he still thought there was not enough screening and was often dissatisfied with the class.

As the lecture hall slowly emptied, Wenton turned to the small table nearby to collect his briefcase. He normally attended the class with the laptop and nothing else, but today he'd returned an assignment and had been forced to use his briefcase to transport the cumbersome stack. The assignment, a research paper on a forensic topic of the students' choosing, had been a failure. Close to seventy-five percent of the students wrote on criminal profiling, a topic he didn't enjoy promoting. It disturbed him that profiling was so much in vogue these days. The field of forensic psychology gained both recognition and infamy by the introduction of the pseudo-science. It was the sensationalistic nature of "profiling" that drew students to forensic psychology and forced Wenton to be overly vigilant in weeding out the inferior applicants in his course.

"Excuse me," a voice broke through Wenton's thoughts as he prepared to leave. "I was wondering if I could have a word with you, Doctor?"

He turned to the student—a pretty female in her early twenties. Her tight T-shirt was mostly hidden beneath an oversized denim shirt that hung down well below her faded jeans. Without realizing, Wenton had pulled his eyes over the length of the student's body as he brought his attention to her. He gritted his teeth in anger over his lapse of concentration.

"Yes," he said.

"I got my paper back and wanted to, maybe, talk about my mark."

"Why?"

The nervous student hesitated but managed to respond. "I guess...I mean, I'd like to maybe talk about what I could've done differently."

Wenton forced himself to concentrate on the student's face, not allowing his attention to drift down her body again. "What topic did you write on?"

She looked away from him and then down to her hands where she held the essay. "I wrote on criminal profiling."

Wenton dropped his body into the oversized chair in his office. The chair matched the rest of the sparse decor: a large desk, filing cabinet, and a bookcase. There was no clutter. His desk was bare except for his computer. There were no knick-knacks, pictures, or other signs of a personal life. He preferred to keep his space clear of distraction. He resisted a need for ornamentation in his work life.

The office matched his personality and appearance. Dr. Wenton was an imposing man, standing six foot four and rarely breaking his neutral expression of distaste. He insisted that all of his dealings with others be professional, almost coldly so. Other staff in the psychology department had no sense of who he was as an individual. Even his past was something of a mystery, although at the age of thirty-seven he'd already established himself as an authority in the field of forensic psychology. He specialized in the study of psychopaths and violent serial offenders and had written landmark books in the area.

He tapped a key on his computer and the screen saver melted away revealing a page of text. It was his latest book project. He was writing the introduction for a book called *Theory and Practice in Forensic Psychology*. It was an easy publication credit. Wenton had invited some of the leading researchers to contribute chapters in their areas of expertise. All he had to do was collect the chapters, edit, and present them to the publisher. It was a suggestion his literary agent had made years before, but that he'd resisted because it didn't feel like real work and he didn't know if he could attach his name to a product that was not entirely his own. He'd eventually given in because the demand for such a text was growing and he knew that some other researcher would take it on eventually.

He stared at the screen:

...within the last decade the proliferation of applied forensic psychology research has changed the face of modern police investigative...

He let his eyes drop from the screen and noticed his left hand lying on the desk. He lifted the hand and turned it back and forth, looking at the back and then the palm. Satisfied with its appearance, he curled his fingers into a fist and watched carefully. His ring finger did not quite bend far enough to complete a fist. Looking more closely, he saw only thin lines of distortion where the bones of two fingers had been forced back into place beneath the skin. It bothered him that he didn't have full mobility, but he thought it appropriate that it was the ring finger that was permanently damaged. Since struggling with sexual addiction early in his career as a psychologist, he'd refused to allow himself personal relationships anyway.

He considered the serial homicide case that had resulted in his disfigurement. Only a few months ago Detective Tim Dallons contacted him for help on a particularly difficult case. A serial killer had murdered five women in the space of about six months. With each attack the violence increased and the killer was getting reckless. Dallons was stuck and needed help, but he'd resisted bringing Wenton in sooner. Although he was a good cop, Dallons hated psychologists. A few years ago his wife had committed suicide while being treated by a psychologist. After that, he'd had no use for the entire profession. To make matters worse, shortly after consulting with Michael Wenton, Dallons' murder investigation came to a shocking head when the serial killer turned out to be Dennis Choler, a graduate student employed for the last three years in the psychology department where Wenton worked. Even more devastating news awaited the detective: Dennis Choler admitted that early in his graduate training he'd attended a practicum in the same clinic where Dallons' wife was a client. While in the waiting room he confronted the vulnerable woman and encouraged, goaded, and harassed her into committing suicide—just another disturbed act en route to becoming a murderer. When Dallons learned the true fate of his wife, he'd been unable to continue. He tried to kill himself, but in an ironic twist, it was Wenton, a psychologist, who knocked the gun out of his hand just in time. The insult of having his own life saved by a psychologist only increased the detective's hatred of the profession, and Dallons ended up on psychiatric ward.

Wenton shook his head. The events seemed so far away now.

three

85th day (friday)

The red and white of the antique barber pole reflected off the glass of the front window of Moe's Barbershop as the proprietor tended to his current customer.

Carl, a regular, sat in one of the chairs that lined the wall under the window. The chairs faced into the barbershop, looking toward the three barber chairs and the storage room in the back. Moe's current customer was a teenager from the neighbourhood who had come in for a trim.

"Damn shame about these girls," Moe said, lifting another strand of hair and making a quick snip with his scissors.

"What kind of sick fuck has to go around raping women?" Carl asked as he dropped his magazine onto his lap.

Moe simply shook his head as he continued to move around his customer, lifting and cutting hair as he went.

"I mean, you gotta be one of them psychos to be going after women like that," Carl continued. "It just ain't right, fer instance. I guess I like the women just as much as the next guy."

"I hear that," chimed in Moe.

"But I can't see me taking no woman in a violent way, fer instance. It just wouldn't do nothing fer me."

"Exactly," Moe said as he leaned over to eyeball the back of the teen's hair. "The thing is that guys like this fuck not only do it, but they get off on it. I mean, come on."

"Well that's what I mean," exclaimed Carl. "It's bad enough to be raping the women, but buddy is liking it and can't stop, fer instance."

"Sure as hell is liking it, Carl," Moe said." I mean how many are we talking about now, seven?"

"I'dsay."

"Feet please," Edward said quietly.

Carl looked up at him and at the broom he held in his hands.

"Oops, sorry there Eddie." He leaned back in his chair and lifted his feet out of the way. Edward swept under Carl's feet, then moved past Carl and continued on his route through the shop.

"Bloody shame," Moe went on, shaking his head. "They should hang this pervert by his balls."

"Yes sir, oughta make an example out of him for the rest of the perverts, fer instance."

The two men lapsed into silence. Moe continued working as Carl lifted his magazine once more.

After a few minutes Carl looked up from his magazine again. He dropped his hands and spoke as if an idea had just occurred to him. "What's your take on this whole thing, Eddie?"

He stopped pushing the broom and leaned against it, not making eye contact with Carl.

"Edward," he corrected.

"Sorry," Carl said sarcastically. "Edward."

Moe stopped briefly and gave a stern look at Carl who shrugged apologetically

"I feel sorry for the girls," Edward said.

"Yeah, but what would you do to the fucker if you caught him?"

"He should die."

"Pretty harsh," Moe said. "No room for leniency or rehabilitation in your view, eh?"

"It's not that," Edward said. "He can't control it."

Moe and Carl waited for him to say more.

Edward began pushing the broom again. "If he could stop doing it he would've. He can't, so he should probably just be killed."

Carl whistled and said, "You're a tough cookie, ain't you?"

Edward had moved to the back of the store and pulled a dustpan off a shelf. He bent and swept the clippings into the pan and stepped quickly through the doorway into the backroom.

"What was that?" Carl asked when Edward was gone.

"Don't know. Never know with that guy. He's got a mental condition, eh? He's on a whack of drugs."

"What kind of mental condition?" asked the young man in the barber chair.

Moe looked into the mirror to see the kid's face. "Don't know. Something like schizophrenia or what have you."

Carl grunted at this and returned to his magazine.

"That about does it," Moe announced to his customer and began brushing the loose hairs away.

four

85th day (friday)

Mitchell Wa couldn't get her words out of his head. It was unlike him not to let his cases drift away when he returned to his personal life. He brought his four-door Saturn to a stop in the driveway and turned off the ignition.

He rested both hands on top of the steering wheel as he composed himself. He was worried about Theresa McDouglas. The way she'd screamed. The things she'd said. He didn't understand what she meant by "I killed my baby." He hoped that he hadn't contacted her too soon. He needed a clear, coherent account to work with. Statements from the rapist's previous victims were already murky enough. The reports all lacked a clear description of the assailant. For some reason the women were unwilling or unable to recollect the guy's face or clothes. Nothing. It didn't make sense to Wa. None of the victims had reported being blindfolded. Medical reports after the fact hadn't identified any drugs in the victims that would account for their disorientation. The physical evidence showed only that they were sexually assaulted. Each victim showed clear evidence of forced vaginal penetration, and the semen residue conclusively identified a single assailant.

When we catch this guy there won't be any doubt, Wa mused. The physical evidence will be indisputable even if the victims can't testify personally, but...what's happened to these women?

"That's it!" he shouted as he banged his hands down on the wheel. He decided to force his mind away from the investigation. He reached to his right, grabbed his briefcase, and stepped out of the car. A glance around the front yard and driveway showed evidence of his three children. A toy truck, tricycle, pail and shovel, some snake thing that might have hooked up to the garden hose, and a well-loved doll that had only a half a head of hair left, were strewn about the immediate area. Wa stepped over the tricycle and moved to the front door of his split-entry home.

He tried the door before putting his key in. The door was unlocked. He made a mental note to mention it to Gloria when they were in bed tonight.

"Dad!" Joshua screamed from the top of the stairs. He scurried around the railing and down the steps two at a time, jumping into his dad's arms.

Wa caught his four year old in mid-air and drew him into a hug. "How's it going, buddy?"

Nicholas and Lisa came over to stand at the top of the stairs and peer down. Two-year-old Nicholas was not confident enough to leap down the stairs, even though he was overcome with excitement and bounced up and down on the spot. Lisa, the oldest at ten, was too mature to bound down the stairs and enjoyed her role as the big sister standing at the top holding Nick's hand.

"Hey kids," Wa said.

"Daddy!" Nicholas said.

Wa returned Joshua to the floor and he scampered off as the other kids returned to their post-supper play. Wa left his shoes at the front entrance and hung his light overcoat on a hook before going upstairs. Gloria stood at the sink rinsing a plate. She looked over her shoulder at him as he entered the kitchen.

"Welcome home Detective," she said.

Gloria was a petite woman with striking Asian features. Her dark hair was pulled back into a ponytail and she wore a plain dress under an apron. Wa knew that Gloria only wore an apron to make spaghetti; she complained of splattering tomato sauce.

"Sorry I'm late, Wife," he said as he snuck in to embrace her from behind. She leaned her head back against him briefly. "Smells good in here, though. The kids ate already, eh?"

She looked at the plates in the sink. "Yep."

As he broke away from her, he asked about her day.

"Not bad. Nicholas still has a cough but he's back to running around like he's possessed. How's your cold?"

"Good. Good," Wa responded as he peeked inside the large metal pot on the stove. As he suspected, tomato sauce bubbled inside, although the pot was now only half full. The strong smell of garlic and spices worked their way through his nasal passages reminding him how hungry he was.

"I waited for you so we could eat together," she said.

"That's nice of you. You didn't have to."

"I know," she said, smiling. "But it's always best to be nice to the cops. You never know when you'll need a favour."

"Oh yeah. What say we continue this conversation down at the station?" he asked, with a mock expression of authority.

She laughed and turned to the cabinet to take out two clean plates. "Speaking of you being a cop, what's up with that rape investigation?" she whispered the word "rape" in case the kids were within earshot.

"Not much," he answered with a heavy sigh. "It's bad. I don't know what's up. There's a team meeting next week to get things sorted out."

Just then a scream sounded from the living room, followed by loud sobs. Wa and Gloria looked at each other with "what now?" expressions and Wa went into the living room to break up the latest misadventure among the kids.

five

88th day (monday)

"You're late," Rhonda Ott, a pretty young nurse with a dark complexion and straight, black, shoulder-length hair scolded as Dr. Brian Claric hurried through the nursing station toward the backroom.

"Nurse Ott," he announced with mock authority, "you should treat your superiors with more respect." He winked at her and stepped into the conference room, shutting the door behind him.

Dr. Claric was the head psychologist at the Maximum Security Psychiatric Centre, the major referral centre for psychiatric patients in conflict with the law. Its layout resembled the prison on which it was based, with four secure units including an assessment unit, short stay unit, and two treatment and rehabilitation units. The MSPC housed three types of patients: remand clients charged with a crime and sent to the psychiatric facility for assessment; clients found not criminally responsible for a crime by virtue of a mental disorder; and prison inmates who transfered for treatment. The mix of patients sometimes proved volatile and staff were always on guard.

Monday and Wednesday mornings the staff of the assessment unit, referred to as North Bay because of the direction the wing pointed, met to review a few clients and update each other on clinical progress and setbacks. This weekly "rounds" meeting was the primary method of communication among the professional disciplines, which included psychology, psychiatry, nursing, social work, occupational therapy, and recreational therapy.

With the door closed, Dr. Claric could still hear Rhonda Ott chuckling in the nursing station. Many of the staff at the MSPC took a casual, friendly attitude toward one another. The stress of the job and the daily contact with violent patients meant they had to keep their spirits up. Having a sense of humour was a prerequisite for success.

Dr. Claric found the conference room full and realized he actually was late. Seated at the table were Dr. Georgia O'Connors, an older, well-respected psychiatrist; Diego Sanchez, recreational therapist; Andy Thomas, the fifty-something social worker who frequently competed with Dr. Claric for best gag honours; and Dorothy Montague, an occupational therapist who was frequently the butt of Dr. Claric's and Andy's jokes. In addition to the clinical staff, two front-line nursing staff sat at the table. Rebecca Ly, a nurse in her thirties, had worked at the MSPC for almost eight years. Finally, Milton Carlisle, a male nurse in his forties who'd served time as a prison guard before returning to school to obtain his nursing degree.

Dr. Claric apologized for being late and sat in the only available chair. A fifteen-year veteran of the MSPC, Dr. Claric was recognized as one of the leaders of the service and was well respected by the other staff. He was of average height and slightly overweight with most of his excess showing in a happily rounded midsection. His traditional work uniform over the years had evolved into a shirt, sport coat, and slacks—no tie. He'd stopped wearing a tie after his second year on the job, when a patient leapt across the room and got a handful of it. It took two staff members to pry the patient's hands free. Dr. Claric promptly went home to throw the rest of his tie collection in the garbage.

After Dr. Claric was seated, Milton began. "All right folks, we have four clients to get through this morning, including one new admission from last week. How do you want to proceed?"

"The new one's mine," Dr. O'Connors announced. As each new patient arrived at the MSPC they were assigned to one of the facility's seven full-time psychiatrists.

"Well, let's run through his file first and then do the others," Dr. Claric suggested.

Milton looked at the names on the spines of the four green binders he had on the table in front of him. He selected one and flipped the chart open.

"Okay, we've got a twenty-two-year-old male, Gary Newcastle, who's charged with two counts break and enter, one aggravated assault, one resisting arrest, and one breach of probation. The charts from the Atlantic Coast Hospital are on their way. I guess the guy has a mental health history."

"He's got a breach of probation which means there were priors," Dr. Claric said.

"We didn't get the police check back yet but were told it would be arriving too."

"What do we know about the charges?" Andy asked.

"His story more or less matches the police report," Dr. O'Connors began. "He was staying in a halfway house and a bunch of the guys decided to have a little party. Gary's probation order says no booze but he had a couple anyway. He was on lithium for a previously diagnosed manic-depressive condition, but he's been sporadic with the follow-up. So the booze went down on top of his meds and he claims to have flipped out. He ended up smashing in the windows of a couple cars on the street just down from the halfway house. I think he was just looking for money or something to steal. Anyway, it so happens that one of the houses nearby was a frat house. The noise roused the drunken university guys who staggered out of the house to see Gary leaning in the window of one of their cars. Well, to make a long story short, Gary didn't look too pretty when he came in here."

A few chuckles circled around the group.

"So the aggravated assault was against the university guys?" Dorothy asked.

"I guess so," Dr. O'Connors answered. "The police report kind of glosses over the whole confrontation, but it would appear that Gary fought back and got a couple of punches in. I'd assume that's the assault charge."

Dorothy raised her eyebrows.

"Anyway," Dr. O'Connors continued, "I've met with the guy once. He's actually not too bad. I'm not sure his mental illness will exempt him from responsibility but I haven't fully decided yet. Seems like the guy just gets himself in bad situations and ends up doing something stupid. I'd like to check out his social supports." She turned to Andy. "Could you maybe see what you can find out in a social assessment?"

Andy nodded.

Then she turned to Dr. Claric. "And I'd like a full risk assessment."

"Sure," he said.

Diego tentatively interjected. "Excuse me," he said in a voice that clicked with traces of a Spanish accent. "I know that Gary has approached nursing staff about participating in gym programs and going to the weight room. Do you want me to hold off or is he okay?"

Dr. O'Connors looked at Milton for input. He shrugged.

"I'd say so," she replied. "He's settled quite quickly so I don't see a problem."

The table fell silent for a moment as Dr. O'Connors waited for other questions or input from the team.

"All right," Milton said. "Let's move on to Ronald Ware."

six

88th day (monday)

"Do you still believe that Satan lives in you?" Dr. Darious asked as he kept his eyes down on the blank pad of paper before him.

Edward hesitated before answering. "No sir. That was illness."

Dr. Darious looked up at his patient with a smile. "Illness, eh? What do you mean by illness?"

"I have a serious mental illness. That's why I take my medication."

"Sounds like a rehearsed answer, Edward. You aren't simply saying what you think I want to hear, are you?"

"No sir."

"Are you sure?"

"Yessir."

Dr. Darious considered pressing the issue but decided against it. He generally followed the modern rule of treating mental illness: insight is nice, compliance is better. As long as Edward appeared to be taking his medication regularly there was no need to dig too deep.

"All right, Edward, what about side effects? Have you noticed anything?"

"No sir. Nothing."

"Dry mouth? Blurred vision? Any movement of your mouth or jaw? Tremors? Any problems with your energy levels?"

"No sir."

Dr. Darious began making a note as he continued. "How's that placement going? You're working at a barbershop?"

"Yessir."

He finished his note and looked up again. He was waiting for Edward to elaborate on his work experience.

Edward remained stiffly in the same position he'd taken as soon as he sat down. Each month he dutifully reported to the community clinic, sat in a full waiting room, then moved into the doctor's office to answer questions and have his prescriptions for quetiapine and respiridone renewed. The years he'd spent visiting psychiatrists had taught him many things. Perhaps the most important thing he'd learned was to keep his head down and answer questions in as few words as possible. Edward knew that fewer words meant fewer questions in return, and fewer questions were always preferable. More than a few brief questions usually meant a trip to the hospital.

"Can you tell me more about your work placement?" Dr. Darious asked at last.

"I sweep. I help out. I do whatever Mr. Crawster asks."

"Are you enjoying your time there?"

"Yes, thank you."

Dr. Darious knew he wasn't going to get any more out of Edward. He finished scratching a note and dropped the pad on his desk. "Well, that's about it then. I'll have the prescriptions called in by the end of the day. You're still with the same pharmacy, yes?"

Edward nodded.

"Good. And as you leave please make an appointment with the receptionist for about a month from now."

"Yessir."

Edward stood and left the room as Dr. Darious watched, shaking his head at his quiet, odd patient.

Edward's small apartment was located over Moe Crawster's barbershop. He hurried up the wooden steps outside the shop and thrust his key into the single lock in the doorknob. He rattled the knob back and forth to get the key to catch but he finally felt the click of the lock opening. He turned the knob and stepped through the doorway.

His apartment was sparsely furnished and reflected a small monthly income. There was a single bed in the corner, a small table with two chairs in the middle of the room, and a black and white television on the floor near one wall. A small bathroom with a shower was located through a door at the back of the apartment. The cramped, dirty kitchen was in an alcove off the main room. There wasn't space in the apartment for full-sized appliances, so Edward made do with a mini-fridge, a sink, and an electric hot plate.

He kicked his shoes off and moved to his bed, lying down on his back and placing his hands over his face.

He struggled to understand why he felt the way he did. Why he lived the way he lived.

He knew that it was only a matter of time before people found out who he was. In fact, he wanted to be caught. He was tired. He didn't understand who he'd become. He didn't understand why he couldn't control himself.

The worst part was the constant fear. He thought maybe, just maybe, if they'd caught him, it would take away the fear.

"Please God," he whispered, and then remembered what he needed to pray for.

He reached under his bed with one hand and found his tattered copy of the Bible. He brought it up and held it tightly to his chest with both hands.

"Please God take me away from this and make me whole again. Please God let me be a normal person. Please God forgive me my terrible sins and let me not sin again. Amen."

seven

89th day (tuesday)

Wa cleared his throat and adjusted the lozenge in his mouth before speaking.

"Thank you for being here," he said. "We need to review where we are with the case and discuss our options."

Four other people sat around the table in the police conference room. Detective Roland Makum, a veteran of the Major Crimes Division, served the first five of his nearly fifteen years on the Narcotics team before being transferred, against his wishes, to Sex Crimes.

To Makum's left sat Detective Margaret Meredith, a stern woman who had a tendency to get personally involved in her cases. Margaret's partner on the Sex Crimes unit was Detective Laurie Abrahms. Laurie was the youngest member of the team, having only recently been promoted from the patrol ranks of Metro Police. The last person in the room was Constable William Lawrence, an energetic officer who wanted to work his way up the ranks to detective. He felt his presence at today's meeting was an important opportunity and had already resigned himself to staying quiet and observing.

"Right down to business, eh Wa?" Makum asked, grinning. "None of that 'How was your weekend,' 'Did you see the game last night' bullshit, eh?"

"These rapes are serious, Detective Makum," Margaret said.

"And I said they weren't?" he asked.

"C'mon," Laurie interrupted. "Let's just get on with this."

Wa nodded at Laurie in appreciation and then addressed the group. "I just want to recap the events so I know we're all on the same page. Over the last twelve or thirteen weeks, seven women have been raped. The last victim was Theresa McDouglas who was attacked in her own apartment five days ago. All the evidence is pointing to a serial rapist. The attacks have happened with incredible regularity. Each rape has occurred on a Thursday and the rapes have been exactly two weeks apart. In each case the victims show clear evidence of sexual assault and so far the physical evidence, including analysis of semen, have indicated a single assailant. Another curious fact is that the victims have sustained relatively few defensive wounds. The medical examinations found hardly any bruising, abrasions, or marks that would indicate the perpetrator battered the victims or physically restrained them."

He paused to give his audience a chance to absorb the details and then continued. "None of the seven victims in this case has reported being blindfolded. Presumably all of them had an opportunity to see their assailant, but so far the statements haven't been very helpful. One of the victims hasn't spoken a word since her attack. Two of the victims have refused to talk about the assaults or stated they don't remember a thing. Three of the victims gave vague accounts of a man in dark clothes who was present in the room but they were unclear about whether he was the man who assaulted them. The last victim, Theresa McDouglas, actually told me she saw a small, naked child covered in blood standing in the room. She was unable to elaborate and she couldn't provide a description of the assailant."

"What the hell do you think she meant?" Makum said.

"I don't know. Initially I thought she meant the attacker looked young but she insisted there was a child there." Wa paused, wondering whether to relate the crazier part of Theresa's story. He decided he needed to tell them everything. "McDouglas told me she thought the child was a baby she aborted ten years ago."

"What?" Laurie said in surprise.

"I know," Wa continued. "That's why I didn't mention it right away. It's just crazy. So I don't know what to make of it." He looked around the table and then addressed Margaret and Laurie. "You've been following up with the previous victims, probing for additional information. Anything?"

"Nothing, unfortunately," Margaret said. "The women are still traumatized by their attacks and I'm afraid there wasn't much to learn. Laurie and I have only seen the first four victims and two of them were still in hospital suffering from what the doctors thought was post-traumatic tress disorder, or, ah, something the shrink called..." She paused to look at her notes. "Stress-induced psychosis."

"Psychobabble for 'they've all turned into whack-jobs,'" Makum mumbled. Margaret frowned at him.

Wa waited for Margaret to continue but she simply shifted, uncomfortably, in her seat.

"Was there anything else, Margaret?" Wa said.

"Well," she began, "one of the women reported something really weird and I wasn't going to mention it but since you brought up the thing about the child in the room..."

"Go ahead," Wa urged.

Margaret looked over at her partner before continuing. "One of the women reported that the attacker was her father. It was kind of hard to get a clear idea of what she was saying, but I think she saw her father either in the room or actually on top of her."

"Does her father have a good alibi for the time?" Makum asked.

Margaret turned to him. "Her father died in prison about six years ago. Carla—the victim's name—was in therapy and recovered memories of childhood sexual abuse at the hands of her father. Because of these memories she had him prosecuted. This was all about seven or eight years ago. The father was found guilty and sentenced to five years but he died within the first year. It was the stress of an old man trying to adjust to prison life."

"Holy shit," Bill Lawrence said.

"So she claims she saw the father but he's been dead for six years?" Makum said.

"Yes."

"You can't beat an alibi like that." Makum chuckled as he shook his head. "Man, it sure sounds like these women are flippin' out."

Margaret looked harshly at him. "These women have suffered probably the most invasive, destructive crime that one person can inflict on another. I think their reactions aren't outside the normal range."

Makum shrugged. "I'm not saying that."

Laurie said, "What's next, Mitchell?"

"I'd like you and Margaret to continue with the follow-up on the victims. There's always a chance one of them will remember some crucial detail that'll make the difference between catching this guy and missing him. Why don't you continue where you left off and interview the three most recent victims. Leave McDouglas until last."

Margaret and Laurie nodded.

"And," Wa glanced quickly at Bill before turning to Makum, "you were going to pull a list of names out of the computer. You wanna let us know where that's at?"

"Bill and I went through the national database on sexual and violent offenders to see who's in our area. We also reviewed recent federal releases of sex offenders to check on any matches to the current MO. It took a damn sight longer than I figured but we eventually narrowed a list down to twenty-four men in and around Metro."

"So I guess our next step is to work through that list. I want to check each guy. Find out where he was on the Thursdays in question. Find out if there's a connection to any of the victims, especially the first. Basically turn their lives inside out and see what dirt drops."

Laurie lowered her eyes to the table, obviously disappointed. She'd hoped there'd be more to report at this meeting.

"You got that list there, Roland?" Wa said. "Let's start dividing them up."

eight

90th day (wednesday)

Dr. Wenton pulled onto the gravel lot of the maximum security federal penitentiary that was located outside the city limits. He parked his black Durango in a space away from the rest of the cars and stepped out. His trip to the penitentiary had become familiar to him and he strode purposefully to the metal gates of the entrance.

Somewhere inside the facility he was being monitored on a security camera and the guard, recognizing Wenton, pushed a button causing the heavy metal fence to slide open. Wenton entered the alcove and ran a hand down his shirt to his belt. His fingers touched his ID badge and he nodded. It'd become habit to check for his ID whenever he was in a secure facility.

After stopping to sign in at the front entrance, he made his way through the inner walls to a long corridor lined with wire mesh. He followed the path toward the Inmate Services building where a number of programs were housed. His destination was the Psychology Department where Dr. Tom Kirkson waited.

Wenton had established a strong working relationship with Dr. Kirkson, the prison psychologist. Initially, he'd only wanted a good contact so he could access a pool of subjects for his research. Over time he'd grown to respect Kirkson and his work at the facility. As part of their working arrangement, Wenton provided consultations, completed risk assessments on clients up for parole, and consulted with Kirkson on various treatment groups. This last was the reason for his visit today.

He found Kirkson speaking to one of the secretaries in the lobby area of Inmate Services.

"Hey, Doctor," Kirkson looked up as Wenton entered.

He nodded in return.

"Ready to get going with our group?" Kirkson said.

"Yessir."

Kirkson thanked the secretary for her help and turned to walk with Wenton back to his office.

Dr. Tom Kirkson was a solid clinical psychologist who'd spent most of his career in the penal system working with offenders. At forty he wore his age gracefully; he'd kept his light brown hair and trim waistline. He valued Wenton's contributions to the penitentiary, especially because Wenton was such a recognized expert in the field of forensic psychology.

After much discussion and debate, Kirkson had finally convinced his administration to fund Dr. Wenton to help lead a sex offender treatment group at the facility. The administration had initially balked at the idea because of the expense and because they felt the treatment needs could be met with their current staff complement, or at the most by hiring an additional psychological assistant. Kirkson insisted that Dr. Wenton would be useful for more than just the duration of the group and argued that learning from his expertise would be invaluable. Kirkson also knew that the prison administration wanted to maintain its professional affiliation with Dr. Wenton and the university. They eventually relented and gave their approval.

The sex offender treatment group had eight members: five pedophiles and three rapists. The group was moving into its fifth week and much of the inmates' resistance over participation, and denial of their offenses, had been resolved. It was the intention of both Dr. Kirkson and Dr. Wenton to move the group into specific treatment areas in today's session.

"Yes, but the sexual urge is only a part of the offense cycle. There are other factors, other things that happen before the sexual offense occurs."

Wenton spoke directly to Rudy, a child molester serving six years for offenses against three different children in the neighbourhood where he used to live.

"I don't know what you mean," Rudy said, lowering his eyes to the floor to avoid eye contact with the others in the room.

The other inmates watched with detached interest. None of them wanted to seem too involved in the discussion in case it drew attention to them and put them on the hot seat next.

"Tell me about a typical week," interjected Dr. Kirkson. "A week that preceded an offense."

"Don't know. Guess I'd get up most mornings. Get dressed. Do a few errands or what have you. I think I mostly went to the video store and checked on what was new or whatever. I don't know."

"What did you do for fun?" asked Wenton.

"Didn't have no fun."

"What did you have?"

Rudy looked up, agitated. "I had shit. Listen man, I wasn't going through life, laughing it up and having a great old time diddling kids!"

"Okay," Wenton said, "I know that. That's what I'm trying to get at."

"Getting at what?" Rudy spat back.

"What you *felt* in the days or weeks before you offended. What you felt, other than sex."

"I felt crap. I felt lonely, angry, and frustrated."

"Why?"

"Because the whole world is shit, man. The whole world already thought I was the king of perverts. I'd been convicted already for being a pedophile. I'd done time. I was out. I wanted to go straight. I didn't want no shit. I wanted to just hide out, be cool, do something, but no fuckin' way. No sir. Once you are a *sex offender* you ain't got choices anymore. So I was fuckin' trapped at home. I was living off my damn social assistance cheques that barely covered rent in the crappy apartment. I was bumming money from people. Nothing."

Rudy stopped talking and took a deep breath to compose himself. He knew he couldn't break down in front of this group. No one could show weakness in prison because it'd be used against you.

Wenton stood and moved to a flip chart. The ten chairs were arranged in a circle leaving the centre of the room clear. The flip chart stood outside the circle on the right hand side of the room and Wenton had to step between two inmates to gain access to it.

"Sexual desire is not the birthplace of your offending," he said and picked up a marker. "Sex is your coping response to negative feelings." He began drawing a simple flow chart to illustrate the general pathway to the offense.

"I never saw women as human," Richard mumbled as he sat with his legs stretched in front of him and his arms folded defiantly across his chest. "I felt like I was always getting fucked around so I could basically do whatever I wanted to get even."

"Including rape?" asked Kirkson.

"Including rape."

"And where did those feelings of anger and mistreatment go after you raped a woman?" Wenton asked.

Richard looked up to the ceiling and blew out a lungful of air as he considered the question. "Don't know. Gone, mostly."

The group was silent waiting for Richard to provide more detail.

"I guess I was sort of messed up afterwards. I still felt angry but for different reasons. Normally, I would sort of just say 'fuck it' and go on with shit."

"So raping someone didn't help you get even?" Wenton said. "It just distracted you for a time, but the feelings of mistreatment would eventually—inevitably—return."

"Yeah."

"And what did it feel like when the feelings returned?" Kirkson asked.

"It made my fuckin' head spin. I couldn't get the evil thoughts out of my head. It felt like I was possessed. All I could fuckin' think about was how nice it would be to pull some dumb bitch's shirt off. See those titties and get caught up in the act. I knew it'd just change me, make me feel alive and whole. I didn't want to do any of this shit, but I felt forced to, like I had to do it one more time just to get the fucking thoughts out of my head."

Other members in the group nodded in appreciation of the description.

"I can't really explain it but when there was shit going on in my life I knew I could just jerk off or get a porn video or go to a strip club or something to feel better. Sometimes that'd just make me more angry and I'd want to have a real woman. I felt like I deserved a real woman and shouldn't be forced to jerk off like some huge fuckin' fag."

"Let's go back to what you said about 'evil thoughts' in your head," Wenton interrupted. "What did you mean by that?"

"Sex can be so strong that it takes control of you. It can make you do things you don't want to do just so they're done. When I started to think about raping someone it took hold of me like I was under the power of some evil spirit or some shit."

"Like you were possessed?" Kirkson said.

"I don't know about that," Richard answered.

Both Wenton and Kirkson knew they should let the silence prompt clarification.

Richard finally continued: "I guess it sometimes feels like you're so full of crap that it has to leak out somewhere and onto someone."

"Like onto the rape victim?" Wenton asked.

"Yeah, but I don't just mean the sex. I think some of the crap gets passed on too."

"Whaddya mean?" another inmate asked, obviously engrossed in the conversation.

"I always thought the chick got more than just the rape." Richard said. "I think fucking her left something psychological in her head. Something bad."

A large black man spoke up. "It fucks them up," he said with some authority.

"Yep," Richard agreed. "It fucks them up."

"Fucks them up how?" Kirkson asked.

"Leaves some of your evil in them," the black man said, nodding. "Leaves some evil, yep."

nine

96th day (tuesday)

Mitchell Wa felt awkward. He'd returned to the Atlantic Coast Hospital but not on official business. It was Tuesday and, if the rapist held his schedule, there'd be another attack in two days. Two days away and the investigation still wasn't any closer to a suspect. The best they could do now would be to plan a major stakeout of the city on Thursday, but even that wouldn't prevent another rape. Not unless they got really lucky.

So what the hell am I doing here? Wa asked himself as he strode down the hospital corridor. *A social call?* He shook his head. He knew it was more than a social call. It was an obligation and maybe something more.

He kept his head down as he walked. It was a path that seemed almost familiar. His presence here today felt urgent, but he couldn't quite put his finger on why. He wondered if there was something unconscious about his motives. He laughed at that thought. He was psychoanalyzing the reason for his trip. Ironic. He shrugged and looked up to get his bearings.

A heavy door stood in front of him. The hospital's activity level dropped off considerably in this area. A sign posted next to the door announced:

Visiting Hours
10:00 a.m (1000) to 12:00 p.m. (1200)
1:00 p.m. (1300) to 4:00 p.m. (1600)
Please Ring Buzzer for Entrance
Please Ensure Door Is Locked Behind You

Wa only glanced at the sign. It was the middle of the afternoon, well within visiting hours. He reached for the console beneath the laminated sign and pressed an intercom button. A scratching buzzer sounded.

"Yes?" a voice said.

Reflexively, Wa leaned toward the speaker before responding, "It's, ah, Detective Mitchell Wa." He coughed and held a hand to his mouth.

A different buzzer rang and the noise held steady, indicating the door was unlocked. He pulled the large handle and swung the door open, stepping quickly through. He guided the door closed behind him and the buzzing stopped.

After taking a deep breath, he strode down the hall of the Psychiatric Unit toward the nursing station.

The nurse on duty looked up as Wa approached. She smiled in recognition and stepped out of the station to greet him.

"Good afternoon, Detective."

He felt some congestion in his throat and cleared it before answering. "Yes, hello."

"He's in his room. It's the same one around the corner toward the end of the hall. Number 312."

"Thanks."

"Oh! And Detective?" the nurse called to him. She started toward him with a serious expression on her face. "We really appreciate visitors on our unit, I want you to know that."

"But?" Wa asked, anticipating a request and trying to hurry her along.

"Nothing, really. I guess I was just going to say our customer," she nodded down the hallway, "should be leaving soon. He doesn't need to be an in-patient any longer and if you can do anything..."

"I'll talk to him," Wa said.

She nodded profusely, almost apologetically, and headed back to the nursing station. He turned and continued down the corridor.

The unit consisted of a series of closed doors along two separate corridors. One corridor led back to the door through which he'd entered. The other corridor led to the back of the hospital and an emergency exit. Alarms would sound if this door were opened. At the centre of the unit was a nursing station enclosed behind Plexiglas windows allowing a view down both corridors and into the common room adjacent to it. At this time of day, half the clients on the unit were off at programs within the hospital. Of the clients that remained, many were in bed. A few sat in front of the TV, while a group of four sat at a table playing cards.

Wa stopped in front of room 312. He knocked solidly and waited.

There was no response or sound of movement from behind the door.

He knocked again, not wanting to intrude. Still no answer.

He knew that it was acceptable to push the door open and look inside. Clients often failed to answer a knock for reasons other than a desire not have a visitor. Wa used the knuckles of a closed fist to slowly push the door open and step inside.

The room was dark. Only light from a slit in the drawn curtains entered to compete with light now streaming in through the open door. Wa left the door open and moved further into the room. He felt a tickle in his throat and wanted to cough but fought desperately to stifle it.

He saw a figure on the bed. His memory flashed to his meeting with Theresa McDouglas and he shook his head to clear it. The large man on the bed had the covers pulled to his waist. The pillows were propped behind him to elevate his upper body. His unshaven face made him virtually unrecognizable.

"Dallons?" Wa asked quietly.

Detective Tim Dallons rolled his head on the pillow and trained his eyes on the visitor. He nodded in greeting.

"How are you doing, partner?" Wa asked. He hoped his tone was soothing.

Dallons shrugged slightly.

Wa searched for something to say. "Thought I'd check up on my mentor, see if there was anything I could do for you."

"No."

He again felt trapped for something to say. "So what's going on?"

Dallons continued to look at his former partner with cool eyes, "Nothing. Nothing at all."

It had been seven months since Detective Tim Dallons had attempted to take his own life. Ever since then he'd been holed up in the psychiatric unit of Atlantic Coast Hospital, refusing to return to active duty, or even leave the hospital.

"The nurse was telling me that you're ready to go, if you want," Wa said.

Dallons grunted but didn't respond.

"I suppose it's about time you got out of this place," Wa added.

"I don't give a rat's ass," Dallons grumbled. "They want me out because they wanna give the bed to someone else."

Wa decided to let the subject drop.

"I'm working Sex Crimes now," Wa said.

Dallons nodded.

Wa cleared a tickle out of his throat before continuing. "It didn't make sense to continue in Homicide without my partner."

"You should've. You're a good detective."

Wa shifted and looked away from Dallons. "If I'm a good detective, I owe it to you. You really showed me a new side of being a cop."

"Bullshit," Dallons said and let his head roll back on the pillow. "What exactly do you want?"

Wa tried to look sincere. "I'm here to see how you're doing. People at the station wanted to know. They ask about you. Kelly's asked about you." He paused and added, "They want to know when you'll be back." He wasn't sure it was an appropriate comment.

Dallons laughed. "I'm not coming back."

"But you don't need to stay here. Why don't you...," Mitchell began.

"I want to be dead."

"Don't say that."

"Then don't ask me personal questions."

An uncomfortable silence fell between them.

Wa's mind drifted away from Dallons. The thought of wanting to be dead struck him as terrible. He wondered how empty a person's life had to be for them to want to die. He thought about his wife, his kids, his family. He knew how devastating it would be if he couldn't see them ever again, worse yet if they were taken away from him. He consciously stopped himself. He didn't want to think about it. Thinking about questions like that made him wish he were an accountant. Seeing his former partner in a psychiatric ward wishing he were dead only made Wa more unsure about his career. He couldn't stand the thought of something coming between him and his family. He decided he needed to leave the hospital.

Dallons spoke first. "I guess you'll be busy the next few days."

Wa didn't immediately make the connection and he looked at Dallons with a blank expression.

"You're Sex Crimes now. That rapist will be back at it in two days, Thursday night."

Wa nodded. "How'd you know the timeline? We hadn't released that, exactly."

"I've seen the papers. I can put two and two together. Just because I'm in this place doesn't mean I've actually gone insane."

"Well, you're right. We're kinda under the gun right now. We've stepped up the investigation but the names we generated off the computer haven't panned out."

Dallons' grunt indicated a distrust of computer-generated lists.

"Our next step is a bit of long shot. We'll be staking out a few locations, keeping an active police presence throughout the city on Thursday night. Don't know what that'll turn up yet, but hopefully we'll get lucky."

"Did you consult Wenton, yet?" Dallons asked with obvious derision.

"No." Wa kept his answer short, not wanting to draw Dallons into a discussion on the merits of using an expert consultant. He quickly changed the topic. "The strangest thing about the case is the inability of the victims to provide a clear description of the assailant."

"Two of the victims are here right now," Dallons said.

Wa hesitated. Protocol didn't allow him to confirm information like that.

"Don't worry about it," Dallons said. "I know you can't say. But I also know two women are in the hospital. I hear the staff talking."

Wa nodded.

"Those girls are pretty fucked up. I'm not surprised that you didn't get a good description. He must torture them."

Wa shrugged. "Not really. There's no evidence of a prolonged physical assault. There's the clear sexual assault, but that's basically it."

Dallons looked at Mitchell. "Is that right?"

Wa nodded.

Dallons couldn't help taking an interest in the case. "Hmm. That's important. This guy's obviously fucking with their heads then. You're looking for a guy that's doing something to these girls beyond the physical rape. He's setting up the room, the situation, to turn the victims inside out. He's probably talking to them, getting way inside their heads and leaving something awful."

He paused and Wa waited patiently for more insight from the veteran.

"If he's that verbal, he's likely smart. You might be looking for an educated rapist. Maybe another fuckin' Dennis Choler."

Wa could sense the anger rising in Dallons with the mention of the serial killer's name. He didn't want Dallons to get too upset, so he intervened to redirect the conversation back to the current case.

"That's an interesting angle. I think we might need to take it back to some of the victims and see what it turns up. It might also help us narrow the search down on the names we have so far."

Dallons' mood shifted and he fell silent. The memory of Dennis Choler had obviously opened a wound.

"Any other thoughts?" Wa said.

The old detective's eyes were blank.

Wa knew that the visit had come to an end. He waited for a moment out of respect.

Dallons continued to stare straight ahead, lost in thoughts about the events that had changed his life, and taken it from him.

"Thanks for your input, partner," Wa finally offered. "I'm going to take off."

There was no response as he left the room and closed the door behind him.

ten

98th day (thursday)

"You working today, Eddie?" Moe asked sarcastically.

Edward stood near the storage room doorway, resting against his broom. He'd been staring blankly at the mirror across from him for a couple of minutes.

"It's Edward," he said in what had become a repetitive game with Moe and his regulars.

Moe stood by a customer with his scissors poised above the man's head. It was 10:15 a.m. and surprisingly slow. No customers were seated in the waiting area.

"You working today, *Edward*?" Moe asked again.

"Sorry sir," Edward replied and resumed pushing the pile of hair in front of him. He stopped sweeping and stepped into the backroom. He pulled a dustpan off a hook, then returned to stoop and sweep the hair up.

"Geesh," Moe said, "I don't know about that kid. Might just be that the medication ain't exactly at the right dose yet."

"I hear ya," Gerry said, and blinked his eyes against the little hairs fluttering down his face.

Edward didn't hear the men. His body reflexively continued on with his duties while his mind clouded over. It was Thursday and today was a day that he feared more than any other. He felt exhausted with his battles against the evil inside him. His stomach churned and twisted and he felt physically ill. He wanted only to be good, safe, and God-fearing but he couldn't escape the darkness inside. His head spun with fear at what could happen. He could feel his sense of balance slowly disappear.

He took the full dustpan into the backroom and emptied it in a large garbage can near the exit. He set the broom against the wall and hung the pan back up. He looked around the storage room, which was jammed with shelves holding hair care products, towels, razor blades. He sat down on the only chair in the room and let his head drop to his chest.

"Please don't," he whispered, not wanting Moe or the customer to hear him.

A dark shape shifted, twisted and disappeared in the corner of the room. Edward tried not to look, but his eyes were drawn to it. The shape twisted and shifted and he thought he saw a face appear. It was the face of an old man. An old man that looked vaguely like him. Dad? He blinked to focus but it was gone. A tear formed in his eye, escaped, and rolled down his cheek. He wiped it away with the back of his hand.

A voice suddenly tickled the back of his right ear. "*Tonight. Tonight.*"

Edward knew not to acknowledge the voice. He prayed. "Please God. Take this obligation away from me and let me be pure and true. Let me not fall..."

"*Edward,*" the voice hissed.

"...victim to the evil that..."

"*Edward.*"

"...surrounds me and makes my every..."

"*Edward.*"

"...thought tainted in the very..."

"*Edward.*"

"...thing that I despise about myself."

"You fucking retard. Do you think that you can change who you are that easily and get rid of me?"

"Stay away from me," Edward growled. A chill swept through his body with such force that he nearly slipped off his chair.

"*No.*"

"I won't be your servant."

"Youwill."

"I'll kill myself. I swear."

"*Fuck them.*"

"No," he whispered, and brought his hands up to cover his ears.

"*Fuck them, you worthless shit eater.*"

"No," he said, louder now.

"*You have to take one of those sluts. I need my sex or I'll fuck your mom again because she's a nice little girl.*"

Edward shook his head slowly. "Leave...me...alone."

"*No.*"

A flash of light made Edward look up. There was one bare window in the back of the room next to the door. Light had been streaming in from the morning sun but now Edward watched in shock as the light moved backwards, gliding across the floor, over shelves, over towels, from between bottles of shampoo, and sucked back through the window. As the light retreated a palpable greyness filled the empty space. It leaked into the room, bubbling through the tiles of the floor, oozing in around the doorway, leaking off the shelves.

He tried to shut his eyes but he couldn't.

The black mark that had been the window bulged and drew his attention. He saw a swirl of darkness glide past in the distance. The darkness outside the window was thick; Edward sensed the shapes that moved back and forth in the inky blackness.

"No. Please don't do this to me. Please don't. Please stop," he whispered.

"Work for me like a good little daddy's boy."

"Please stop."

Pressure gripped the sides of Edward's head and dropped down around his neck. He felt hands encircle his throat.

"Work for me."

The dark shapes from outside the window disappeared from sight for a moment and then burst with incredible speed through the window and into the storage room. The formless textures of darkness swirled through the greyness before finally descending upon to Edward.

"Work for me."

The blackness moved over him. A cold sensation began at his head and drew down over his face. Tentacles of darkness slipped into his eyes, his ears, his nose, his mouth and retreated leaving a tingling sensation of cold sweat. The blackness continued down his body, massaging, pushing, pulling, and exploring. It melted through his clothes at every point and dragged down his bare skin. The blackness wrapped around his genitals, squeezing his balls, stroking his penis until he was hard. It continued down his legs, through his toes and away into the floor leaving Edward covered in sweat and limp from exhaustion. Voices continued to batter him:

"Work for me."

"Take their bodies; fuck them until they are one of us."

"Let me fuck them."

"Let me have them so you can escape and be free once more."

Edward's mind floated and he wished for unconsciousness. He felt helpless and couldn't find the strength to fight, couldn't find the strength to protest anymore.

"What the fuck is going on in here?" a voice boomed into the back of his mind.

Edward blinked and looked up at Moe. The barber stood in the doorway of the storage room looking at him with disgust. Edward was reclined in a chair, one hand hanging limply at his side and the other slowly massaging his erect penis. His pants were unbuckled and unzipped only enough to allow him to pull himself out of his jeans.

"What in the fuck do you think you're doing?" Moe screamed again.

Edward quickly sat up, slipping his penis back into his pants. He stood and pulled his zipper up, covering himself.

"I want you out of here, now!" Moe barked.

With his pants done up, Edward didn't even look at Moe. He grabbed his jacket and slipped out the back door. As the door closed behind him he could hear Moe mumble, "Crazy fuck."

eleven

98th day (thursday)

"This is futile," Makum said to Wa.

They sat in an unmarked police car parked on 18th Street, in an area that formed a border out of the downtown core. It was this street where business towers gave way to the residential districts and apartment complexes.

Wa didn't respond to the pessimism of his fellow detective. He pressed a button and spoke into the handset he held in his right hand. "Meredith? Abrahms? You set?"

A slight pause and then a voice crackled back through the speaker. "Ready, set, go. We're in position on the East side. It's a busy night. There's lots of traffic. Over."

Wa glanced at his watch before responding. It was 5:30 p.m. He pressed the send button. "Sure is. Lots of traffic at this time of day. Lots of people heading home. We'll keep in touch, but I want you to maintain radio silence until there's word. Over."

"And out," responded Detective Meredith with a click signaling the end of the transmission.

Out of the corner of his eye, Wa could see Makum shaking his head. Wa pulled a tissue out of his pocket and held it to his nose.

"It's a long shot," he said, "but we need to take a chance. Someone's going to be raped tonight and I want us out on the street in full force."

"You sure you got enough cops out here?" Makum asked sarcastically.

"I want a strong presence tonight. It's not just about being in the best position to respond to a call, it's about showing the rapist that we're here. Maybe the guy sees a cop car, gets spooked, and decides it's too risky to get his rocks off. That's fine with me. We just prevented a rape."

"Hey,don't get me wrong. I understand the theory of this little operation, but I still think we're set up like fuckin' cub scouts on a bird watching expedition. I mean we sat here two weeks ago, and two weeks before that, and if I recall correctly, two fuckin' weeks before that. What'd we get then, eh?"

"And we might be here two weeks from tonight, but if that's what it takes—that's what it takes," Wa said.

"Yeah, all right," Makum said. "I just know that we never get the fuckin' 9-1-1 until the next day. The call always comes in too late to get us to the scene to grab this fucker. He's always long gone and the women are fucked up. I don't think tonight's gonna be any different."

Wa ignored him. He knew that Makum was right but he didn't want to believe it. He hoped they'd get a break. He hoped the rapist would make a mistake, get sloppy, let them get to a crime scene early. It might be their only shot at catching him.

twelve

98th day (thursday)

The street was a whirring hum of motion. The five o'clock rush had started and business people in suits and long jackets filled the sidewalks. Edward was drawn into the masses of people. The crowd seemed like a refuge because of the anonymity it promised. He wanted to be anonymous.

Across one shoulder he carried an old, stained backpack, one of few possessions he'd managed to retain over his years in and out of hospitals. He walked slowly, but steadily, his head hung to avoid eye contact. His thin frame was well suited to darting between the throngs of commuters as he made his way down the street. He wore his only jacket, a thin cloth one that served him through every season. In his panic to flee the barber shop, he'd neglected to pack any other clothes. As he walked, he briefly allowed himself to regret not bringing a change of clothes.

His backpack was empty except for his Bible and his prescriptions. He didn't want to be without either of these items and even through the haze of his panic he knew enough to pack them.

The keys! he thought, and quickly patted the front and then back pockets of his blue jeans. He felt only his thin wallet, nothing else. In his haste he'd somehow left the keys for his apartment behind.

What does it matter? he told himself. He knew he couldn't return to the apartment. He knew that the scene in the storage room ensured that he'd be kicked out of the work program, kicked out of his apartment. He knew that.

My life is coming apart, he thought. *I can't fix it. I can't fix anything. It's just not worth it. I should be dead.*

His pace slowed, but he continued to walk through the thinning crowds. The business people were slowly filtering out of the downtown core. They slowly found their buses, or found their car pools, and the streets became increasingly quiet.

Edward didn't have anywhere to go. He didn't know if there were any safe spots. He considered checking into the hospital, telling them he was ill and needed help. He couldn't do that. He'd tried before and been turned away. "We don't have any beds," he was told. "Can you try a hostel?" and "This isn't a hotel, Edward," the staff would tell him. "Unless you're really sick we can't just let you stay here."

But I am really sick, he thought.

He shook his head and continued to walk.

His head felt light and full at the same time. He felt dizzy and off-balance. As he walked he couldn't be sure his feet were connecting with the ground. It was a strange sensation like sitting still in an IMAX movie and feeling like the room was spinning anyway. He had to concentrate in order not to lose his balance completely.

As he worked to maintain his composure he was forced to keep his head up and look at his surroundings. Only a few people remained on the sidewalks. Reflexively, Edward began focusing on each face. He found he couldn't help himself. His eyes were drawn to theirs. Each set of eyes he saw were dark, black, lifeless. The people all looked at him, through him. Each set of eyes accused him and judged him. These people knew Edward was the one responsible for the evil in the city. *They knew!*

He could feel his sense of panic return. His heart thumped with increasing speed and urgency. His head darted back and forth to see each passing person. The faces turned to watch Edward as they moved. The eyes burned into him.

And then one of the pedestrians leaned toward him and the face changed. The man's features melted into a gaping mouth of black filled with poorly spaced teeth. A voice hissed at Edward, "*Find someone.*"

Edward's breath sucked in so quickly, sharp pains creased his chest. He pulled his eyes away from the thing and another person leaned into him. This time it was a woman and her features instantly twisted until her face became a gaping black mouth. "*Find me someone to fuck,*" it snarled in low tones.

"No," he said quietly and stumbled with the effort of moving. *Please God don't do this to me.*

A large woman in a fashionable brown overcoat approached him, veering only at the last moment before walking into him. As she passed, Edward couldn't help but turn to watch. The woman looked back at him and revealed a distorted mouth of black with yellowed teeth where her face should be. But then the face swirled and took on new features. It was vaguely familiar to Edward. Was it his real mother? No! *My real sister?* As the woman's body continued to move, the head remained fixed on him and the mouth gaped, choking out its words, "*Find someone, you worthless fuck.*"

"I won't!" he screamed as his tears broke free.

His words drew the attention of the few people on the street. Pedestrians stopped, heads turned to look at the spectacle, and he felt exposed. He quickly glanced at the crowd through a fog of tears and saw only dark, black eyes looking through him. He pushed his way past the eyes and turned down an alley between the buildings.

He slumped against a wall, dropping his backpack, and slid down until he rested on his heels. He brought his elbows to his knees and held his head in his hands.

"Why?" he asked and his tears were joined by heavy sobs as he covered his face.

A cool breeze made him stop and he sucked his breath in and held it. The slight breeze wafted beneath his feet and around his legs. He turned to look down the length of the building, to what he thought must be the source of the breeze. The light that spilled in from the street only travelled part way, and the rest of the lane was black. The strange breeze blew out from this blackness. He continued to watch as the breeze became cooler and moved up and down his body like someone waving a flashlight over him.

"No God," he whispered.

The blackness shifted and the breeze became cooler still. He continued to watch as the back of the lane began to breathe. The walls of the buildings on either side twisted and arched as the blackness drew in air and expelled it.

"Please," Edward cried softly.

A swirl began in the centre of the shifting black. A swirl that soon overpowered the heaving of the buildings. Edward watched in terror, unable to move, unable to escape. The swirl slowed its circular motion and opened wide to reveal a mouth that parted into a gaping maw and shot forward so quickly it shocked Edward off his heels. He dropped back onto his buttocks and the oversized mouth came to a sudden stop next to his face. The stale breath of death lapped at him as a voice entered his mind.

"*I want sex. I want sex tonight.*"

"Never. Not again. Not ever."

"*Serve me.*"

"Please no."

"*Serve me.*"

"Please."

"*Now.*"

Edward bowed his head for a moment but felt a presence in front of him. He looked up and saw a man standing across the alley. The man was standing overtop of a girl. The girl was familiar. She crouched on the ground, cowering, trying to protect herself from the man. *Who was she?* The man was pointing a rifle at her. *My sister, my mother? Is that man going to shoot...*

"NO!" Edward screamed, but it was too late. The man pulled the trigger and the girl's head exploded. Edward closed his eyes, unable to bear the sight.

Everything fell silent for a moment, but then someone kicked his foot. He forced his eyes open and saw the man standing in front of him, pointing the rifle down. "*BANG*!" the man said. "*Goodbye my bastard son.*"

"NO!" Edward cried and closed his eyes tightly.

"Hey!" a voice called to him and he felt someone kick his foot again. "Are you okay buddy?" The voice reached him through a thick cloud of darkness.

He looked up, expecting to see his father. Instead he saw a man he didn't recognize. The man held a large bulky briefcase under one arm and wore a dark coloured suit with a grey wool overcoat. His expression showed genuine concern.

Edward looked across the alley for the girl's body, but there was nothing. Down the lane he saw only the dark recesses of the alley. He looked back at the man. "I'm fine. Just felt dizzy."

"Do you need some help or something?"

"No. I'm okay now."

"Be happy to get you a cab."

"No. I live close by. I just needed to catch my breath."

The man nodded. "All right then. Take care." He stepped out of the alley and disappeared down the street.

Edward gazed after him. Something about the man seemed odd, out of place. He couldn't quite figure it out, but... The hat! The man wore a baseball cap that seemed inconsistent with the business suit. Edward shook his head. It didn't matter.

He stood and looked down at his backpack. He lifted a foot and kicked it, sending it skidding away from him. He turned and walked out of the lane. Nothing mattered anymore. He was ready to accept his destiny.

"I need to find a bitch for my daddy," he said quietly to himself.

thirteen

98th day (thursday)

The bus driver moved one hand over the other as he turned the large steering wheel. He successfully maneuvered the forty-foot city bus around a tight corner by swinging out wide into the opposite lane. After he'd finished the tight turn the entire bus rocked from side to side before the heavy-duty shocks stabilized. As they continued down the road he took a quick look into the passenger mirror affixed over his head. None of the passengers behind him had hit the floor. *The expertise of the business commuter*, he smiled to himself and pressed down the accelerator.

The familiar sound of the bus engine groaning as it picked up speed crept into Kathy Fineman's consciousness. She looked up at the other passengers briefly before turning to the window next to her. It was already growing dark outside. She didn't like arriving home from work this late. She gauged their location and the distance to her stop. About another five minutes, give or take. It wouldn't leave her much time to unwind before she'd have to drop into bed. She sighed.

Kathy returned her attention to the book she held in both hands. It was a paperback edition of John Grisham's latest novel. She was drawn to Grisham's novels partly because she worked as a receptionist in a law office, but mostly because she liked the stories. Soon she was lost in the book and oblivious to the constant movement around her.

Kathy Fineman was twenty-six years old with light brown hair and dark eyes. She was somewhat plain looking; her most noticeable feature was a slightly hooked nose. She'd often thought about getting a nose job but knew she had neither the money nor the stomach for the surgery. She worried about other physical features as well. She felt overweight and wanted to lose at least twenty-five pounds. She'd also inherited her mother's ample breasts and was sure they made her look even more overweight. Finally, Kathy hated her clothes. She never felt comfortable shopping and had no idea how to create *outfits* out of her random acquisitions.

She'd worked late tonight. There was a big case coming up at the firm and she'd been asked to stay and finish typing a few letters that, according to Bob, a junior partner, "Absolutely had to go out right away." Kathy resented working late but always agreed anyway. She found it difficult to assert herself because she worried about looking mean, or worse yet, like a *bitch*.

She glanced outside again to check her surroundings. It was only seven o'clock but some of the streetlights were already flickering to life.

Through the hazy darkness she saw Pizza Pete's familiar red awning. It was her favourite pizza place and it was located in the bottom of a high-rise building one block away from her apartment.

She reached for her bookmark and paused before she stuck it into the spine. Somehow, her bookmark had ended up being a creased, faded picture of her and her ex-boyfriend, Murray. She frowned at it and automatically lifted her middle finger. "Son of a bitch," she muttered, feeling foolish for even keeping the picture. She hadn't seen him since their abusive relationship had ended a couple of years ago. *Good riddance*, she thought.

She slammed the book shut and looked out the window again. She was nearing her stop so she pulled her Discman earphones out of her ears, letting them hang down over her shoulders. She reached up to pull the cord.

As the bus slowed to a halt, Kathy dropped her book into the large bag that sat between her legs. She snapped the top together and stood. The driver watched in his mirror as Kathy walked to the back doors and exited.

Stepping down onto the pavement, she looked up and down the street. The rush hour pedestrian traffic had disappeared by this time. She saw only empty sidewalks in both directions except...

She snapped her head back, peering into the darkness behind her. Somewhere in the shadows she'd seen something. Was it a person standing in the shadows? The light from Pizza Pete's didn't quite reach the end of the building. She peered into the void and saw only darkness. She assumed it was nothing.

Edward's breath came hard and heavy. The blackness that circled him made him pant like a dog. He hated that. He wanted to feel relaxed, confident. He swallowed but there was no moisture in his mouth and he almost gagged.

The corridor where he stood was empty. Although the lights were on, he found it difficult to see. Something swirled around each light, something dark. It circled slowly around the sunken pot lights and made little diving, biting motions. It looked as though the darkness was attacking the very light itself.

He didn't know how long he'd stood in that spot. His stomach growled in protest, urging him to give up his vigil. Edward knew he couldn't.

He looked over his shoulder and down to the end of the other corridor, still empty, still quiet. He knew something was wrong.

He'd seen people here. A couple in their forties had passed him about twenty minutes ago. They'd moved down the hall and gone into one of the units, a nice working couple arriving home after a hard day on the job. But they weren't right.

He'd seen a younger man arrive home. He was heavyset and in his early twenties. Edward had trouble figuring out what was wrong with him when he'd gotten off the elevator. It took a second to realize the man was carrying a bike over his shoulder. He wasn't right.

The only other person he'd seen in the hall during his vigil was an older lady, who must have been in her late sixties. Edward had moved toward her but the voices had said, "*No.*"

Now he waited for another. He knew he was in the right hallway. Someone would come.

Kathy shrugged and headed down the street. *Don't be paranoid*, she scolded herself. She walked quickly, purposefully, as she always did. There was a chill in the night and she didn't care to waste time. She found it so hard to unwind at the end of the day anyway. She always worried about the work to be done tomorrow—the work she hadn't done today. She came to a stop at the intersection and waited for the light to turn. She watched the walk/don't walk sign casually.

A strange feeling suddenly made the back of her neck tingle. She turned quickly and scanned the dark street. A car passed and continued down the street but there was no other movement. Still...she felt like she was being watched. It was a strange feeling—more of an intuition—that there was someone else there.

She turned back to the light and noticed that it had changed. She stepped into the street and hurried across. As she reached the curb on the other side, she again glanced back. Nothing.

Relieved, she continued down the street. The entrance to her building was only a short distance ahead. She half-walked, half-ran the last few steps and then went up the stairs two at a time.

She shook her head as she arrived at the door. *Why am I so jumpy tonight?*

She fumbled with her keys until she found the right one. She inserted it into the lock and turned, using the key to pull the door open. She caught the bottom of the door with her foot and held it while she removed her key and stepped inside.

She grabbed the handle of the large glass door and brought it shut, satisfied with the click of the lock. She stood for a moment looking out into the dark street. She still saw nothing, no one. She grunted and turned to head into the building.

"It's Thursday night!" she blurted out as if she'd finally remembered the answer to a riddle. *I shouldn't be out tonight. The police issued a warning about the rapist striking tonight, Thursday night. No wonder that idiot Bob was so hesitant and nervous about asking me to stay late. He knew it was Thursday night and he didn't say anything.*

Fear and anger stirred inside her as she arrived at the elevators and pressed the *up* button.

That bastard! she thought. *I should say something to him tomorrow.* She knew she wouldn't say anything.

She glanced back at the door. The corridor that held the elevators led straight back to the main entrance. The light from inside made it difficult to see out, but she could discern the outlines of shapes outside the building: a plant, a parked car near a light pole...and then a figure lurched into view.

She sucked in her breath and held it.

The dark figure bounded up the steps to the doorway and peered inside. Kathy's head shot back to the elevators. She looked up at the digital display that was counting backwards from six. "Come on, come on," she said under her breath as she reached out and pressed the *up* button a few more times.

She looked back to the doorway. There was no one there. She peered more closely. Still nothing. The dark figure had disappeared. She slowly released her breath as her shoulders relaxed.

Click.

Kathy froze. The cold metallic click of the door lock reverberated through her mind. Someone had unlocked the door and was coming into the building. She slowly turned her head back to the entrance. Still nothing.

Ding!

Kathy jumped at the sound of the elevator. The doors dragged opened and she leapt into the car, desperately punching the button for her floor—eight—then the *door close* button. As the elevator doors shut, she placed her hand on the hard plastic facade and pushed, attempting to speed the doors closed. She watched the narrow entrance grow smaller and smaller. She half-expected a hand to shove through the doors and stop the elevator at the last second. She'd seen it in countless movies. Her heart pounded so hard she found it difficult to think.

Edward struggled to keep his eyes open. His head pounded and spun and he leaned heavily against the wall. A constant presence sent shivers up and down his body. Each time his head drooped to his chest a voice would hiss into the back of his mind:

"Be patient."

"Watch."

"It's time—find her."

"I am thirsty."

After what seemed like an eternity, the doors finally pushed together and the elevator bumped to a start. Kathy watched the numbers above the door light up in sequence showing her their upward progress. She breathed another sigh of relief and dropped her shoulders and head. She felt a tension headache bubbling and knew she was going to be a bundle of nerves once she got into her apartment.

Finally the voice hissed, "*It is her.*"

"Where?" he whispered back.

"*There.*"

He felt his attention drawn to the arriving elevator. He stood four doors away and watched the elevator in anticipation. A leg lifted through the opening and someone stepped into view. He'd seen enough and dropped back. "It's her," he whispered with a weak smile.

He heard the woman moving toward him. He held his breath, worried that she would come too far and see him in the doorway. She didn't. She stopped in the doorway next to him. He heard her keys rattle and he stepped out of his hiding place. He could barely see the woman's back inside her doorway. He moved quickly down the hall and stood next to the entrance. His thoughts were completely erased by the monster he served. "*It's her. It's her,*" it screamed. "*Get her! Get her!*"

He hesitated. His hands shook violently and his head pounded until he thought it would split in two. Then her face appeared.

The elevator shook slightly as it stopped at the eighth floor. The doors pulled apart and she stepped out, looking down one hallway and then the other. It seemed okay. She walked down to her suite, number 829. It was a small apartment, but the rent was good and the building was well kept.

She held her small key ring in one hand and looked down to find her apartment key. She located it as she came to a stop in front of her door. Each door was slightly offset into the walls of the corridor and she stepped forward to slide the key in. She turned the knob and pushed the door open. Light streamed along the floor into her dark suite. Everything seemed in order. She leaned back slightly to take one last peek down the corridor. As her head passed the edge of the doorway she found herself face to face with a man.

fourteen

98th day (thursday)

The woman looked straight at Edward. Her eyes were swirling circles of black. She snarled at him, barked, and snapped her fangs. He reached out in panic and gripped her shoulders. With a strength he didn't know he had, he flung the woman into the apartment. He stepped into the doorway.

The woman lay on the floor beneath him. She looked up at him and the shadows from the light that crept around him played across her face. The woman's face distorted and shifted as she looked at him. He wanted to hide his eyes from her but couldn't. She opened her gaping mouth and made a high-pitched screech that pierced Edward's ears until he was sure they were bleeding. The shadows continued to play across her face and he felt as if he might be sick. He reached back and shut the door to cut off the light.

When he looked back the woman had flipped over and was moving across the floor. He leapt after her and straddled her back. He dropped to his knees using his weight to bring her to the ground. She twisted and writhed like a snake and he knew he needed to contain her. He used his legs to pin her arms while continuing to rest most of his weight on her back.

Her head twisted and in the dark of the room he could see the gaping mouth drip with venom. A terrible screeching again rang in Edward's head and he leaned down to speak into the woman's ear:

"*Facini*."

The word was not his own. The evil used his body now. He could feel it becoming a part of him, using him like a toy. He wasn't even sure if he was speaking English.

"*Blackened side*."

The words tore out of him, stinging his senses. He could feel them gurgling and bubbling inside his throat and eventually spilling out but he couldn't control them.

"*Facini entfaste blackened side*," he hissed.

The words seemed to have a life of their own. They fell from him and circled through the air, looking, watching, seeking out the woman on the floor. She continued to howl and screech with an ungodly ferocity.

Edward needed to lean closer to her. He needed to make sure his voice found its way inside her head. "*Facini entfaste blackened side*."

The woman's high-pitched screams echoed through the room.

He drew back suddenly. "SILENCE!"

"*Good*," a voice cheered him on.

The voice made his stomach retch and he almost vomited. He choked and swallowed hard.

"*Take her, you fucking worthless fuck!*" he screamed. The words were not his own. His eyes flooded with tears and he leaned to her ear again. "*Bitch-whore. I know everything you are. There's nothing pretty inside you. Nothing left that anyone wants. I know what you are and now you'll know. You'll see the black as I do and taste the evil that flows out. Prepare to be opened wide. Prepare to feel the heat of death.*"

The words continued to pour out of Edward and he felt the woman's body go limp.

Kathy was helpless against the onslaught. She lay pinned to the floor as the voice dug into her mind. The strange phrase the man repeated twisted and pushed deeper and deeper until her head was bursting. The enormous pressure made it difficult to think.

The voice continued and she knew she wouldn't make it. She was sure she would die. She wanted to be dead. She wanted the words to die. She wanted the pain inside her head to end. And most of all, she didn't want to face the horrors that the voice promised.

"*It's pain because you won't let go and accept what you already know is true.*"

She felt a hand stroke her hair. A cold, lifeless hand working its fingers through her hair and stroking her scalp as the words continued to bite into her mind. The hand felt suddenly different. The way it stroked was oddly familiar.

The darkness of the room soaked through her and held her. She couldn't find anything solid to focus on, anything to hold her mind in reality. The position of her head didn't allow her to see the demon that rested on top of her. Out of the corner of her eye she thought she could see something. It was dark and black. It had the texture of hardened tar. It could have been the dimness of the room playing tricks on her, but the thing didn't have a permanent shape—it continuously shifted and moved. She strained to see what held her. She twisted and squirmed until she finally caught a glimpse of something hovering above her. It was her ex-boyfriend, Murray. *That's why the hand felt familiar!* It was the son of a bitch who had cheated on her. The man she'd contemplated killing so many times. The bastard that berated her until she was so confused she'd actually purchased rat poison to use on him, or herself. He was here—in her apartment! And he was grinning at her.

She struggled harder now. She wouldn't let that bastard hurt her—not again, not ever again. "Get off me you son of a bitch!" she screamed as she twisted and kicked.

She felt Murray's hot breath as he leaned to her ear, "*Kathy. Don't fight like this. Don't fight like this after what you did to me.*"

"Did what?" she screamed. "You're the one that ch—" She stopped in mid-sentence as she caught another glimpse of Murray. This time he wasn't grinning. His face was a strange grey-green colour. His eyes were sunken in his head. There was a strong smell of decaying flesh. She gasped for air at the sight.

"*Do you see what you've done?*" Murray whined at her through brown misshapen teeth.

Kathy opened her mouth to scream but nothing came out. Her eyes were locked on the living corpse of her ex-boyfriend. Suddenly, Murray gagged and his throat spasmed.

"*You put rat poison in my coffee,*" he spat, as saliva dripped down to settle on Kathy's forehead.

"No," she pleaded. "I never...I don't think I..."

"*You did. You wanted to kill me. I was sick for a month. I threw up until the stomach bile destroyed my throat. I can still barely talk because of you.*"

"No, I didn't..."

"*You fuckin' bitch. You killed me.*"

"Didn't... You're not dead."

"I wanted to be dead. You made me so sick I wanted to be dead." He retched again and brown mucus tinged with blood shot past his rotted lips and splashed down into Kathy's right eye and onto her nose.

"No, please," she whimpered as she blinked to clear her vision of the sticky fluid.

"*I'm going to fuck you,*" Murray whispered, and then stood.

She flailed wildly, desperate to escape, but a voice slipped into her mind. Murray was saying something she couldn't understand.

"*Blackened side facini facini facini entfaste blackened side.*"

The strange words chilled her and the spasm in her body stopped.

She didn't understand. Was it English? She couldn't even tell if the voice was actually Murray's. She risked another look but couldn't see him. But there was something in the room with her.

Her breath sucked in. *What was in the room? Where was Murray?*

She wanted to run. Hide. She wanted to get out but couldn't find the strength. Panic swept over her so completely that she felt exhausted beyond all reason. Her head swam. She closed her eyes, unable to fight, unwilling to see anymore of the horror.

"No more," she said weakly.

Something grabbed her and held her tightly. "*You want me to fuck you, to hurt you, to tear you apart.*"

"Please. No more," she begged.

"*Facini entfaste blackened side.*"

"No."

"*Blackened side, blackened side.*"

"Don't do this. You don't need to," she pleaded.

"*Blackened side.*"

"Please," she said as her head spun violently. She thought she was going to be sick.

The thing's voice changed, became lower, deeper, darker. She knew now that it wasn't Murray.

"*You want to be violated, torn apart, fucked, fucked, fucked...*"

"No. Please."

"*Be fucked, get fucked, let the insect crawl into you and face your black inside.*"

Her ears rang out with the pressure in her head. She just wanted to pass out. The pressure was so painful, so intense. She couldn't bear the thought of being conscious any longer. Please God.

"*Peel your skin away and be free to take the fuck and be fucked and be evil, take evil.*"

Finally she felt the sweet relief of her consciousness slipping away. The world began to strobe with flashes of black. The constant words, the constant breath across her face was overcoming her. Her final refuge would be to descend into unconsciousness. But her escape didn't come. She remained conscious.

She felt hands slipping down her body, working into every crevice, slipping into her clothes, down her pants.

"*I have to fuck you!*"

Hands taking her throat, fingers moving over her legs, taking her shoes off.

"*Accept it and take me.*"

She no longer felt any weight on top of her. He moved freely around her, exploring her. Her body twitched at the cold touch of whatever it was, but she didn't have the strength to resist. Not anymore. Not after what she'd seen. Not with the pressure inside her head.

She felt him grip her ankles and lift her legs from the floor. He began dragging her and she was powerless to stop him.

He pulled her into the bedroom, roughly picked her up, and dropped her onto the unmade bed.

She felt hands touch her as her clothes were removed. With each new length of exposed skin cold tentacles caressed her, explored her, penetrated her. She shivered with pain and terror as her body was opened. She felt a swirling mist enter her eyes, her nose, her ears, her mouth. She tried one last time to cry out, but couldn't. Something rubbed against her breasts and down over her stomach. She felt hands touching her vagina, spreading her lips and touching her. Her body tensed against the intrusion and something entered her. There was no heat, no sensation except for a cold that penetrated every part of her nakedness.

The darkness moved in and out of her, fucking her. Weight pressed her into the bed and pushed the air from her lungs. She felt her legs being lifted and spread apart as something continued to rape her. Her body was helpless to the intrusion and she once again wished for death. Her mind wouldn't be released. She couldn't slip into unconsciousness. She was forced to endure the violation as it went further and further inside her. Until each thrust felt as though it pushed into the back of her throat. She felt her stomach churn and barely resisted an urge to vomit. She couldn't tell if her vagina was tearing, but felt the warm sensation of fluid trickling into her anus.

She forced her eyes open and saw a face close to hers. It was a distorted face that screamed in pain. It was her ex-boyfriend with trickles of blood seeping from his eyes. "*Why did you do it?*" he cried. "*I was sick for months!*"

"I didn't," she whispered and he disappeared. The rape continued. Her body convulsed with each thrust. She looked around the room in desperation and again saw Murray. He was standing next to the bed, watching. His face was a jagged mess of skin, and bloody vomit still clung to his chin. She looked at Murray for help. He leaned over and brought his putrid mouth to hers.

And then it stopped. The blackness pulled out of her, deflating her like a balloon. She felt the weight lift from her body and disappear. She struggled to open her eyes and saw only her bedroom. She looked down over her naked body and knew it wasn't a dream. Suddenly, she couldn't breathe.

She clawed at her throat, trying to suck in air. She knew she'd pass out if she didn't draw a breath into her lungs. She couldn't. Her arms flailed out to either side and she kicked and rolled on her bed until she managed to find air.

She panted in short bursts as her mind raced. Every time the horror of the attack slipped into her consciousness, she forced it out. She clung to her sanity, barely.

She knew she needed to do something. She had to try and do something. She leapt to her feet but as soon as she did, her balance left her and she reached for the bedside table to support herself. After a moment she staggered again, wanting desperately to get to the other room, to find her phone. She took one uneasy step and then another. She walked like a toddler just getting used to her legs.

When she finally arrived in the living room she fell against the desk where she kept the phone. The desk shook precariously under her weight and the phone slid off the edge, crashing to the floor.

She could hear the buzz of the dial tone as the receiver dislodged from its cradle. She dropped to the floor and groped for the phone with one hand. She found it and dialed 9-1-1.

"Police, fire, medical—how may I direct your call?" a voice answered.

"I've been raped," Kathy managed before the phone slipped out of her hand and she finally fell unconscious.

fifteen

98th day (thursday)

"We've got him," Wa announced after taking the call from dispatch. A woman in the downtown area had just called 9-1-1 claiming she'd been raped. The caller hadn't identified herself or her address, but because the call hadn't been disconnected it was easily traced.

Wa pressed the button on his handset and spoke. "This is Detective Wa. We have a go on 1818, 25th Street East, the Lancaster Arms apartment complex. I want the special teams units assembled around that point as planned. No one leaves the area without identification. Let's not be sloppy. Out."

The extra patrol cars in the downtown core tonight had been monitoring a special frequency waiting for this message. Earlier, Wa had briefed them on the specific plan if a sexual assault call came in. Each unit had a designated position to take within a certain distance from point zero. Wa's plan was to respond quickly and shut the streets down: if they were lucky, they could trap the perpetrator near the scene. Only individuals who provided proper ID would be allowed to leave the area. That way there'd be a record of everyone.

"We don't know if this is the guy yet, Wa," Makum said, attempting to keep his partner's expectations in check.

In what seemed like a single motion, Wa started the car, put it in gear, and pulled away from the curb. "I know."

They arrived at the victim's address in under two minutes. Detectives Margaret Meredith and Laurie Abrahms were already parked in front and were walking up the steps to the building's entrance. A patrol car was pulling up from the opposite direction; the two officers inside it would soon set up a checkpoint on the street to control traffic. Another patrol was scheduled to arrive any moment.

Wa brought his car to a rough halt against the curb and threw it into park before it stopped rocking. He and Makum jumped from the car and ran up the stairs to meet the other detectives. Police badges hung from their sportcoats and bounced as they moved.

Detective Meredith was already speaking to a man in his late forties. He was short, stocky, and balding. He'd obviously been settled into his apartment for the night. His clothes were in disarray, his shirt only half tucked into loose jogging pants. He wore imitation leather slippers over his bare feet. A length of graying hair had fallen away from its position across the top of his head and gave him an almost comical look.

Margaret nodded at Wa and Makum. "This is the superintendent, Mr. Yago. We've explained the situation to him."

They acknowledged the man without the common conventions of exchanging names or a handshake. There was no time for cordiality.

"Let's go. Apartment 829," Wa spat. He coughed and gritted his teeth against the tickle in the back of his throat.

The group turned and headed for the elevator, which stood open and waiting.

As they stepped in, Margaret spoke. "I had Mr. Yago bring his key and lock the elevator off for us."

Makum smiled.

Wa complimented her forethought. Laurie turned the key in the panel and pressed the button for the eighth floor.

"Who's in that apartment, Mr. Yago?" Wa asked as the elevator lurched upwards.

"Just Ms. Kathy Fineman. She's a good sort. Quiet. Polite. I think she works at a law firm."

"No one else in there?" Makum asked.

"No one."

"Boyfriend?" Wa asked as he rubbed his nose roughly.

"I don't think so, but I couldn't be sure. I don't really keep track of such things."

"Fine." Wa turned to address his fellow detectives. "This is an entry situation. I'll lead. I want you to hold off until we know what's going on in the room, though."

"Got it," Makum said as the other detectives nodded. Each of them retrieved their service guns from hidden holsters and held the weapons in check.

The elevator came to a stop and the doors slid open. Laurie turned the key on the panel to lock the elevator out of service again.

Mr. Yago went to take a step out and was pushed back by Wa's straight arm across his chest. "Hold on a second."

He stepped to the edge of the doors and took quick, careful looks in each direction. Next he took longer looks down each corridor. "Fuck," he spat under his breath.

"What's the matter?" Makum said.

"Fuckin' building has recessed entrances to each unit. I can't tell if the hallway's clear."

Makum glared at Mr. Yago, willing to blame the closest person to him.

Going down the hallway now meant they could be walking into an ambush.

Wa shook his head in frustration and then turned to Mr. Yago. "Okay, we're going to do this but we're going to have to take it pretty slow. I want you to wait here. Don't go anywhere or do anything unless we tell you. Got it?" Mr. Yago nodded so Wa continued, "Now, I'll need the master key for the suite."

Mr. Yago fumbled in his pocket and pulled out a large key ring. He flipped through and found a key which he presented to Wa. "That's it."

He took the key and then turned back to Yago. "Apartment 829 is right or left?" Wa asked.

"Right."

The detectives stepped out of the elevator and moved down the hallway. They came to a stop in front of 829. The door was closed. Wa knocked sharply. "Police. Open this door."

No response. They listened for movement but there was none.

Wa knocked again, with more force. "Police. We had an emergency call from this unit. Open this door."

No response.

Wa looked back at his team and nodded. They took positions against the walls immediately outside the entranceway. Wa turned back to the door and put the key into the lock.

"POLICE!" he announced loudly. "We're coming in!"

He turned the key and shoved the door, releasing it. The apartment was black. "POLICE!"

Wa hated entry situations. There were too many unknowns and the chance of being hurt was high. Try as he might, he couldn't help but think of his wife and kids every time he took a step into a dark room. He didn't need that kind of distraction.

He took a careful step forward, viewing the room over his gun and outstretched arms. He swung from side to side trying to pick up any movement, his eyes hunting for any people who might be in the room. He saw nothing but furniture. He glanced over his shoulder and saw the light switch. He took his left hand off his wrist and punched back at the wall. Light flooded the room. He took a quick swipe over the room again with the increased visibility. Still nothing but a furnished apartment.

Using small, shuffling steps in order to maintain a sturdy shooting stance he moved further into the apartment, keeping his gun locked in front of him. He could see into the small kitchen through a large nook. Next to the kitchen were two doors at the rear of the apartment. One door was wide open and he could see a sink and tub inside. The other door was partially closed and must have been the bedroom.

"POLICE! Is anyone here?"

No answer.

"CLEAR!" he yelled back to the detectives. They charged into the room, taking up positions to complement Wa. He turned back to them and silently motioned to the kitchen, bathroom, and bedroom. They nodded.

With expert precision, Laurie and Margaret quickly moved to the kitchen and bathroom while Wa and Makum prepared to enter the bedroom.

Wa stood next to the bedroom doorway. "POLICE! We're going to enter the bedroom."

He turned and crouched, shoving the door open.

"She's here!" a voice suddenly called.

Wa didn't let his attention stray from the room. He didn't see anyone in the bedroom either. He stood and reached for a light switch on the wall next to the door. The light came on and Wa quickly checked beside the bed and in the closet. Makum backed him up from the doorway. Satisfied that the bedroom was empty, Wa moved back to the main room.

They found Margaret in the kitchen, crouched beside a naked woman in her twenties. The woman lay on the linoleum floor and a drawer was open above her head.

Laurie stepped into the kitchen with a large towel in one hand. "Bathroom's clear," she announced to Makum and Wa. Margaret reached and took the towel, covering the woman.

"She conscious?" Makum asked.

"Barely," Margaret said.

Wa glanced into the open drawer. It was full of utensils, mostly kitchen knives.

"Roland," he said, "go get the paramedics up here. They'll be downstairs waiting."

Makum turned and hurried out of the apartment.

"This is the police, sweetie," Margaret said softly. "We're here to help. You're okay now."

Wa crouched beside the woman.

"Has she said anything?" he asked.

"No."

The woman shifted slightly and moaned.

"It's okay," Margaret said, taking the woman's shoulders gently. "The paramedics are on their way up."

"Can you tell us what happened?" Wa asked, looking at the woman with a concerned expression.

Margaret frowned at him, but he ignored her.

"Hmm?" she mumbled. "What?"

"What happened?" he repeated.

"I...I shouldn't have tried to kill him."

"Kill who?" he pressed.

She burst into tears. "My boyfriend raped me. Or not my boyfriend...something that used to be him. I wanted him dead for what he..."

"What do you mean? Your boyfriend raped you?"

"I'm not a murderer!" she screamed.

Margaret held the woman's twisting body. "Sh, it's okay. You're safe now."

The woman relaxed against the floor.

"Who opened this drawer?" Wa asked quietly, not wanting to upset her again.

The woman's eyes flickered as she looked toward the drawer. "I did."

He nodded, "Okay. Okay, and were you trying to get something?"

"A knife."

"To protect yourself against, ah, him?" he asked and coughed.

"No."

"It wasn't to fight off your attacker?" Wa asked.

"No," she said with glazed eyes that seemed unable to focus on the room or the detectives. "He was gone. It was gone."

Wa could hear the rattle of the stretcher and paramedics approaching. "Why did you want the knife then?"

The woman's lip began to tremble as she contemplated her answer. Laurie, Margaret, and Wa leaned forward to listen.

Tears welled up in her vacant eyes and she raised her hands to cover her face. "To kill myself. I wanted to kill myself."

The paramedics turned into the doorway. "Is it safe?" they asked before entering. Laurie, who was still standing in the entrance to the kitchen waved them in.

"Why?" Wa asked.

"That's enough for now, Wa," Margaret said.

He ignored her. "Why did you want to kill yourself?" he asked more urgently.

The paramedics stepped in front of Laurie and asked for the other detectives to step aside.

As they stood to move away, the woman uncovered her face and looked at Wa. Her eyes locked on his with incredible intensity. "I wanted to kill myself because the evil is in me now," she said in a voice without emotion.

sixteen

98th day (thursday)

The detectives watched the paramedics wheel Kathy Fineman down the hallway to the elevators. Mr. Yago waited nervously by the sliding doors in his new position as the elevator operator.

Wa shook his head in concern as he watched the stretcher disappear into the elevator.

"Another one. Fuck." He pulled a tissue out of his pocket and wiped it across his nose.

"So she's talking weird shit like the others, eh?" Makum asked no one in particular.

"Yep," Laurie said.

"What the hell is going on here?" he asked, the frustration obvious. "Why're all these women going cuckoo?"

"Have you ever been raped, Detective?" Margaret replied.

"That's enough," Wa said. "Let's get moving on this one. I want each of you knocking on doors. Someone saw something."

"No one's ever seen anything before," Makum said. "My fucking knuckles are sore from knocking on doors each time."

"Then wear gloves. Let's go. Laurie, that hallway," Wa said, pointing. "Margaret the other side. Roland and I will go down the other corridor."

The commotion in the hallway meant that the detectives didn't have to knock on a lot of doors. Many of the residents stood in their doorways watching the events with curiosity.

Wa approached a man who looked to be in his early twenties. He was heavyset with young features. His broad face was pale and there was no trace of a mustache or beard. He was dressed casually in a plaid shirt and pale cargo pants.

"Excuse me sir. I'm Detective Wa with Metro Police. Can I ask you a few questions?"

"Sure. What's going on?" the man asked.

Wa ignored the question. "Do you live in this suite?"

"Yes."

He jotted down the apartment number. "Can I have your name and occupation, please?"

"Roy Eckland. I'm a junior accountant just finishing articling."

Wa made another note. "And do you remember seeing anything

unusual tonight? Anything out of the ordinary?"

"How do you mean?"

"Did you see anyone you didn't recognize? Hear any unusual sounds?"

Roy thought for a moment and then looked up at the detective. "Is this about Kathy? Is she all right? I saw her go out on the stretcher."

"I can't talk about the specific details of the case sir. Did you see or hear anything tonight that struck you as unusual? Anything at all?"

"Yeah well," he said slowly, "I guess. Yeah. When I got home from work. There was some dude in the hallway. I remember because I had to squeeze to one side to get past him. I was carrying my bike."

"Some dude?"

"Yeah, some guy I hadn't seen before. He was sort of wandering down the hall like he was looking for an apartment. I was out of breath because I rode my bike from work. Otherwise I would've asked if he needed help or whatever but..."

"What time did this happen?"

"Well," Roy said, thinking, "it would've been between six o'clock and six-fifteen. I get off work at five and by the time I get changed and down to my bike, I don't get home until then."

"Did you get a good look at him?"

Roy again contemplated the question before answering. "Yeah, actually, I'd say so. He was kinda odd looking. Thin and dressed a little sloppy. He might've even looked a little nervous."

Wa could barely contain his excitement. It was their first break. If they could finally get a physical description of the assailant they'd have something to work with, somewhere to start.

"That's great, sir," Wa said. "We'll need you to come down to the station to complete a full statement. What you've told me could be very helpful."

By the end of the night the detectives had discovered that an unusual looking, nervous individual had been seen by four people on Kathy Fineman's floor: the junior accountant, an elderly lady who lived just down the hall, and a couple in their forties.

Wa refused to let this break slip through his fingers. All four tenants were escorted down to the police station to provide full statements. Before the end of the evening he also called in a police artist to produce a composite sketch of the suspect from the descriptions of all four witnesses.

It was mid-morning on Friday before Mitchell Wa finally returned home, exhausted, but satisfied that they finally had a break: a clear picture of the rapist.

seventeen

99th day (friday)

The light from the fridge was all Dr. Michael Wenton needed as he stooped in front of its open door. He reached for the flat cardboard box which lay on the bottom self. As he turned away from the fridge, he caught the door with the back of his leg and it swung shut with a rattle of bottles and jars.

With the fridge shut, the only light that filtered through to the kitchen was a green flickering haze from a large-screen TV in the living room. The size of the screen nearly dwarfed the condominium. It was a luxurious apartment in an expensive fifteen-storey complex. The building was close to the university, which suited Wenton. Although the apartment's design was spacious and open, he'd stuffed it with oversized furniture and an impressive entertainment centre. Shelves held speakers that provided full THX surround sound and an enormous bookcase was packed with the colourful cases of DVDs. It was the only luxury, the only indulgence, that Wenton allowed himself.

He dropped the pizza box on the kitchen counter and flipped the top back. He questioned the wisdom of eating it. It was three nights old and he knew that the jalapeno, ham, and black olive pizza shouldn't be kept too long. He shrugged and pulled the last two pieces out of the box, dropping them onto a plate. He turned and went into the living room.

He paused in front of his bookcase, scanned the titles and stopped at *Pulp Fiction*. The Quentin Tarantino film suited his mood tonight—violent, fast-paced, and full of dark humour. He set his plate down on the coffee table and slid the disc into his player. He dropped back onto the couch and automatically adjusted the pillows until he was perfectly comfortable. He reached for a large remote that controlled the TV, DVD player, and the sound system. Soon, the scream lit up with the familiar scene of a couple in a diner discussing a "robbery."

The phone's shrill ring sounded a second time and Wenton frowned. It was unusual for him to receive a phone call at home. There was no answering machine to pick up the call. Wenton avoided systems that obligated him to return calls. He didn't like commitment.

The phone rang a third time and he stood. He walked slowly into the kitchen and retrieved his cordless phone from a cradle on the wall. It was the only phone in his apartment. He looked at the call display on the receiver; the call was listed as "Out of Area."

He waited for the sixth ring before he pressed the answer button. "Wenton."

"Michael?" a surprised female voice questioned.

"Yeah."

"Hi there," the voice replied, more friendly now.

"Who is this?" Wenton refused to play games and did not like his privacy invaded.

"Marion Thomas," she answered, taken aback by Wenton's abrupt tone. "Um, I work in the main office."

It was a receptionist from the Department of Psychology. "What's the matter?" he asked without emotion.

"Oh, nothing. Nothing's wrong, Dr. Wenton," she replied. "I just wanted to call and talk to you."

Wenton didn't respond. He didn't want to encourage conversation.

"Anyway," she continued, "I just wanted to say hello and ask you about something."

Wenton hated the tentative manner in which she was approaching whatever she wanted to ask. "Yes?"

"Yeah, well, I, I mean, my husband and I were going to go out tonight for a drink and, well, I have this really great friend, Angela, who I wondered if..."

Wenton's head began to pound. He carefully selected his words. "How'd you get this number?"

She hesitated. "Why?"

"My number is unlisted."

"There's, ah, staff lists."

"You used a staff list to call me at home and try and set me up on date?" he asked through clenched teeth.

She hesitated again. "I'm sorry. I hope I didn't upset you. I never intended to..."

"Marion," he said deliberately emphasizing her name, "my personal life is mine."

"I know, sir," she said becoming overly deferential. "I sincerely apologize for—"

Wenton hung up and stood for a moment attempting to regain his composure. He knew that he shouldn't be angry with the receptionist. There was no harm intended by her call, but he insisted on a strict division between his personal and professional life. A mistake early in his career had forced this rigid separation. He would never allow such a mistake again.

He shook his head to clear it of doubt over the exchange. He returned to the couch and restarted *Pulp Fiction.* John Travolta's character had just accidentally shot the head off the young passenger he and Samuel L. Jackson had been driving with.

eighteen

100th day (saturday)

"So another girl got it last night, eh Moe?" Melvin asked nonchalantly as he sat in one of the waiting chairs. He was holding a newspaper Moe provided for his customers.

Saturday was a busy day at Moe's Barbershop. Many customers with steady jobs waited for the weekend to make their visit to Moe's. At that moment, Bill Maple was in Moe's barber chair.

"Wasn't last night," Moe answered without missing a click of his scissors. "It was Thursday night."

"Moe's right," Bill chimed in.

"Whatever," Melvin continued. "Damn shame I'd say. Should castrate this guy if they catch him."

"Oh, they'll catch him soon enough I suppose," Bill said.

"You figure?" Moe asked as he leaned over to eyeball his work. He made a quick snip and took another look, peering across the back of Bill's hairline.

"Damn sure," Bill replied. "I heard on the car radio on the way here that the police finally got a picture of the bastard."

"You don't say," Moe replied. His attention became fixed on the finishing touches on top of Bill's head.

"Damn right. They say they finally got the break they needed because a few people saw the guy at that woman's place on Thursday. I guess they got one of them police drawings."

"That should help."

"I heard it's in the damn paper there." Bill turned his head suddenly. "Melvin is there a picture in that paper?"

"Hey!" Moe scolded as he pulled his scissors away from Bill's twisting head.

Melvin scanned the front page of the paper, then flipped it open to the second. An odd expression crossed his face as he stared at the page. "Yep," he finally said. "It's here."

"So what's he look like?" Bill asked as he settled back into the barber chair.

Melvin hesitated before he responded. "Say Moe, what happened to that retarded guy that swept the floors?"

Moe paused and turned to him. "He wasn't retarded. He was mental and I don't know what happened to the bastard. He took off out of here a couple of days ago and hasn't been back. Good riddance, I say."

Melvin pursed his lips and nodded, his eyes fixed on the paper.

Moe didn't return to Bill's hair, but waited for more of an explanation.

"What was that kid's name?" Melvin finally asked.

"Edward something. Why? What the hell's gotten into you?"

Melvin stood and walked over to Bill and Moe. He held the paper out and they all stared at the black and white drawing of the suspect in the serial rape investigation. There was no mistaking the man in the picture. Even though the drawing was a composite based on several people's verbal reports, the image was undeniable. It was Edward.

nineteen

100th day (saturday)

Late Saturday Moe Crawster phoned the police station. He claimed that the composite drawing in the newspaper looked very much like an assistant he'd had working at his shop. The call was immediately transferred to Detective Margaret Meredith, the only member of the investigating team who was at the station. She insisted that Moe come down in person to provide a full statement and then paged Mitchell Wa who arrived fifteen minutes later.

Soon, Wa and Margaret were seated in an interview room with Moe Crawster. They quickly learned that an individual named Edward Carter was placed at Moe's Barbershop as part of a community reintegration work program from the Regional Mental Health Initiative. He began work almost five months ago, either late December or early January, but had recently disappeared. With some reluctance, Moe told the detectives about discovering Edward in the backroom, "jerking off." He denied having ever witnessed any other deviant behaviour, sexual or otherwise. He reported that Edward was a strange fellow, but then again, he didn't know what to expect from "a mental patient."

"All right, Mr. Crawster," Wa said. "Thank you for your time tonight. One last thing, though, how confident are you that this picture is Edward Carter?" Wa held a copy of the composite drawing. "The man who worked in your shop?"

Moe pursed his lips and stared at the picture for a moment. "Listen," he began, "I ain't saying that Edward's a rapist or anything—don't get me wrong—but that drawing may as well be a portrait of the guy."

Margaret and Wa looked at each other with something bordering on excitement and relief. She stood to escort Mr. Crawster out of the interview room.

As the two left, Wa leaned back in his chair and held the drawing up. "Hello, Edward. I think it's time we met."

102nd day (monday)

Wa felt an incredible sense of urgency. They had a name for the face in the composite drawing; he wanted to find out everything he could about Edward Carter. What he wanted to know most was where in the hell Edward Carter was. He disappeared from Moe's Barbershop last Thursday, the date of the most recent rape. A search of Edward's apartment hadn't provided any clues. There was no evidence that he moved out, but apparently Edward was not one to collect a lot of personal items. Moe Crawster had informed police that he found the keys to Edward's apartment in the lock Thursday night. He'd gone up to Edward's suite with the intention of kicking him out, but discovered it was unnecessary—he was already gone.

After taking Moe Crawster's statement, a police notification was sent out to bring Edward Carter in for questioning. By Sunday afternoon the investigating team was actively trying to track down any information that might help determine his whereabouts. With great difficulty Wa managed to contact a representative from the Regional Mental Health Initiative on Sunday afternoon, who informed him that Edward had no immediate family in the city and advised the police to speak to Dr. Leonard Darious, Edward's community psychiatrist. After a short argument with Dr. Darious' answering service Wa was connected directly to the psychiatrist. They arranged to meet first thing Monday morning in his private office.

When Makum and Wa arrived at Dr. Darious' office they were greeted by a receptionist, who sat behind a small Plexiglas window in an office adjoining the waiting room. There were no other patients: Dr. Darious had explained, "I don't normally work on Monday mornings."

"Hi." Wa said leaning over to speak to the metal grid fixed in the middle of the Plexiglas window. "This is Detective Makum and I'm Detective Wa. We're here to see Dr. Darious."

"Yes sir," the receptionist said quickly. "He will be with you right away."

Makum couldn't resist. "He musta pulled you in this morning special, eh? Since I guess you don't usually work on Monday mornings."

"No sir. The office staff is here to book appointments, catch up on paperwork, and so forth. It's just Dr. Darious who isn't normally here."

Her quick answers and uneasy tone suggested that she wasn't used to speaking with the police. Wa tried not to be overly suspicious.

Just then an older man opened a door next to the receptionist's office. He was of average build with graying hair receding across the top. He wore dark slacks and a sport coat with a wool sweater vest beneath. He nodded at the detectives.

"Gentlemen, I'm Dr. Leonard Darious."

Wa took a step toward him holding out his hand. "I'm Detective Mitchell Wa and this is my partner Detective Roland Makum."

Darious shook the detectives' hands and then waved them down the corridor.

Soon they were seated in his comfortable private office. A large oak desk separated him from the two leather and wood seats where the detectives sat. The room was furnished with heavy wooden pieces and a large wood and glass bookshelf. There was a window behind Dr. Darious' desk. The office smelled of dust and worn leather. Wa noticed a leather couch hidden in the back of the room and smiled at the image of psychiatrists and their trademark couches.

"So gentlemen," Dr. Darious began, "you're here because of Edward Carter, are you?"

"Maybe," Wa replied as he reached into his jacket and pulled out the composite drawing. He unfolded the paper and handed it across the oak desk to Dr. Darious. "Can you identify the man in that picture?"

Darious looked at it with a passive expression and then handed it back before answering. "It could very well be Edward."

"Fair enough. We'd like to ask you a few questions about your patient."

Dr. Darious leaned back and folded his arms across his chest. His large oak chair creaked beneath him as he sighed. "There's a little matter of patient confidentiality."

Makum grunted and Wa looked quickly at him to silence his partner. He looked back at the psychiatrist.

"Dr. Darious, Edward Carter is the prime suspect in the serial rapes that have been terrorizing the city every second Thursday for the last four months. We want to locate him in order to eliminate him as a suspect or to further investigate him for the crimes. Either way we'd appreciate your help."

Darious frowned and looked away from the detectives. He turned his chair with a creak and stood. He clasped his hands behind him and took a leisurely step or two out from behind his desk. Wa and Makum watched with some confusion as Darious strolled over to his bookcase and looked through the glass panes as if he were searching for a book.

Makum turned to Wa with a *what the fuck?* expression. Wa shrugged.

"Gentlemen," Darious said finally as he spun to face them, "I must weigh the welfare and confidentiality of my client against the safety of the community. It is a difficult role for a psychiatrist to be in. One must never break the sacred bond of patient–doctor lightly." As he spoke, he moved back to his seat and sat, dropping his arms on top of the desk with his fingers together. "However," he continued, "in this case I am sure that there is some gross misunderstanding, some case of mistaken identity. I have worked with the individual in question for the last five months since his discharge from hospital. My time with Edward overlaps completely with the dates of the crimes and I must assure you that he is no rapist."

"That's really very encouraging," Makum said with more than a hint of sarcasm. "But our job forces us to actually talk to the suspects in person."

Dr. Darious ignored the comment. "I will provide you with information on Edward Carter because I believe it is in his best interest. From what you told me on the phone he is currently missing from his work placement and I believe that he needs to be found for his own sake. He is too fragile an individual to survive on the streets. I am confident that the misunderstanding about Edward and these rapes will be resolved shortly after he is located."

"We really appreciate your willingness to help," Wa said. "We'd like to get some information on his history, his family, and anything else that might help us understand who we're looking for."

Darious took in a deep breath before responding. "Well, diagnostically, Edward meets criteria for schizophrenia—paranoid type."

"So the guy has multiple personalities," Makum said.

"No. That's a common misconception about schizophrenia. The disorder is distinct from multiple personalities or, as the current diagnostic system refers to it, dissociative identity disorder. In schizophrenia there are prominent hallucinations or delusions, but there is nothing about multiple, distinct personalities. A true case of dissociative identity disorder, or multiple personality, is extremely rare—much more so than schizophrenia which affects somewhere between one and two percent of the population over their life span."

"Bottom line is that this guy's crazy, right?" Makum retorted, feeling somewhat like a student who'd just gotten a question wrong in front of the whole class.

Dr. Darious laughed softly and shook his head. "Crazy is such an awful term. But yes, Edward Carter suffers from a serious psychiatric condition that requires pharmacological intervention in order to maintain an improved state of mental health."

"He's crazy," Makum said flatly and nodded at Wa.

The psychiatrist ignored the comment and directed his attention to Wa. "Edward was an extremely sick individual while in hospital. He was found to be somewhat unresponsive to many of the traditional neuroleptic medications but eventually was stabilized on a dose of a newer medication: quetiapine at two milligrams per day."

Over the next two hours the detectives learned that Dr. Darious liked to talk. With only a few questions to redirect the psychiatrist, they learned a great deal about Edward Carter. His mother, Carmen Carter, was a teenage girl from a fundamentalist family. Her unwanted pregnancy was carried to term because the family's religious views did not permit abortion. Complications at birth led many doctors to predict that Edward would be developmentally delayed, possibly mentally retarded. This was never the case, but the family insisted on institutionalizing the infant anyway. They were unwilling to take the chance of suffering the double indignity of raising a mental retard who was also a bastard.

As Dr. Darious continued to describe Edward's history, the detectives learned that his institutionalization as an infant may have, temporarily, saved him from the dark secrets of his fundamentalist family. Only two years after giving birth to Edward, Carmen Carter hanged herself with an electrical cord in the family basement. It was soon discovered that her staunchly religious father had been sexually abusing her for years and was actually Edward's father. After her daughter's suicide, Mrs. Carter finally spoke out against her husband and admitted that Carmen had never been allowed boyfriends. As rumour and allegations flew around the Carters, Mr. Carter reached a breaking point. The police were on their way to the family home to begin preliminary inquiries into the allegations of abuse, when three blasts resounded through the neighbourhood. Mr. Carter shot and killed his wife and eight-year-old son, then put the rifle in his mouth and pulled the trigger. It was less than two weeks after Carmen's suicide.

By this time, Edward was in a foster home. The Social Services agency in charge of his placement decided that the young child was better off not knowing what had happened to his biological family.

Although the doctor's predictions of developmental delays never materialized, Edward's childhood was difficult. He was moved from foster home to foster home until, at the age of thirteen, he was placed with a solid couple in a middle-class neighbourhood. The couple explained to Edward that they couldn't have children and that it was their duty as Christians to help the less fortunate. They considered their participation in the Social Services placement program to be a way of living up to their duty, and it justified God's decision to leave them without their own children. Edward soon became a regular churchgoer and student of the Bible. Without realizing it, he'd found his way back into a fundamentalist family.

Dr. Darious paused and asked whether either detective wanted something to drink. They each agreed to coffee and the psychiatrist picked up his phone to connect to the receptionist. After speaking briefly to her he hung up and continued.

Edward was deeply drawn to the religious views of his new family. It gave him a meaning and focus that was lacking in his life. As a young child he'd struggled with answers to questions about why he should shift constantly from family to family, community to community, without ever finding a place to call his own. Just as he was beginning to feel totally lost he found his new family. By the age of seventeen, he'd established an entirely new identity. He was a devoted son to his foster mother and father. He fully endorsed their conservative social views and strong religious idealism. He spent many hours after school reading the Bible and eagerly anticipated the day-long church services on Sunday.

"And then it all went fell to pieces," Dr. Darious said with a frown of concern.

He explained that Edward had suddenly become curious about his origins. To this point he knew nothing of his real mother and father or the reasons he'd been put up for adoption. With some assistance from his foster parents, he contacted Social Services. Having kept his last name he was able to more easily bypass some of the obstacles to identifying his biological parents.

"Naturally," Dr. Darious continued, "he eventually contacted someone at the Child Welfare office who knew the true story. At that point Edward was shut down hard and fast."

The Child Welfare worker saw the red flags all over the Carter file and quickly told Edward that there was no information available and he shouldn't pursue it. The intensity of the response left him even more curious about his biological family and he decided to continue his search for answers. He encountered nothing but roadblocks at every level of Social Services and decided that he needed a different approach. One day he told his foster parents he was going to the public library and headed out. He pulled some old microfiche of newspapers from around the time he was born. He was probably looking for a birth announcement that could help narrow the search. He wouldn't have found anything in the newspapers at the time of his birth for obvious reasons. But somehow, and no one knew how, he stumbled across the articles on Carmen's suicide and the subsequent murder-suicide of the rest of the family by Mr. Carter.

"Well, poor Edward lost it. His religious beliefs crashed headlong into his family origins. He was the bastard child of the incestuous union of his grandfather and mother. More than that his whole family had died at the hands of his father-grandfather." Darious paused and shook his head. "It makes my head spin just trying to explain it."

The detectives learned that Edward had his first psychotic break in the library that day. With the newspaper article still centred in the microfiche machine, he'd gone on a rampage, pulling down bookshelves, attacking staff, and shouting, "I am Satan. Satan commands me." He was apprehended and sent for a psychiatric evaluation. Under the circumstances, no charges were laid for the damage in the library. Edward was committed to a psychiatric facility and remained there in a semi-catatonic state for two years. Shortly after his admission to the hospital, his foster parents broke off contact with him. They felt unable to cope with the news of Edward's origins and his current mental illness. They blamed Social Services for not providing more information when they had first become involved with him.

Edward didn't respond well to any medication during this time and the medical staff were at a loss for what to do. After approximately two years he slowly came around, but remained plagued by severe hallucinations. Psychiatric staff always experienced difficulties in clearly identifying Edward's symptoms since he refused to talk about them in detail. His vague descriptions only indicated that he heard voices somehow linked to Satan and that he was somehow under the control of evil. At best, medication had only been able to suppress the hallucinations and allow him to live a semi-normal life. Edward was now twenty-seven years old and had spent as much of his adult life in psychiatric hospitals as out.

Early last year he was living in a group home with other psychiatric patients when he was attacked by a roommate. The other patient had stopped taking his medication and quickly decompensated. Edward was knocked unconscious during the assault but otherwise not seriously hurt. There was no evidence of a concussion. Unfortunately, the incident temporarily disrupted the delicate regimen of pharmacological intervention that kept Edward mentally healthy. As a result he too became ill and was re-admitted to hospital until his psychiatric medications could be adjusted. At the time, Edward was on fifty milligrams of loxapine but for some reason it appeared to lose its effectiveness and he began developing side effects such as involuntary movements of his mouth.

Dr. Darious demonstrated by rotating his jaw in random jerking motions before continuing.

"That's why Edward was started on the quetiapine. It was hoped that he wouldn't experience the same side effects and overall it appeared to work. Edward was discharged after Christmas last year when the hospital team got him hooked up with RMHI. You indicated that you already spoke with them. They basically try to get patients back into the community as quickly as possible and hook the patients up with people who are willing to give them work. That's how Edward got the job with Moe Crawster at the barbershop."

"Any comments on Edward's relationships with women?" Wa asked.

"Of course," Dr. Darious nodded intensely as though he'd forgotten something obvious. "Sex. A natural question given the circumstances." He leaned back in his chair to consider his answer. "You have to understand, gentlemen, that schizophrenia is a complicated disorder.

Generally, we see two types of symptoms. Positive symptoms—these are the active psychotic symptoms like the hallucinations or delusions. Negative symptoms, those of mood and interpersonal orientation. Individuals with schizophrenia are typically quiet with depressed mood or flat affect. They don't feel or express emotion in the same way as you or me. They struggle with their relationships with people. They typically retreat from the world and fear interaction with others. It is a scary experience to be mentally ill, and those suffering from earlier onset schizophrenia often have immature, socially-delayed personalities that further restrict their ability to establish relationships with others. Edward was a shy, quiet individual who wanted nothing more than to do his job and return to his apartment to read his Bible. He never expressed any interest in sexual or intimate relationships nor was he ever suspected of any deviant sexual arousal. Nor, for that matter, did he ever express any violence or aggression toward others. He has always been very passive and cooperative." Darious sat up in his chair and looked intently at Wa. "You see Detective, that's why I say you have the wrong guy. He's had a tremendously tough go of it but he is certainly not a cold, calculating rapist who preys on women every Thursday night."

"Every second Thursday," Makum corrected him.

Dr. Darious looked briefly at the Detective to acknowledge the comment and then returned to Wa.

"Where might he go now, Doctor?" Wa asked.

"I think that if Edward was in trouble he might return to the hospital or wind up in a homeless shelter. Or he might contact me." He paused. "Or he might just keep running. If he is getting ill again he might be too disoriented to formulate a plan. I really don't know, Detectives."

"If he does contact you...," Wa began as he reached into his jacket to retrieve a business card.

"I know. I know. I'll contact you immediately."

"We'd appreciate that," Wa said as he handed the business card across the desk.

twenty

102nd day (monday)

Edward squinted up at the sign. The afternoon sun flickered off windows on the surrounding buildings, making it difficult to see. The faded sign hung on two small lengths of chain and read Second Chance. He pushed through the set of double glass doors into the single-storey building.

The building was a modified warehouse that stood in contrast to the large apartment buildings and office towers nearby. Edward was in an older part of the city where years of neglect had left most of the buildings in poor condition. Second Chance was a non-profit shelter for homeless people. According to its mission statement, it provided temporary lodging and meals for people "down on their luck." The passage of time and government cutbacks had left Second Chance somewhat the worse for wear. The warehouse was divided roughly down the middle with half of the area serving as the kitchen and dining area and the other part a makeshift sleeping area with cots occupying virtually every square foot. The room smelled faintly of urine and had a strong smell of body odour. A poorly constructed check-in was located next to the front doors and a young man in his mid-twenties stood at the desk. He was thin and tall with a permanent expression of concern etched on his face. He watched Edward enter and remained silent as he looked around the room.

"Don't recognize you," the young man finally said.

Edward turned to him.

"I don't often see new faces down here I'm happy to say."

Edward simply stared at the young man.

"*He's a fucker*,"the voices screamed at him.

"Having a bit of a hard time, eh?"

"Don't talk to this motherfucker."

"It doesn't suit us."

"Take us away."

"Yeah," Edward said after a slight hesitation.

The man mistook Edward's awkwardness for embarrassment—not an uncommon feeling for first time visitors.

"Hey, listen," he said coming out from behind the desk, "things'll work out. You probably just need a breather while you get back on your feet." He came up beside Edward.

"*Don't let the fucker touch us*," the voices screamed in his head.

The young man put his arm around Edward's shoulders.

"*Ahhhhhhhh!*"

"Come on in. Grab a cup of coffee." The young man led Edward into the kitchen and up to a table with a massive aluminum coffee urn. He sat Edward down nearby and then grabbed a chipped, stained cup, filling it with coffee. "Cream or sugar?"

Edward could barely understand the man's question. He shook his head.

The young man handed the coffee to Edward.

"*Throw the coffee in his fuckin' face*," the voices screamed.

Edward looked down at the steaming mug he held in his hands and then back up to the young man. The man's eyes sunk away into his head and left gaping black holes. A dark ooze leaked out of the sockets and twisted and slithered down the man's face. Edward quickly looked back at his cup.

"You'll be fine," the man said in a comforting voice. "You're safe here."

twenty-one

103rd day (tuesday)

Detective Mitchell Wa settled into a chair in the familiar conference room. The other members of the investigative team were present, including their liaison to the officers, Constable Bill Lawrence.

"All right," Wa began, "we appear to be making some progress here. We have a name for the suspect—Edward Carter. He was initially identified by his former employer, Mr. Moe Crawster, and then Roland and I had a very interesting conversation with Edward's psychiatrist yesterday." He looked at Makum who nodded. "I've called this meeting just to make sure we're all on track and to give you a more complete update than our informal chats yesterday." He paused and lifted a glass of water to his mouth.

"First off, Dr. Leonard Darious turned out to be reasonably helpful. He gave us a quick history of this Edward character. Apparently, Edward is certifiably insane and needs medication. Since he disappeared under somewhat stressful circumstances, it's more than likely that the guy's off meds. This means he's likely not mentally stable and should be approached with extreme caution." He looked directly at Constable Lawrence to emphasize the message that needed to get out to the ground troops.

"Sorry sir," Bill interrupted. "What were the 'stressful circumstances' of his disappearance?"

"Right," Wa said as if he'd just remembered. "In Mr. Crawster's statement he told us that he'd caught this Edward guy masturbating in the backroom of the barbershop. It was right in the middle of the day—Thursday—the day of the most recent rape. Well, I guess old Edward took off after he was caught and didn't return."

"Thanks," Bill said nodding.

"So on the advice of Dr. Darious, we're keeping a watch on the hospital and community clinics. Edward might go to a place he considers safe, a place that's familiar to him—the psychiatric ward. We've started circulating his picture to the clinics and asked them to contact us if he shows up. I guess Edward might also go back to Dr. Darious, who's agreed to contact us in that event."

"Hey Mitchell," Laurie asked, "were you going to tell us about the guy's mental illness?"

Wa shook his head. "I'm rambling. Sorry. Dr. Darious tells us that Edward is a paranoid schizophrenic."

"Which doesn't mean he has two personalities," Makum interjected, smugly.

Wa smiled. "Right. Schizophrenia is more a classic kind of crazy—like hearing voices and seeing weird shit. Darious didn't really have a lot of information about exactly what Edward's hallucinations and delusions were. The guy keeps to himself mostly, but apparently there are some religious themes to his illness—something about how his family was evil."

"Really?" said Laurie with obvious interest. "*Was* his family 'evil?'"

"In a way. His birth was the result of the sexual molestation of a young woman by her father. When the scandal of the abuse broke the father ended up killing the family, but not before Edward's mother hanged herself."

"Holy shit," Bill breathed.

Wa shrugged, unsure of what else he could add. After a moment he turned to Bill. "Why don't you give a quick update on the search of the city."

Bill nodded and straightened in his chair. Being included on this investigative team was a big step toward moving up in rank. It was part of a grooming process and he wanted to be thorough and professional. "Well, we have a grid for the city, and uniformed teams within each grid. We're focusing most of our attention in the downtown area because transients more easily lose themselves there. We've got extra teams out patrolling these areas, talking to people on the street, and circulating the composite drawing."

Wa interrupted. "We're trying to get a real picture from the hospital chart at Atlantic Coast but there have been a few snags getting in that area. Sorry, go ahead."

"So, we're showing the composite around and trying to get at least a sequence of events, a timeline for where the guy's been or who he's seen. So far nothing. He seems to have left the scene of the assault and vanished."

"Well let's keep digging," Wa said with a neutral expression.

"We're in the shelters too?" Makum asked, indicating the police search should include the few homeless shelters and soup kitchens in the downtown core.

"Yep, they're in specific grids so they get covered as part of the natural search pattern."

"Okay. He's going to pop up soon. I can feel it." Wa looked to Laurie and Margaret. "And you've finished talking to the victims. Any updates there?"

The two detectives looked at each and Laurie motioned for Margaret to take the lead.

"I've never seen anything like this," Margaret began with an expression of concern. "Each of the women is truly disturbed by her experience. None was able to provide a coherent account of the crime. We did show the composite drawing to the last few we interviewed and they didn't react. They looked at the picture as if they were seeing it for the first time. Nothing."

"You mean he's not our guy?" Makum asked with impatience and frustration.

"Not exactly. The victims partially recognize Edward's picture, but insist that there were other people involved. We're still getting strange stories like an ex-boyfriend, old family members, or some other bizarre person being involved in the rape." She smiled an awkward smile of discomfort.

"Let's remember that it's entirely possible that he's not our guy," Wa said firmly. "At the moment we simply have him identified at the scene of the most recent rape. Nothing else. We want him for questioning. In fact, his psychiatrist virtually swore that there's no way Edward Carter is the rapist."

"Well," Margaret continued, "we'll submit a report on the interviews with the victims. I wish there were more to give you today. I think it's going to help to get this Edward guy in here and have a chat, but whoever this rapist is, he's fucking these women up in ways I didn't think possible."

The table fell silent as each thought about what that meant.

twenty-two

103rd day (tuesday)

"He's acting pretty strange," Larry, the young man at the front desk at Second Chance told Laura.

Laura had just arrived to relieve Larry at the homeless shelter. At each shift change, staff would update each other on new clients, any difficult situations that were developing, or whatever else was happening at the shelter.

"Do we have his name or anything yet?" Laura asked with concern.

"No, he's been pretty quiet. I think he's got some issues that he needs to work out. He's not real comfortable being here."

"Yeah, I noticed that last night. He wouldn't even go for dinner. He just lay in a bunk all night staring at the ceiling. Some of the guys around him reported that he was mumbling to himself."

"Yeah, I heard that today too. Anyway, keep an eye on him."

"Will do," she said and stood straight to offer a mock salute.

Larry grinned at her. "I'll see you later." He turned with his jacket in hand and stepped toward the door. He hadn't taken more than a few steps before he turned back.

"Oh, and Laura? The cops were here yesterday. I forgot to tell you. They're shaking down the whole neighbourhood..."

"LAURA!" a voice from the kitchen screamed. She turned to look and saw one of the cooks standing with her hands on her hips in a defiant pose.

She turned back. "What's that? Sorry, Larry."

"Nothing, I was just saying the police dropped off this picture yester—"

"LAURA!" the cook yelled again.

Laura turned back to the cook and waved her away, indicating she'd be right down. She looked back to Larry. "I gotta go."

"Yep," he said. "I was just saying the cops left a picture of the guy they're looking for. It's in the desk here. I never even got a chance to look at it."

"Good, thanks," she called back over her shoulder and disappeared into the dining area.

Larry shrugged, turned, and headed home.

Edward's body was soaked in cold sweat. Every few moments a chill shook him so violently he thought it might be a seizure. He'd left this small bed only once today to eat lunch. The voices had driven him out of bed because they didn't want him to die. Edward wanted to die.

He stared at the rough ceiling with numerous burned out fluorescent tubes. He tried little tricks to take his mind off the evil that lived in him. He counted the number of burnt out bulbs, then counted them again. He counted the number of times a particular light flickered in one minute. Nothing helped.

"Why are we here?" the voices asked.

"We don't belong here with these fucks."

"Take us away."

Edward softly argued against them. "Leave me alone."

Another resident of the shelter rested in a cot next to Edward. Henry Yargurl was a large, burly man in his early forties. A thick beard covered his face and his long, naturally curly hair was a mat on his head. He lay with his arms behind his head and his eyes closed. At the sound of Edward's soft voice he rolled his head to look at him. "What'd you say?"

"*Take us away.*"

"No more," Edward answered the demons in his head.

"You talking to me?" Henry asked more loudly now.

A chill shook Edward violently and he turned to see the man. Through a haze he saw only black eyes staring at him and a thick covering of writhing black hair. He looked up and down the man's body and saw the large frame bubbling and shifting like a tarp blowing in the wind. He closed his eyes against the horrible sight and rolled over.

"Fucker," Henry announced and turned away from Edward.

"Lights out," Laura called to the room. The sleeping hall was still teeming with motion as people tucked coffee mugs away, finished making plans for tomorrow, and settled into cots. At curfew the lights were shut off. The shelter's program included strict policies regarding hours. Everyone was in bed by 10:30 at night. This meant everyone was up early in the morning. The goal was to discourage a comfortable routine where people used the shelter for a prolonged period of time.

With a minimal amount of grumbling the room quieted. Laura turned to the wall and flicked a series of light switches. Darkness descended, leaving only the light from the kitchen to filter in and cast shadows throughout the room. She headed back to the desk where she would read under a small desk lamp until her shift ended at midnight.

Henry rolled onto his side and closed his eyes. He decided tomorrow was the day. He was going to get himself off the streets once and for all. He had a lead on a job and he wasn't going to let this one slip through his fingers.

He began drifting off to sleep.

"*Facini entfaste blackened side*."

Words slipped into Henry's consciousness but he couldn't quite make them out.

"*Facini entfaste blackened side*."

He continued to doze as the words slid over him.

"*Facini entfaste blackened side, blackened side, blackened side*."

The words were like a hum or a buzzing that he couldn't shake. It held him in that place between being awake and being asleep. He strained to understand what the words were saying.

"*Please don't, Daddy*," a small child's voice cried.

Henry's eyes shot open. It was the sound of his daughter. He listened closely but heard nothing more. He closed his eyes, figuring it must have been his imagination playing tricks on him.

The moment his eyelids shut an image flashed through his mind. His oldest daughter was standing naked in front of him with tears streaming down her face. He gasped and opened his eyes again. The image slowly faded and he felt his body shake as though he were having a convulsion.

"*Facini entfaste blackened side*."

That voice again. He didn't understand. He tried to block it out.

"*Facini entfaste blackened side*."

He couldn't.

"*Facini entfaste blackened side*."

FUCKING VOICE! Henry screamed in his head.

He peered through the darkness. He was sure it was the new guy mumbling, and he was going to shut him up. What he saw drove the air out of his lungs like someone had punched him.

Across the room he saw his two little girls walking toward him. He sat straight up and watched in amazement. The girls continued moving in a slow, awkward fashion, barely shuffling their feet, gliding along effortlessly. Henry's heart pounded in his chest as the girls came closer and closer. The girls were also speaking to him:

"*Daddy, please don't. It hurts, Daddy*."

"I didn't...," he started, but choked on his own words.

"*No Daddy, I don't like it*."

"Please stop, I never did it. I love you," Henry whimpered.

The girls were close enough that he could see them clearly. Their faces looked old and worn. Tears streamed down their cheeks. The girls were both completely naked and their skin was wrinkled and grey. Henry could barely stand to look at them.

"Why?" he whispered. "What happened?"

"*Daddy?*" the girls said as they came to a stop. "*No more*."

"I can't," he screamed, and fell backwards onto the bed. He closed his eyes and brought his hands to his face. He pressed his fists into his eyes until he saw bright specks of light. He didn't want to open his eyes again.

"*Facini entfaste blackened side.*"

He gagged but couldn't find any air to replace his breath. He felt panic sweep over him. He strained to listen for the sound of his girls but heard nothing. He wondered whether he should risk opening his eyes again.

He lifted his hands away and his lids opened a crack. He rolled his head to the side to look for his girls. He saw only a faint outline of a face, a pitch-black face, blacker than the night around it. The face was close enough to his own that he should have been able to feel the heat of its breath. He felt only a cool, wet presence against him.

"*Facini entfaste blackened side.*"

He tried to open his mouth to scream for help. He simply couldn't breathe, couldn't find any strength to bring air into his lungs. He wanted to reach up and push the black face away from him but he couldn't raise his arms. He felt an urgency, a desperation that he'd never experienced before. He wanted to escape.

"*Facini entfaste blackened side*."

Then he noticed two strands snaking away from the black shape in front of him. The two tentacles circled through the air and attached themselves to his neck, wrapped around him, choking the air from him. From somewhere inside he found the strength to move his arms. He lifted them to grab at the monster. His hands touched something cold, something wet and he held on.

"*Facini...*"

The voice stopped. The tentacles uncurled from his throat and he choked as air returned to him. His hands went limp, releasing the strange, wet thing. It faded backwards as if it were escaping into the darkness of the room. He watched in reluctant amazement as the thing sunk onto the cot of the man next to him. He was about to scream for the man to run when the haze of the room lifted slightly.

He craned his neck as he stared at the cot. He could see a man lying on his side. The man stared back with a blank expression. To Henry, the man could have been dead. The eyes burned back at him with a vacancy that made him shiver.

And then the man smiled.

Laura settled into her seat at the front desk. The room was dark and she could hear the sounds of sleep beginning to creep in. She picked up the book she'd left on the desk. She was finally reading something that had been on her list for years—Truman Capote's *In Cold Blood.* It fascinated her.

Someone in the room coughed and gagged. She looked up briefly but didn't see any obvious motion inside the shelter. She returned her attention to the book. People had often questioned her about her decision to work at the shelter. Given the higher percentage of male residents, many of her friends thought she would be unsafe. She'd shrugged off their concerns. She always told people that she wasn't alone. There was always staff in the back. But every once in awhile she got a creepy feeling.

Another strange gagging cough sounded from somewhere in the back of the hall. She dropped the book to the desk and looked out over the room. It was dark and difficult to tell where things were. She thought she saw motion on one side but wasn't sure. She continued to watch and listen, but heard nothing else.

She was really feeling tense and jumpy tonight. She wondered if her unease had anything to do with her choice of reading material. She shook her head, telling herself that she was being silly, and picked up her book. Before she found her spot on the page she remembered something that Larry said just before he left. Something about a picture of a guy the police were looking for.

Laura grabbed her bookmark off the desk and stuck it into the book's spine. *Now where did he put that picture?* she wondered as she pulled a drawer open.

The black and white drawing sat on top of other papers in the drawer. She picked it out and held it near the light to look at it.

Wow, she thought. *He's familiar.*

She looked at the picture more closely and scanned the bottom. There was a large warning printed at the bottom of the page: "MISSING. WANTED FOR QUESTIONING. MAY BE DANGEROUS. PLEASE CONTACT POLICE IMMEDIATELY IF YOU HAVE ANY INFORMATION ON THIS INDIVIDUAL." She looked at the picture again and sucked in her breath. Her head shot up and she looked into the dark recesses of the room. She did know the man in the picture. He was sleeping in the far corner of the room right now.

twenty-three

111th day (wednesday)

Dr. Brian Claric settled into a chair in the conference room of the North Bay unit at MSPC. He set his stainless steel thermal coffee mug down on the table and offered a smile to his colleagues seated around him. It was only shortly after nine in the morning and rounds were about to begin. The room was unusually quiet. There was no friendly banter being exchanged between Dorothy and Andy, nor was Diego telling stories of his most recent athletic adventure. Even Rhonda and Milton were silent.

"I can only guess that your mood this morning means you know who arrived yesterday," Dr. O'Connors announced as the meeting began.

Diego stood and closed the door to the room.

Dr. O'Connors continued, "We got Mr. Edward Carter yesterday. He's the suspect in a highly publicized serial rape case. I don't think I need to tell any of you the details on that one."

The team nodded in unison. The recent rape cases had obtained some notoriety in psychiatric circles because of the after-effects the victims were left with. Word of mouth had spread quickly that each of the rape victims experienced some type of mental disorder in the wake of their assaults, and some of the victims even met criteria for a full-blown schizophrenic diagnosis.

"I'll give you the lowdown on Mr. Carter's recent history."

Dr. O'Connors went on to describe Edward's recent difficulties at Moe's Barbershop, and his subsequent disappearance. She explained that the day he left his work placement was the day of the last rape—two weeks ago, tomorrow. He was discovered at a homeless shelter, Second Chance, by one of their employees. He was arrested without incident. He was formally charged and provided with legal representation from legal aid. The preliminary hearing was scheduled immediately. He was unable to instruct his lawyer and the court decided a psychiatric evaluation was necessary to determine his mental capacity to stand trial. The court was also interested in the question of criminal responsibility.

"So his preliminary hearing was yesterday," she continued, "and we got him yesterday afternoon. The jail was happy to dump the guy on us because there's some ugly press happening. I don't know if you noticed the media vans outside this morning." She paused to look around the table and saw the acknowledgments of a few. "I saw Edward right away and he wasn't particularly cooperative. There was evidence of loose associations along with prominent delusions and hallucinations with strong religious themes of persecution. He has a long mental health history with a primary diagnosis of schizophrenia—paranoid type."

Dr. O'Connors paused to take a breath. "We've already started him back on quetiapine—the medication he was on before he left the barbershop. Dr. Leonard Darious, Edward's psychiatrist in the community, called me yesterday afternoon shortly after Edward was admitted. He had some strong opinions about the whole situation. He's asked to come in and speak with me and I may do that on Friday." She turned to Andy. "I'd like you to speak with this Dr. Darious. From my previous conversation I think that the family of origin is going to play a big role in our psychiatric formulation." She next turned to Diego. "Nothing for the guy," she said, indicating that Edward should not have access to recreational activities. "Nor you, Dorothy," she said turning to the occupational therapist.

"Um, Dr. O'Connors," Rhonda interrupted, "I know from talking to the other nursing staff that there's a lot of nervous people here. There've been some pretty freaky stories going around about this case."

Her expression was one of serious concern. "You're the primary nurse, right?"

Rhonda nodded.

"Which makes you the associate, Milton?" The psychiatric nursing model of care that the MSPC used was a two-tiered system in which one nurse was identified as the primary who followed the client's care throughout, and a second nurse was designated the associate who also followed the client's care closely and provided back-up to the primary.

"I'm the associate," Milton said.

"I want this guy on close observation," Dr. O'Connors said firmly. "There need to be consistent checks on this guy at all hours of the day and night. I'm worried about suicide and I'm worried about the safety of the other clients."

"He's on close obs already," Rhonda stated as she checked the green chart that lay open in front of her. "He's been on them since admission."

"You want me to get involved at all?" Dr. Claric asked.

"Not yet. He's not stable. And, as I said, he's not really cooperative at the moment." Dr. O'Connors paused. "But if he responds quickly to the medication I'd like you to prepare a sex offender profile and perhaps a risk assessment. I think something on personality might also be helpful."

"I'll keep checking back then," Dr. Claric offered.

"Good, thanks."

The table fell silent for a moment as people digested their own involvement, or lack thereof, in the case.

"There's one other thing," Rhonda said tentatively.

The table turned to her.

"You mentioned that tomorrow is exactly two weeks since the last victim. His timeline has been one rape every two weeks. He rapes on every second Thursday, and tomorrow is Thursday."

The expressions from the other staff indicated that many were already contemplating that timeline. Until Rhonda mentioned it the table had generally avoided broaching the topic.

"I'd thought of that," Dr. O'Connors finally replied. She looked around the table. "Suggestions?"

"I guess we just follow the close obs order," Milton offered.

Dr. Claric added, "I'd suggest that all night checks be done with two staff. I wouldn't want anyone poking their head in his room all by themselves."

"He's in a single room, eh?" Dorothy asked.

Rhonda nodded. "Yeah, we figured that was easier and safer for everybody."

"So two staff on night checks?" Milton asked to confirm the order.

"Yeah, I think that makes sense. I'll make a note in the unit book," Dr. O'Connors answered.

The table fell silent again as the team members considered the decision.

twenty-four

111th (wednesday)

Detectives Mitchell Wa and Roland Makum parked across the street from the Second Chance shelter. Without a word, both exited the unmarked sedan and headed across the street. They both casually glanced around the street before entering.

An older woman stood behind a desk near the entrance. She nodded as the detectives entered. She knew immediately that they weren't prospective clients of the shelter.

"What can I do for you gentleman?" she asked.

"I'm Detective Wa and this is Detective Makum." Both showed their identification. "We're here to talk to the employee who called in the suspect the other night."

"Oh, you mean Laura," she said. "She and Larry are in the dining room." She slipped off a stool and stepped out from behind the desk. The detectives followed her around the corner and she pointed to two individuals.

Laura and Larry sat in the back of the dining room having coffee. The detectives approached the table and introduced themselves. Wa had called earlier in the day to arrange the appointment.

"Yes, we've been expecting you," Laura said. "Have a seat."

The detectives sat on the opposite side of the table facing them and Wa pulled a notebook out of his sportcoat.

"There shouldn't be too much, Ms...," he hesitated, waiting for a name.

"Garrauche," she said. "It's French." She spelled the name as Wa copied it into his book.

"Thanks. Anyway, we shouldn't be long. We just need to ask a few questions for the report. For instance, how long had Edward Carter been here? Has he been a resident here before? Et cetera."

"I don't have much to say," she answered with some disappointment. "He only arrived a day before we realized he was the suspect. That was the first time we'd ever seen him." She looked at Larry for confirmation and he nodded.

"Did any of the other residents seem to know him?" Makum asked.

"Not really," again she looked to Larry for more information.

"He really kept to himself," he added.

"When you say he 'kept to himself', what do you mean?" Wa asked.

"He really didn't talk to anyone. He just sort of..." Larry's voice trailed off.

There was movement behind Wa and he turned to see a bearded, rough looking individual.

"Can we help you, Henry?" Laura asked, addressing the man.

He'd been staring at the detectives and now he looked over at Laura. His expression was blank, as if he didn't understand what he'd been asked.

"We're kinda in the middle of something here. Could you give us a minute, Henry?" Larry asked patiently.

Henry turned his head to look at Larry. He stared at him with the same blank expression.

The detectives looked at each other and then turned back to the table.

"Are you okay, Henry?" Laura asked with a concerned expression.

"I'm evil inside," he said softly.

"What's that?" Larry asked with surprise.

"He let the evil out of me."

Wa and Makum exchanged glances and Wa turned to look back at the man again. Makum rolled his eyes and sighed.

"Okay," Laura said sympathetically. "We'll talk about it later. Why don't you go lay down?"

"He showed me my evil and now it doesn't matter anymore."

Larry stood and looked down at Laura. "I'll deal with him. You go ahead with the Detectiv—"

Before he could finish Henry raised an arm and swung at Makum's head. The glint of a kitchen knife sparkled as the end of the blade sunk into Makum's neck. Makum spasmed and reached up with both hands, trying to grab his attacker. Henry pulled back. The knife dragged away and Makum grabbed only air. Blood quickly began spewing out of the wound. Within seconds, Makum's hands were soaked in blood.

Wa was the first to react. Before Henry could strike again, he leapt out of his seat and tackled the man across the chest. He brought Henry hard to the ground and reflexively caught the knife hand, pinning it to the floor. The impact caused the knife to spin away harmlessly.

"Call 9-1-1 now!" Wa screamed as he struggled to hold the large man down. "Tell them an officer's hurt and we need back-up."

Laura and Larry stared at the scene. It had happened too quickly for them to fully comprehend. There'd never been such graphic violence at the shelter before. Residents frequently yelled and fought with each other but no one had ever been seriously hurt.

"NOW!" Wa screamed.

Larry, who was already standing, broke free of his shock and bolted away from the table heading for the phone at the front desk. Makum slumped against the table gripping the wound in his neck. Blood was pulsing out through the space between his fingers and his hands were already bathed in dark red. Laura reached out to put a hand on the detective and then pulled away. Her emergency first aid and CPR training hadn't prepared her for this gruesome scene.

Wa roughly flipped Henry over onto his stomach and held him with a knee against his back and one arm twisted behind. He looked to his partner. "FUCKIN' HELP HIM!" he screamed at Laura.

Laura finally reacted and pulled a towel off a nearby table. She pressed the towel on the wound but the blood instantly soaked through. She tried to speak softly, to encourage the man. "You'll be okay," she said. "It's going to be okay."

Wa watched helplessly as the young woman struggled with Makum. He turned angrily back to Henry and wrenched the man's arm further up his back. Henry called out in pain but Wa didn't release the pressure.

Makum's body slumped further forward and then began to slide under the table as he lost strength. Laura tried to hold the detective up without letting the pressure off the towel but it was no use. Makum flopped to the ground and Laura tumbled after him.

"Fuck!" Wa yelled. He was going to handcuff Henry, but decided on a quicker route. He grabbed Henry by the back of the head. He lifted the man's head and in one motion cracked it against the hard floor. With Henry unconscious, he leapt over to Makum and leaned in close, pushing the frantic Laura to the side.

"Roland! Roland! Talk to me, man. You'll be okay."

Makum's eyes fluttered open but Wa saw only the whites before they shut again.

"ROLAND!" Wa screamed.

Wa, Laura, and Larry watched the paramedics wheel Detective Roland Makum out the front doors. Henry was already in custody in the back of a police van.

As they stood in the entrance to the shelter there was a heavy silence among them. Large patches of blood had soaked through their clothes during the ordeal making it feel as though they had put their clothes on over wet swimsuits. Laura shivered.

Police still drifted through the facility but purposely avoided contact with Detective Wa. No one wanted to disturb him yet.

Finally, Wa spoke. His words were stilted, unnatural. "Who was that? What the fuck's the matter with him?"

"I don't know," Laura said shaking her head. "He's been here a few times and never been a problem. We had no idea."

They were silent again.

"Why?" Wa asked.

There was no answer.

"I don't know what happened," Laura said softly. "That wasn't Henry. Not the Henry I knew."

Wa turned sharply to her. "What the fuck does that mean?"

"Henry was the kind of guy I thought would protect me if something bad ever happened. He was great. I trusted him."

"Then what the fuck just happened?"

"He'd been quiet for the last few days. Ever since that Edward character got arrested."

Larry nodded. "You're right," he said. "He's been different since Edward was here. He's been really moody and quiet."

Wa looked back and forth between them. "Did this guy have contact with Edward?"

"I never saw them talking or anything," Larry answered.

"Me neither," Laura added and then paused before she continued. "But their cots *were side by side*."

"Their cots?" Wa asked.

"Yeah," Laura said. "They slept next to each other."

twenty-five

112th (thursday)

"I don't know why you guys are making such a big deal," Rebecca Ly scolded her night shift partners, Carl and Samantha.

The three nurses sat in the nursing station on North Bay. A fourth nurse, Nicholas, was on his break, sleeping in a staff room down the hallway. It was fifteen minutes before midnight. A security guard sat adjacent to them in a station filled with monitors showing various strategic locations within the unit.

"Well," announced Samantha, "for one thing the entire city has pretty much been shaking in its boots every second Thursday for the last three or four months. You may have seen it on the news. It was a pretty big deal."

Samantha was another young recruit to the MSPC. She was twenty-five and slightly overweight. She'd recently graduated with a nursing degree and taken a job with the forensic service as a starting point in her career. Her light blond hair was a stark contrast to Rebecca's jet-black hair. Samantha had quickly made a name for herself among her colleagues as being somewhat theatrical and prone to exaggeration. The veteran nursing staff attributed it to her inexperience in the area of forensics.

"Innocent until proven guilty," Carl reminded her. "We're just doing an assessment on someone. He isn't necessarily a rapist."

"Whatever," Samantha replied.

Her casual but dramatic approach annoyed Carl. He'd worked as a nurse in psychiatric facilities for close to eighteen years and always approached the job professionally. He had no time for staff who didn't share his approach.

"It's check time," Rebecca stated as she looked at the clock high on the wall.

Carl leaned across the desk and pressed a button on an intercom. "How we doing out there?"

Darryl, the security guard, replied through the static of the speaker. "All quiet."

Carl pressed the button again. "And Carter?"

"Nothing," came the reply.

He turned to the other nurses and nodded.

"It's a visual check right now for close," Rebecca said with an expression that resembled a smug little girl who'd just come up with a correct answer.

"Fine, go ahead," he said shrugging.

"Yeah, but it's like almost midnight and then this guy misses his deadline for Thursday," Samantha said with an exaggerated tremble. "We can break the curse!"

"Give it a rest," Carl said.

"Odds and evens," Rebecca announced. It was a common method for solving minor disputes on the night shift.

The three nurses each held up a fist and in unison they counted off, "one, two, three" pumping their arms on each stroke. On the third stroke each of them extended either one or two fingers.

Carl extended only one finger and smiled.

Both Rebecca and Samantha extended two fingers.

"Fine," Samantha fumed and grabbed a clipboard off the wall.

Rebecca stood, took a flashlight off the desk beside her, and followed Samantha out of the nursing station.

There were three patients who required visual checks for close observation. Rebecca and Samantha checked the other two, leaving Edward Carter to last. Close observation meant a client got checked every fifteen minutes and a note was made on a special form. The nurses stood outside the last room on the wing. It was Edward's single room.

"You check," Samantha hissed in an urgent whisper as she busily looked at the clipboard in her hands.

Rebecca shrugged and stepped toward the door. The hallway was dark but not pitch black. Evening running lights remained on in tracks that ran along the ceiling. The lights provided enough illumination to maneuver safely through the hallways. Each of the patients' rooms, however, was black inside. Someone decided that it would be a violation of patient rights to force them to have lights on while they were trying to sleep. No amount of reasoning could convince the hospital administration differently.

Rebecca quietly pushed the door open and peered inside. She could just barely make out a shape beneath the covers in the bed. Without more light it was difficult to identify the patient as Edward Carter. Besides, close observation demanded a check of *vitals* at each interval—the nursing staff had to make sure the patient wasn't dead. Most staff simply opened the door and shone a flashlight at the patient until they verified what they needed. A patient would swear, or roll over, and thus confirm they weren't dead. Rebecca preferred a less intrusive approach.

She looked back at Samantha who stood impatiently in the hall looking one direction and then back the other way. Rebecca moved further into the room and peered toward the shape in the bed. The covers were still. She kept one hand on the door and held a mini-flashlight in the other as she leaned toward the bed. As she did so, she thought she heard a soft murmur come from Edward's direction.

"*Facini.*"

She strained to listen. She wondered if he was speaking in his sleep or whether it was just snoring.

"*Blah blah side.*"

It was definitely words that Edward was mumbling. "Edward?" Rebecca asked tentatively. There was no answer. She stared into the darkness, squinting her eyes to try and see the movement of his chest under the covers. She could only see a shapeless mass beneath the sheet. It was not enough to count as a thorough check, and she wasn't about to have something go wrong on her watch.

"*Blah and blah reside.*"

Again, she heard the mumble of words but it didn't make any sense. She leaned further forward and called again, only louder, "Edward? Are you awake?"

No answer.

She looked back at Samantha who was standing in the hall with her hands on her hips. She was staring into the room with impatience. Rebecca decided this was silly and she let go of the door, stepping closer to the bed. The door eased shut on its heavy springs and she consciously slid her fingers over the switch of the flashlight. As the light came on she covered the brightness with her palm to prevent disturbing Edward.

"*Facini entfaste blackened side.*"

This time she heard the words more clearly but they still didn't make sense. She used her hand to allow a thin beam of light out and directed it toward the bed. Her flashlight moved up the length of the sheets to find Edward's face—only it wasn't Edward. She gasped as the light stopped on the face of an ex-client, Morgan Whitler.

It can't be, she thought. *He's gone.*

She stared at Morgan's face. It was definitely him. She let the flashlight fall slightly and noticed that the covers were now thrown aside. Morgan lay on the bed naked. Her flashlight moved down his body and stopped at his erect penis. It stood straight out from his body and she swallowed hard. It couldn't be. That was in the past. He was a mistake. She closed her eyes tightly and reopened them.

Morgan was still in the bed. She still couldn't breathe. The sight of him was beyond comprehension. Morgan was a patient of the MSPC less than a year ago. He was a good-looking, smooth-talking criminal with a long history of convictions. In the end the MSPC assessment found no evidence of mental illness and Morgan went to the correctional centre, but not before something had happened between him and Rebecca.

Why is he here? she thought, almost asking the question out loud.

Without thinking, she took a step toward the bed. She moved the flashlight away from his penis and back to his face. It was definitely Morgan. He'd arrived at the centre at a time when Rebecca and her boyfriend were not getting along, a time in her life when she was vulnerable. She'd tried to forget about that time of weakness and passion. She knew she could've been fired for having sex with a client but the sight of him now still made her palms sweaty. He was dangerous and there's something about dangerous that's sexy.

This isn't right, she thought as fear crept through her. *He can't be here. I must be sick.* She looked again at Morgan's face but it was gone. Morgan's face was no longer there, but neither was any other. The thing that lay on the bed lacked substance, lacked form, lacked any trace of being human.

She sucked in her breath and turned to run out of the room. A hand met her face as her body turned and cold fingers clamped over her mouth just in time to stifle a scream.

Words leaked into her ear. "*Facini entfaste blackened side facini entfaste.*"

She shook as spasms of terror gripped her. She reached up to grab the hand that covered her mouth. The wet, cold of the skin her fingers touched sent chills through her. Her eyes were open and wild with fear but she couldn't see who held her. It had to be Edward.

"*Facini entfaste blackened side.*" Words seeped through her again. They somehow had a texture, a palpable sensation that left a trail down the canal of her ear. She felt her mind spin as the words penetrated her.

It took a moment to recover enough to begin struggling. She tried to kick her legs, to bite at the hand, to swing her elbows back at her assailant. But it did nothing.

"*Fuckin' whore! Facini entfaste blackened side.*"

She felt her mind cave away and her body went limp. The sheer exhaustion of her terror had eaten away her strength before she'd had a chance to fight back. She hung in her assailant's arms and prayed that Samantha would open the door.

"*Facini entfaste blackened side.*"

The tip of a cold tongue snaked inside her ear and moved deeply down. She desperately wanted to scream as the tongue made its way past her eardrum and continued to drill deeper into her mind. She could feel her sanity sink away as the cold, wet thing slithered inside her. It was not human. She knew something else was with her now.

"*Facini entfaste blackened side*."

Something ran up the inside of her leg, making a circular trek around her skin until it reached her underwear. The thing was cold and left her leg shaking with spasms. In one motion the thing slipped beneath her underwear and worked between the lips of her vagina. She moaned as it entered her. She felt her vagina become full as the thing expanded and pushed deeper. She didn't think she could stand the pain of the intrusion and thought that she would tear apart. Soon she felt the thing push past her stomach and up toward her lungs and throat. She felt nauseous as her stomach shifted to one side to allow the slithering thing access to the deepest recesses of her body.

Rebecca was on the verge of complete collapse. She felt her bowels about to release, bile was rising through her throat, and she wanted to vomit. The thing that entered her ear had wound through her mind and was now dripping down the back of her throat to meet the dark thing that was raping her from below. Her mind fluttered as consciousness began to fade.

"*Facini entfaste blackened side*."

She wanted to be dead and escape this pain.

"*Facini entfaste blackened side.*"

She knew she was about to get her wish.

"*Facini entfaste blackened side*."

And then another voice broke through her fog. "Let's go, slow poke."

Rebecca opened her eyes and blinked. Her arms were hanging at her sides and the flashlight dropped through her fingers and banged against the floor. She turned her head to the door and saw Samantha looking at her with an expression of concern.

Her head shot back to the bed and she watched Edward roll over and look up at her.

"Is everything okay?" he asked softly.

She stared back at him. Edward lay in bed with the covers pulled up to his neck.

"Rebecca?" Samantha said urgently from the door. "Let's go."

In a sleepy, dreamlike fashion, she turned to Samantha and nodded slowly. She turned back to Edward and looked at him. He stared at her with a passive expression. She leaned over to retrieve her flashlight from the floor. The beam still shone out and was directed beneath the bed. As she moved down she kept her eyes on Edward. He watched her without expression. As her head came level with his she saw his expression change. He smiled at her, a slight grin with a trace of derision. Rebecca couldn't pull her eyes away from him and she froze in her vulnerable position, bent halfway to the floor. She watched as his eyes sunk away and vertical slits of black opened and closed where his pupils should have been.

She shivered so violently she was worried she wouldn't be able to stand. Somehow she forced herself to break free of his eyes. She grabbed her flashlight and walked purposefully from the room, pushing past Samantha.

"Hey," Samantha said and looked back at Edward before she stepped out of the room and let the door ease shut.

Rebecca was already halfway down the hallway heading toward the nursing station.

"Wait up," Samantha called and jogged to catch her.

Rebecca reached the door to the nursing station just as Samantha caught her. "What's up?" she asked with concern.

Rebecca stopped and looked at her. "Nothing," she said flatly.

"Did that motherfucker say something to you?"

"No."

"Well what was going on back there? You looked pretty freaked out or something."

"Nothing. I just...I mean, nothing."

"Come on," Samantha pleaded. "If that fucker said something then you've got to tell us. It could be important."

"Listen," Rebecca said with anger and urgency, "nothing happened. I just spaced out for a second. No big fucking whoop."

She stepped back into the nursing station.

"Fine," Samantha said shrugging her shoulders and following.

twenty-six

113th day (friday morning)

"You're uncharacteristically quiet, Rebecca," Nicholas observed.

The four nurses were nearing the end of the night shift. They sat in the nursing station with Carl hard at work on the computer checking e-mail. Samantha was in the backroom combing through charts, adding blank paper, putting misplaced documents in the right spots, and doing other routine maintenance. Both Nicholas and Rebecca sat at the front desk facing the Plexiglas window. From this vantage they could see straight down one of the hallways, with patients' rooms on either side. Rebecca had been staring down the dimly lit corridor for quite some time while Nicholas read the newspaper.

She didn't react to Nicholas' observation.

He set the paper down on the desk and turned to her. "You feeling all right? It's not like you to be so quiet."

She continued to ignore him and maintained her concentration on the hall.

"Okay," Nicholas said finally and picked up his paper again.

Rebecca Ly's boyfriend, Marcus Hoang, stepped out of the shower and reached for a towel.

"Son of a bitch!" he screamed as he saw a figure standing in the doorway of the bathroom.

He quickly covered himself with the towel and ran a hand over his face to clear the water droplets away. He finally realized he was looking at Rebecca.

"Shit, Rebecca. You scared the crap out of me."

She didn't respond. She simply stared at him with a blank expression, as if he was a piece of art hanging in a gallery and she wasn't impressed. Her arms hung at her sides and she stood very straight.

As the fear faded away, Marcus felt anger sneak in to replace it. The anger helped restore his confidence. "What the fuck are you doing?"

Without a word she turned, stiffly, and walked away. Marcus grunted and finished toweling off.

Marcus Hoang was a young professional working at an architectural firm. He lived by strict routines and rigid schedules. His career goals included opening his own firm before the age of thirty-five and he knew that left little time for foolishness along the way.

Marcus and Rebecca had moved in together sixteen months previously. They'd been dating for a few months before that and it had been his idea that she live with him. He thought that Rebecca was a good match since she was also very dedicated to her career as a nurse. Financially, the arrangement worked very well because his apartment had been a little bit out of his bachelor price range. With Rebecca's financial contribution they lived quite comfortably. At this point both were happy with the common-law arrangement.

The apartment was a spacious condominium-style building on the outskirts of the downtown core. It was a modern looking building with sharp angles and exaggerated features, like oversized windows. Marcus liked the layout and had decorated the apartment in glass and black metal, giving the place a stark feel.

Having dried and put deodorant on, Marcus was ready to shave. He needed to be at work in forty-five minutes and his schedule didn't allow for interruptions. When Rebecca was coming off a night shift the routine generally included her arriving home as he was getting dressed and just dropping into bed. He would sneak into the bedroom before leaving and give her a quick kiss. This morning he had a feeling that the routine was going to be sacrificed.

He looked down at the marble-top sink and his safety blade. He sighed, and tightened the towel around his slender waist, and went out to check on Rebecca.

He found her sitting in the middle of the black leather couch. Her back was straight and did not come into contact with the leather. She rested her hands softly on each knee and stared straight ahead at the TV. Marcus glanced at the TV. It was off.

"Honey?" he said tentatively.

She didn't move.

"Hey," he said as he came around the couch and faced her, "you sure gave me a start. I'm sorry I snapped at you back there."

Nothing.

He frowned. "Is everything okay?"

She continued to stare straight ahead.

"Can I get you something? A coffee, maybe?"

He began to feel impatient. He didn't know what was wrong with her but he knew he didn't have time for games like this.

"Did something happen at work?"

Still no answer. He sat down on the couch beside her and put a hand over hers. He looked at her with concern. Her expression remained blank and she continued to stare straight ahead.

"Did you eat anything yet?" he asked finally as he ran out of ideas.

Her head turned slowly until she was looking straight at him. He couldn't read her expression and it concerned him. He frowned.

She blinked and shook her head violently, clenching her eyes shut and turning her head away.

"Come on," he said. "Let's go into the kitchen."

He took hold of her hand and stood. He pulled her gently to her feet and led her into the kitchen. She went compliantly.

The kitchen was located behind the living room in an open-concept area. Only the small dining room table separated the space. Rebecca moved into the kitchen and stood still when Marcus released her hand. He took a coffee mug out from a cupboard above the counter and set it beside the sink. He pulled the coffeepot out from its spot beneath the cupboards. It was already full of steaming coffee, as part of his morning routine.

He poured her a cup and turned back to the counter to retrieve the sugar. Rebecca took her coffee with sugar—no milk.

"It's in me," Rebecca said softly.

Marcus turned sharply with the sugar spoon still in his hand. "What's that?"

"Nothing," she said and dropped her eyes down.

He finished stirring the coffee and handed the mug to her. She took it in both hands and stared at it as if she didn't know what to.

"You should have something to eat too," he said. "Go sit down and I'll grab some of that banana bread."

He put an arm around her and led her to the table, pulling a chair out for her. She sat and continued to hold the mug in both hands without drinking. He went back to the kitchen and pulled a wooden breadboard out of a cupboard. It was the kind with the wooden rack on a tray so that bread crumbs would drop through and be captured. He looked around briefly for the bread knife and realized it was in the dishwasher. He pulled a large butcher knife out of a wooden block on the counter instead. He came back and set the knife and board on the dining room table near Rebecca. He noticed that the mug of coffee was now sitting at the edge of the table. He gently pushed it back and returned to the kitchen to grab the cloth bag that contained the fresh banana bread.

"I think you'll feel better with a little coffee and some food in you," he announced as he came to stand at the table beside her.

She didn't respond as he pulled the bread out and laid it on the wooden rack. He reached for the knife—but it was gone.

He turned to look at Rebecca for an explanation. She sat with her hands beneath the table and her eyes red with tears. He instantly became concerned.

"Come on, honey, what's wrong?"

"I cheated on you," she said painfully through the tears.

"What?" he demanded.

"I'm sorry," she said so softly that he could barely hear her.

"What?"

"I'm not what you think."

Tears flooded out and rolled down her face.

"No, sweetie. You're just upset," he said sympathetically and leaned forward putting his arms out to embrace her.

"Stay away!" she shouted and recoiled. She raised her arms to block Marcus and he screamed at what he saw.

The butcher knife dropped from her right hand and fell onto the floor. Her left hand was soaked in blood which continued to pour out of a massive wound on her wrist sending a shower of blood onto the table. She held her hands out toward him, trying to push him away. Marcus froze at the sight of her blood. The fingers on her right hand were spread out in her effort to stop him but the fingers of her mutilated left hand hung limply. Severed tendons were visible inside the gaping wound on her wrist.

"What have you done?" he screamed and leapt away from the table.

"I have to kill it," she cried and let her hands drop. Blood had already pooled on the table and her hands slapped against it sending drops of dark red out in all directions.

Marcus felt faint and stumbled back into the kitchen. He shook his head to clear the fog and grabbed a kitchen towel. He ran back to her side and smothered her left hand. He wrapped it tightly around her wrist and pressed so hard he thought he might break her hand off. Even through the thick towel he could feel the open wound and it made him gag. He prayed that he wouldn't do any damage by pressing it.

"Somebody help me!" he screamed as he stood by her side. He felt something warm and sticky under his feet.

"No," she pleaded. "Let me die." And then she fell unconscious from the loss of blood.

twenty-seven

113th day (friday morning)

The security guard finished running the electronic wand down Dr. Leonard Darious' right leg and stood. "You're clear, Doctor."

Dr. Darious grunted in disapproval.

He was standing in the main foyer of the Maximum Security Psychiatric Centre. One security guard sat behind a large, round desk situated in the middle of the lobby. It was an oversized entrance that had four locked doors leading off in each direction. Dark Alley led away to the right and took its name because it was an administrative area housing the doctors and other clinical staff, and as such, it was the only wing that was dark at night. The locked doorway to North Bay was directly behind the round desk. Near North Bay was the entrance to West Bay, which held the mentally ill prison population. Closer to the front entrance was the final doorway, leading to South Bay, which was for the long-term forensic psychiatric population.

The guard who'd completed the security sweep on Dr. Darious turned to his partner behind the desk. "Buzz me into Dark Alley and I'll escort him down."

The guard at the desk nodded and looked down at his soft graphic display of doors and corridors. He touched the screen on a door marked Administrative Corridor, an electronic hum and metallic click sounded in the lobby. The guard stepped ahead of Dr. Darious, pulling the Dark Alley door open.

"Welcome, Dr. Darious. I'm Dr. Georgia O'Connors, team psychiatrist and the clinical leader on North Bay," she said as she opened her office door. "Thanks, Tim," she nodded at the security guard and he turned to leave.

"I don't feel welcome," Darious said caustically as he stepped into the office.

Dr. O'Connors backed away to allow him entrance. "Oh, I'm sorry, is there something the matter?"

Andy turned from his seat near Dr. O'Connor's desk.

"I didn't expect to be treated like a criminal," Dr. Darious said.

"Treated like a criminal?" Dr. O'Connors said.

"Yes. Scanning me for weapons."

"It's policy," Andy offered.

"Dr. Darious, this is Andy Thomas, our social worker. He'll be joining us today," Dr. O'Connors announced. "And yes, it is policy to have all visitors, regardless of occupation, scanned. I apologize for the inconvenience. Would you like to have a seat?"

Dr. Darious sat next to Andy and Dr. O'Connors returned to her desk. Her office was arranged to provide as much open space as possible. Her desk was against one wall in the corner. Her chair and a small coffee table were against the opposite wall, closer to the door. There were three chairs in addition to hers, which sat in a semi-circle facing the back of the room. Dr. O'Connors sat and addressed Dr. Darious. "So you wanted to talk to us about Edward, is that right?"

He cleared his throat and straightened in his chair. "Yes, I felt it was important to speak on his behalf. Are you his treating psychiatrist?"

"Yes, and Andy is the social worker assigned to the case."

Darious smiled and nodded at Andy but was obviously much more interested in directing his comments to Dr. O'Connors. A professional bias.

"Edward Carter is not the serial rapist," Darious said. "I would stake my career on it."

"Strong words. Why the conviction?" Dr. O'Connors asked.

"I've worked with the man for the entire time that these horrible rapes have been committed. I would have picked up on something if Edward were involved. He's not. Edward is a timid, awkward individual who has suffered tremendously. He wouldn't have the strength, or the inclination, to be involved in such a horrendous series of crimes."

"I appreciate your input. However, it isn't really the goal of the Forensic Service to determine guilt or innocence. That's the role of the court."

"I realize that," Dr. Darious said, looking down and shaking his head impatiently. "But I also realize that the report you prepare influences the court. A personality assessment, a risk assessment—whatever goes on—has an impact."

"We'd like to think so," Dr. O'Connors said with a smile.

"Fine then. I'm asking that you give this man the benefit of the doubt and try to help him refute these awful allegations. He's a delicate person. A sensitive person."

"We adopt a similar level of care with all our clients," Dr. O'Connors said coolly.

"I'm not implying that you don't. I just feel that Edward's arrest for these crimes is a horrible injustice and I want to see it cleared up as soon as possible."

"I'm sure it will be."

There was a slight pause before Dr. Darious continued with urgent concern. "Do you know his history?"

"We've seen the charts from Atlantic Coast's psychiatric unit. We have some of the history."

"This man suffered tremendously, literally from the moment of birth." He looked back and forth between Andy and Dr. O'Connors and continued. "Child Protective Services shuttled him around to keep him away from the truth of his horrendous family. The abuse. The incestuous birth. And then he discovered it on his own. It broke him. It literally brought on his psychosis. His adoptive family disowned him. They couldn't handle the press, the stigma, of having this horrible bastard child in their clean, Christian family. That drove the knife of mental illness deeper into Edward. He lost everything and has reclaimed nothing since."

"That was actually a question we had," Andy interrupted. "We wondered about contact with the adoptive family or siblings. There's little information on the hospital charts."

"There's little information because there isn't any." Dr. Darious said. "Edward won't talk about it. He won't talk about his family of origin, his experiences in foster care, or his last placement with the Christian family."

"So, there are no family contacts?"

"None. We don't even know the name of the adoptive family. In fact, we aren't sure whether he was legally adopted at all. Social Services has been remarkably unhelpful with any requests. I've always thought that they felt somewhat responsible for how things turned out and just washed their hands of the whole thing."

"What about other community support?" Andy asked.

"Like what? Friends? Co-workers?" Dr. Darious chuckled. "He had nothing. You must understand that it was a struggle for Edward to get out of bed in the morning. He simply had no resources, social or otherwise, to get him through the tragedies. As a result he turned off inside. Being turned off protected him."

"What do you mean 'turned off?" Dr. O'Connors asked.

"Edward was grossly psychotic after he discovered who is real parents were. The clash of his fundamentalist religious beliefs, and the realization that his family of origin was so twisted, broke him. His psychosis became fixed on religious themes. He believed he was the product of an evil union. He thought that he somehow was a focal point of everything evil. He felt tormented to the point where he withdrew from the world. At times he needed to force his mind to turn off in order to cope. He was constantly plagued by thoughts of his dark secrets, his evil origins, and his failure as a Christian. While he was diagnosed and treated quite quickly, he did not respond well to medication. It took years before a medication was found to treat the delusions and the voices. But as you know, Dr. O'Connors, it is generally only the positive symptoms that respond to medication. Edward also suffered from tremendous negative symptoms: lethargy, inability to concentrate, lack of affect. We couldn't help him with those."

He took a breath before continuing. "The resulting social malaise was equally as great a problem as the schizophrenic illness. Edward was turned off to the world. I don't believe he's ever had a significant relationship—platonic or otherwise. In fact, in all my dealings with him I've found him to be completely asocial. He has absolutely no interest in social matters."

"He had a work placement?" Andy asked.

"Yes, the community reintegration work program of the Regional Mental Health Initiative placed him. The hospital insisted on it before he was discharged the last time. He ended up at that barbershop, but I don't think he had any social contact with the owner or the customers. He kept to himself. Did his work and hid in his apartment."

"And you know of no other acquaintances in the community? No one we could check for collateral information?" Andy asked.

"None," Dr. Darious said, shaking his head. "Edward was asocial, asexual, and without motivation. It is such a shame that this whole rape charge has happened to him."

"Asexual?" Dr. O'Connors asked, raising an eyebrow.

"Completely."

Dr. O'Connors looked at Andy, who shrugged his shoulders.

"Dr. Darious," she began, "what would you say if I told you that Edward had been fired from his work placement for sexually inappropriate behaviour?"

"I would say that's impossible," he said.

"Well the reports we've received from the police suggest otherwise. Apparently, the owner of the barbershop caught Mr. Carter in the backroom, masturbating."

Dr. Darious stared at Dr. O'Connors for a moment, trying to assimilate the information. "What do you mean 'caught'?"

"The owner went into the backroom for something and found Edward with his pants down."

"That doesn't sound like Edward," he said shaking his head.

"We appreciate you coming in to see us," Dr. O'Connors said and began to stand.

"That doesn't change my opinion." Dr. Darious said, waving a dismissive hand. "Edward had nothing to do with the rapes. You mark my words on that."

"I'll head out," Andy said to Dr. O'Connors, indicating he would escort Dr. Darious off Dark Alley.

"Thanks again," Georgia said extending her hand.

Darious took her hand, and then turned to leave with Andy.

"Well that was interesting," Andy said as he returned to Dr. O'Connor's office.

"Very," she said.

"Still want me to track down family or community contacts?"

"Yeah. Why don't you see what you can find out? I'm not sure I believe everything Dr. Darious tells us. You should probably talk to Edward and see what else you can dig up."

"I'll talk to him this afternoon."

twenty-eight

113th day (friday afternoon)

"Come on, girl," Marcus said softly as he sat on the edge of Rebecca's hospital bed.

The diminutive nurse looked even smaller tucked into the coarse sheets of the bed. Her arms lay on top of the blanket and her left wrist was heavily bandaged.

Marcus' constant vigil at her side had so far proved fruitless. To this point, Rebecca had been unable or unwilling to respond to anyone. As she lay on the bed now her eyes were wide open, staring at the ceiling.

"How can I help you?" Marcus whispered urgently and reached for her hand again.

She did not react to his touch, but continued to lay motionless.

"Excuse me," a voice sounded from behind him.

He turned to see a doctor in a white lab coat standing at the doorway. "Yes?"

"Are you Mr. Hoang?"

"Yes."

"Could I speak to you for a minute?"

Marcus gently lay Rebecca's hand down on the bed and stood. He moved to the doorway and followed the doctor into the hall.

"I'm Dr. Merrick from neurology." He extended a hand, which Marcus took. "I've been asked to consult on this case and I wanted to touch base with you. I understand that Rebecca has no other family in the area, is that correct?"

"Right."

"And she hasn't responded since the accident this morning, is that correct?"

"Right."

"I'm sure you've been asked some of these questions before and you're probably getting tired of talking to doctors but I'll really need to go over a few things with you. Can you come to the group room down the hall?"

Marcus nodded and the two of them walked down the hospital corridor a short way before turning into a room. The room was a casually furnished waiting room. Most nursing units had similar rooms that served numerous roles. Marcus stepped inside and sat on the dull brown couch against the wall. Dr. Merrick closed the door and sat in a chair adjacent to the couch.

"This has been a tremendously stressful time for you," he said with a concerned expression.

Marcus nodded. He felt compelled to hurry through this interview and get back to Rebecca's side.

"Let me tell you where things are, and why I'm going to be involved." He drew in a deep breath and continued. "Rebecca did tremendous damage to the nerves and tendons in her arm. It was a deep laceration that's going to require further surgery to make sure she gets a full range of motion back. However, things are a bit complicated by the fact that she hasn't responded to anyone since the accident. In most cases we'd want to do an examination of the hand while she's conscious in order to ascertain the exact nature of the injuries." He paused and looked at Marcus for an indication of his understanding. Marcus nodded.

"All right," the doctor said. "The thing is, the staff are pretty much stumped about why Rebecca has stopped responding. She's not in a coma. That was ruled out quite quickly. You've already told us that she didn't strike her head at any time during the accident. Do you know if there were any head injuries prior to the accident?"

Marcus shook his head. "I don't really know. She came home from the prison acting strange and wouldn't tell me what was wrong."

"When you say 'prison' you mean the forensic facility?"

"I'm sorry, yes. I've always called it a prison."

"Is there any way to confirm with the forensic facility if she sustained any injury at work?"

"I already called. I spoke to the charge nurse and she said there was no record of anything. I didn't probe too much though because I didn't want to tell them what happened. I just told them it was an accident. Anyway, there was nothing on the incident report. The charge nurse said she'd try and check with one of the nurses who worked with Rebecca that night and get back to me. I haven't heard anything."

"Please let me know if you do hear something," Dr. Merrick said. He looked at a pad of paper he'd been carrying. "Was there any history of diabetes or epilepsy?"

Marcus shook his head.

"Has there ever been anything like this before?"

"No."

"Had she complained of headaches or blurred vision?"

"No."

Dr. Merrick went on to screen for other medical conditions but discovered nothing new.

Finally, Marcus interrupted. "How many more questions are there?"

Merrick checked his notepad. "I guess that's about it."

"Well, what do you think is going on?"

"It's impossible to say without more tests."

"What would you guess? I mean, she's never been like this. Out of nowhere she tries to hack her hand off. I don't know what to do."

"We're going to check out every angle. The big thing we need to do today is get her ready for surgery and we need an MRI."

"An MRI?"

"Yes. There's a possibility she's suffered a stroke or some other type of neurological injury. We need to find out what we're dealing with."

"A stroke," Marcus said incredulously. "Isn't she too young?"

"I'm not saying it is a stroke. I don't know at this point but we want to be thorough in our checks."

Marcus nodded.

"And if we don't identify any physical explanation for her condition we might consult with psychiatry."

Marcus snapped his head up to look at the doctor. "Because she's gone insane?"

"No," Dr. Merrick said quickly. "But the trauma she's suffered might have left her in a serious state of shock. There are psychiatric conditions that result from serious trauma."

"That could..."

"What were you going to say, Mr. Hoang?"

"I've wondered if she somehow, I don't know, snapped."

"Why do you say that?"

Marcus dropped his head down onto his hands and rubbed his eyes before he looked up at the doctor again. "It's the way she looked at me. The way she was acting. For heaven's sake—look at what she did to herself!"

Dr. Merrick looked at him with concern and waited for him to continue.

Marcus looked squarely at the doctor. "And it's what she said. She kept saying something about 'it' was in her and she needed to 'kill it.' I don't know..."

As the words left him so did his strength. His fatigue, lack of food, and the stress finally caught up with him and he started to sob. He sank back onto the couch and covered his face with his hands.

twenty-nine

113th day (friday afternoon)

Andy Thomas, social worker, and the associate nurse, Milton Carlisle, walked down the hallway to Edward's room.

"Did you hear about Rebecca?" Milton asked.

"No, what?" Andy responded with concern.

"Guess she's in the hospital. Some kind of accident or something at home. No one really knows but we're sending a card over."

"Is she okay?"

"I guess. I think the word is that she's stable so..."

"Wow. And no one has any idea what happened?"

"It was early this morning when she got off the night shift. No one knows for sure but her boyfriend took her in to Atlantic."

"That's too bad," Andy said sympathetically as they stopped in front of Edward's door.

Milton knocked and pushed the door open with his foot. He stepped into the room and called out. "Edward, Mr. Thomas is here to see you."

Edward was on his bed with the covers pulled to his chin and only his face exposed. He began moving at Milton's first word and was now sitting on the edge of the bed.

"You want to come down to the interview room with us, please?"

Edward stood and dutifully shuffled out of the room behind Andy and Milton. They escorted him down the hall to a small interview room near the nursing station. The room contained a small table and four plastic chairs. Security staff monitored the room through a camera in the corner.

"Have a seat," Andy said gesturing to the chairs as Edward entered.

Andy and Milton sat on chairs opposite Edward. Andy set his pad of paper on the table and pulled a pen out of his shirt pocket. "Thanks for meeting with us, Edward. As Milton mentioned, I'd like to talk to you for a little bit. My name's Andy Thomas and I'm a social worker on the service. I'll be asking you a few questions about your placement in the community, and if there are any contacts we could make on your behalf. What I mean by that is I'd like to find out if there are any friends or family that we can speak to."

Edward didn't respond. Once he was seated he dropped his head and stared at his lap. He didn't attempt to make eye contact and clasped his hands tightly together. He was dressed in a hospital issued gown and dirty socks without shoes. His hair pointed out in various directions indicating that it hadn't been combed since he'd woken up. He looked pale and gaunt in the loose outfit.

Andy continued. "So, your name is Edward Carter, correct?"

"Yeah."

"What's your date of birth?"

"April 11, 1974."

"Now Edward," Andy began quietly, "I know that your early history is rough, so I want to talk about more recent times and then move us backwards. You let me know if you feel uncomfortable, okay?"

Edward didn't respond.

Andy carefully documented Edward's recent movement from his work placement at Moe's Barbershop back through the hospitalizations and various group homes. At no point did Edward offer more information than he was asked for, and he denied ever having any intimate or friendly relationships.

"So over the last six years or so, where was the best place you lived?" Andy asked.

"I don't know. Maybe the last place. Over the barbershop."

"Good. And what made that a good place."

"Don't know."

Just then a loud scream sounded out on the unit. Andy looked over at Milton. Nursing staff needed to respond to potential problems but the plan had been to keep two people with Edward at all times.

"Go," Andy said.

"You sure?" Milton asked with concern.

"Yep. We're doing fine," he nodded at Edward.

"I'll be right back Edward," Milton said carefully and then stepped out of the room, letting the door close behind him.

"Anyway, where were we? Right, you were saying you liked the place at the barbershop."

Edward didn't respond and kept his head down.

"Let's go back a bit further, if you don't mind," Andy continued. "Do you remember the family you were living with before you began having problems?"

"Yeah."

"Do you remember their names?"

"No."

"I need to confirm a few things for our own record. It would be helpful if you could remember their names, even their last name."

"I can't."

"I know it's a difficult topic for you."

"I disappointed them," he said quietly.

"No, Edward. What happened wasn't your fault. Mental illness is no one's fault."

Edward was silent.

"Do you think you let your foster parents down because of your illness?"

"No."

"What then?"

"*I don't have a mental illness*."

This surprised Andy. Reading old hospital charts had led him to believe that Edward readily accepted his diagnosis and actively sought help for his mental illness.

"I'm sorry. What's that, Edward?"

"Nothing."

"You don't believe you have a mental illness?" asked Andy quietly.

Edward shrugged. "*You are what you are*."

"I don't understand."

"*I know.*"

Andy frowned. He hadn't expected this kind of difficulty with Edward. He didn't know if he was playing games or whether he was too ill to answer coherently. He decided to keep trying. "Can you help me understand what you mean?"

Edward's head turned up slightly until his eyes made contact with Andy. A strange smile broke over his lips. It started slowly in the corners and spread across the middle until his face changed noticeably. "*Well sure, Andy. I'd love to help you out.*"

Andy shifted uncomfortably in his chair. The sudden change in Edward's demeanour wasn't a good sign. It was probably an indication of active symptoms. He considered ending the interview unless Milton returned shortly.

Without warning, Edward reached across the table and placed a hand on top of Andy's. Andy's hand had been resting palm down on the table and Edward simply placed his overtop. The sensation was as shocking as if Andy'd placed his hand in freezing water. Edward's hand was incredibly cold and slightly damp. Andy attempted to pull his hand back but Edward gently held it in place. He looked up to find it was no longer Edward sitting across from him. It was a pasty, plump man with sweat streaking down his face. The man looked familiar. Andy tried to speak but couldn't find his voice.

"*Don't reject me,*" the man said in a voice of mock sadness.

"Who...," Andy began but couldn't finish.

"*Let's jerk each other off, quick, before someone else comes in. This is a busy bathroom*," the sweaty man said and licked his lips with a nervous tongue.

"Let go of my hand!" Andy yelled and looked toward the door then back up at the security camera. He couldn't believe what was happening.

"*I want to touch you*," the fat man whispered urgently.

"How can...," Andy began. He stopped in mid-sentence because he finally saw the man more clearly. The man's puffy, white face dripped with sweat but that wasn't what he noticed. There were sores around the man's eyes. Large, open wounds that oozed with pus. The man pleaded with Andy. "*Come on, I want to suck your cock*."

Andy couldn't speak, couldn't answer.

The fat man leaned forward, still holding Andy's hand firmly. His tongue rolled out between his lips and snaked back to lick a circle around his mouth. The man's tongue was also riddled with painful sores. *Herpes!* Andy thought. *That's what it looks like*.

"*I'm so horny*," the man panted.

"Let go," Andy whispered and tugged weakly. He looked down at his trapped hand and gasped. More sores were evident across the back of the man's hand. Andy could feel the herpes wounds being ground down onto his hand. He shuddered at the thought.

"I don't want to...," Andy tried.

"*Oh please, let's cum together*." The man looked at Andy with such an expression of urgency that Andy didn't know how to respond.

Suddenly, the man stood and released Andy's hand. As the man's waist passed the edge of the table his hard penis came into view. Andy stared at him. His penis stood straight out, pointing toward him. As with the rest of the man, sores covered most of his erection. The sight of it sickened Andy. He wanted to turn away but couldn't. He felt a strange surge of warmth inside his own pants. He let one hand fall below the table and found a bulge.

He looked back at the man, but he was gone. Only Edward sat in the chair across from him. There was no man, no sore-covered penis, only Edward. And he still held Andy's hand against the table.

"Please," Andy said calmly even though his heart was pounding so hard he worried it would escape his chest. "Please let go."

"*I want to ask you something*," Edward whispered, ignoring the request. He leaned forward and gently massaged the back of Andy's hand as he moved. "*Does you wife know who you really are? That you gave her herpes?*"

Andy had trouble concentrating. He was resisting the impulse to scream and rip his hand away from the disgusting, cold grip that held it. He barely heard Edward's words but forced himself to focus on him rather than his trapped hand.

"Please sit back in your chair and let go of my hand," Andy said again. His voice remained calm and patient, not betraying his near-hysteria. He knew that he couldn't let Edward know how scared and confused he was. Losing control of emotions meant losing control of the situation. *The situation*, he thought in a flash. *Shit!* He suddenly realized that he and Milton had inadvertently sat on the wrong side of the table—the side furthest from the door. A fundamental rule of interviewing in the field of forensics was to make sure you had unrestricted access to the exit. Andy would have to go around the table and past Edward to get out.

"*Don't be nervous*," Edward said softly. "*I won't rape you.*" He smiled a hideous smile and stroked Andy's hand again.

"That's it," Andy said and pulled hard on his hand. Edward gripped it firmly.

"*I'm not finished with you*," Edward growled.

"The interview is over," Andy announced and tried to stand.

Edward released his hand and reached out suddenly. With both hands he gripped the sides of Andy's head and pushed him back to his seat. The cold, wet hands slapped him like lifeless objects and stung Andy's skin. He instinctively reached up but Edward had already released him. Andy's ears rang from the contact and he slumped forward against the table for support.

Edward leaned forward and spoke into Andy's face. The putrid smell of his breath made Andy gag.

"*Facini entfaste,*" his voice gurgled but Andy couldn't understand him. "*Blackened side*."

Andy stared at him with a blank expression.

"*I don't think I have a mental illness. At least, I don't think I have anything different than anyone else when you get right down to it. It's just that when I stop my medication a lot of things get much worse.*" He paused and then repeated himself for emphasis, "*Much worse.*"

Andy's head spun violently. He thought he might be sick and he knew he didn't have the strength to get out past Edward. He hoped that security was watching the room on camera. He hoped Milton would be back soon. For some reason he couldn't concentrate. He couldn't form a thought.

"*You're not paying attention*," Edward growled. "*Facini entfaste blackened side.*"

Andy's mind tried to fight off the confusion. He was lost. "What? I don't understand..."

Edward stared hard at Andy. "*You know everything you need*."

Andy swallowed with difficulty. He didn't understand why Milton hadn't come back to the room. He didn't know where the security staff were. He needed to get out of this room. He was close to panic.

Edward dropped his head, releasing his lock on Andy's eyes and mumbled something.

Andy stared at him, unable to understand what he was saying, unable to understand how he'd gotten into this situation.

Edward looked up suddenly. His eyes locked onto Andy again and he spoke in a clear, deep voice that resonated through the room. "*I don't have a fuckin' mental illness*."

Something was wrong with the room. Andy's heart pounded and his head spun. Edward's words had texture and substance as they escaped his mouth. Andy could feel them sinking through his eardrums, piercing his mind. He shook his head, wanting to dislodge the sensation moving through him. His mind reverberated with each of Edward's words. "*I...don't...have...a...mental...illness.*"

"I...I..." Andy tried to speak, tried to pull himself away but couldn't.

Edward reached forward and punched one hand through Andy's chest. Andy gasped with the extreme agony. He felt Edward's hand grip his racing heart. He choked and fought for air but was powerless to stop the attack.

Edward leaned and looked into Andy's panicked eyes. "*Face the black inside, motherfucker,*" he said softly.

Andy could only watch as the words again took form leaving Edward's mouth. They became dark, black, wormlike shapes that twisted and writhed in the air between them. Then, without warning, the shapes stiffened and shot into his face. Pain burned through him and he opened his mouth to scream but couldn't. He could only stare straight ahead at the dishevelled, thin man in front of him. Edward's wild eyes watched with intensity. His unkempt hair swayed in the air giving his appearance an even more feral look. Andy smelled something that reminded him of a cross between foul body odour and horrendously bad breath. He choked.

"*Face your blackness, worthless old man,*" Edward whispered in a throaty voice that again sent spiraling black worms out in front of Andy. As the dark shapes twisted through the air, Edward quickly changed his grip, pulling his hand from Andy's chest and using both hands to tightly hold Andy's head again. He thrust an index finger into each ear canal and forced them down. The pain exploded through Andy but he found himself unable to scream. With his mouth opened wide Edward leaned forward, chasing the black shapes as they darted into Andy's mouth. Edward's mouth opened over Andy's and the foul smell burned into him. He felt as though something was penetrating him, reaching down the back of his throat, spreading out through his body.

And then it stopped and he slumped back into his chair, barely able to stay upright. The door to the room opened and he turned in an almost dreamlike state to see Milton standing there.

He looked back across the table and saw Edward sitting with his head down, hands in his lap.

"Sorry about that," Milton announced. "It was nothing." He quickly reclaimed his seat beside Andy and looked across at Edward.

No one spoke and Milton's expression changed to one of concern. "Is everything okay in here?"

Andy turned slowly to look at him. He searched for words but found none.

"Andy?" Milton said becoming increasingly concerned.

Andy looked around the room. He put a hand on his chest and felt only the strong pounding of his heart. There was no gaping hole where Edward's hand had penetrated him. He looked back at Milton with a pale, blank expression. The degree of concern on Milton's face was almost comical but Andy couldn't find strength to smile.

"It's fine," Andy eventually managed to say. He took a deep breath and looked across at Edward. "We just finished, that's all."

Edward remained motionless.

"You're done?" Milton asked with surprise.

Andy hesitated but responded. "Yeah."

Milton shrugged. "Okay, I guess you can head," he said nodding at Edward. "I want you to go straight back to your room."

Edward nodded and stood. He made no attempt to look at either Andy or Milton and left.

The room was silent for a moment once Edward was gone. Milton was still trying to assess the situation. "Did you get what you needed?" he asked.

Andy shook his head. "There's nothing. He doesn't have a history."

Milton frowned. "Really?"

"Yeah," Andy said flatly and then turned away from him to stand. As he did so, Milton noticed something.

"Hey, Andy," he said, "there's something on your ear."

Milton stood to look more closely. "It looks like blood. Did you hurt yourself?"

"It's nothing," he said shrugging off the attention and leaving the room.

113th day (friday evening)

"Where have you been?" Donna asked with concern.

Andy pushed past his wife and into their home. "Sorry," he mumbled.

She turned to watch him kick his shoes off and move into the living room.

"Is that it?" she asked with her hands on her hips. Her expression changed suddenly and she leaned to smell the air around him. "Have you been drinking, too?"

"I went to the pub with a couple of guys from work."

She frowned. "You've never gone to the pub after work. What's going on?"

"Listen," he said impatiently, "it was just a really bad day. Can you give it a rest?"

"What's the matter with you, Andrew?"

"Nothing."

"What happened today?"

"It was just a bad day, that's all. Now drop it."

She looked at him for a few more minutes as if she were thinking of asking another question. She finally decided it wasn't worth it and turned to head upstairs.

thirty

115th day (sunday)

It was so black. It hurt his eyes when he squinted through the darkness.

And cold.

It was freezing in this room.

What room?

Andy didn't know where he was. Was he at home? Was he at work? On the street?

He felt a surge of panic mount inside him. It was as if he'd been rolled inside a large rug and the feeling of having his arms trapped at his sides made him want to scream uncontrollably.

He knew he just needed to relax, calm down, move slowly—unroll the rug.

But it was so black.

And so cold.

He spun around, hoping to catch a glimpse of something, anything that would tell him where he was. By now his senses were so numb that he couldn't even tell if he'd moved. The air was so thick in here.

"Hello?" he called.

He expected to hear an echo ricochet around the empty space. There was nothing. His words seemed to slip out of his mouth and fade away almost instantly.

Panic again flooded him. It swelled up through his chest, choking his breathing and speeding up his heart. He felt beads of sweat form over his forehead.

"Hello?" he called again, louder this time.

Still nothing.

He felt too vulnerable standing in the dark. He crouched and placed a hand on the floor. It was cool and damp. He thought it might have been some kind of tile. For some reason it made him think of the hospital.

The hospital! he thought. *Maybe I'm at the hospital*.

He fell forward onto his hands and knees and felt outwards. The floor stretched away but revealed nothing else. He inched forward carefully, determined to find something that identified this place.

As he crawled, he closed his eyes. The strain of trying to see through the blackness made his head pound, and his eyes were useless anyway.

Shortly, his hand bumped into a wall. He ran his hand up the wall, feeling for something, a window, a light switch, anything. The wall was slightly soft to the touch but still cool. As his hand slid his body followed and soon he was standing. He opened his eyes briefly to confirm that the room was still pitch black. It was. He reached out with both arms to try and cover as much of the wall as possible. His hands drifted up and down over the soft surface.

Then his nostrils reacted. Being this close to the wall he could smell something, a strange but familiar odour. He took in a deep breath to try and capture the scent.

Urine!

The room had the vague smell of urine. And something else.

Disinfectant!

Urine and disinfectant. It smelled familiar to him. He couldn't quite place the smell but he knew it from somewhere. He moved slowly down the wall, feeling with his hands as he did so. He knew, sooner or later, there would be a door.

Within moments he'd reached a corner. The dimensions of the room were small. He frowned. It was familiar to him but he couldn't place it.

He turned the corner and slowly worked his way down the next wall.

Andy couldn't understand why he was here. He knew now that it wasn't his bedroom, it wasn't his living room or his office at work. He didn't understand.

Then he stopped.

He remembered where that smell was from. Urine and disinfectant. He knew.

He opened his eyes and looked up. He wasn't sure but he thought he could detect the outline of a roof a few feet over his head. He turned his head to look at the corner of the ceiling. It was black. He slowly turned and looked across the room to the other corner. Nothing. He began to turn his head—but wait! He looked back at the corner and there it was.

A slow, blinking, red light in the corner of the room. He focused on it until his eyes burned. He thought for a moment that it didn't exist, because the room seemed to swallow the light shortly after it pulsed. But it was there. A security camera.

Andy realized he was locked in the quiet room. A room at the MSPC reserved for violent, out-of-control patients. The padded walls absorbed sound just as they would absorb the impact of a body.

But why was he here?

He moved across the room, trying to stay focused on the blinking light. He stood directly in front of the camera and waved his arms. "Hey," he yelled. "Hey! Get me out of here!! It's me, Andy Thomas! Hey!"

The light continued blinking. He dropped his arms to his sides and continued to stare at the ceiling.

He didn't know why someone didn't come for him. The room was under constant surveillance. A monitor was dedicated to it in security control.

He felt panic return. He knew he shouldn't be in this room. He knew the room shouldn't be this dark. There was something wrong.

He wondered if there'd been some accident, some problem on North Bay. *Maybe a riot or something? Did I get locked in here during the skirmish? Is the unit deserted?*

"Hey! Help! Someone!"

He told himself to stay calm. He knew he was safe for now.

"Help!"

The door! He remembered that there was a small window in the door for visual checks. He knew that the door was on the opposite wall from the camera. He spun and stared into the darkness. He couldn't see the door. The darkness wouldn't allow it. He stretched his arms out and took a tentative step forward. The movement of his arms and his small steps sent chills through him. He noticed that his body was covered in sweat and he shivered violently.

Finally his hand touched the wall and he brought his head close to look down its length. He could see nothing. He moved to his right, assuming the door was more toward the middle of the wall. He moved carefully, slowly, not wanting to encounter something unexpected. Not wanting to trip, fall, injure himself.

His right hand crept out in front of him, hugging the soft wall. His fingers slid over a groove and he knew he'd found the door. He stepped across to stand squarely in front of it. The small Plexiglas window was just below his head. He dropped a hand to find the doorknob and turned it. It turned easily. He pressed against the door but it didn't move. He leaned into it with his shoulder and pushed again. Still nothing. It was bolted on the outside.

"Fuck," he whispered under his breath, trying desperately not to lose it.

Andy crouched slightly to bring his head even with the small window. He peered through and it was dark in the corridor, but not as dark. There was a slight glow that barely cut through the rest of the black.

But the hallway was empty. There was no sign of a riot, no bodies, no debris. He pressed his face forward, straining to see down the corridor in both directions. It was empty.

He felt his legs quiver as if they would drop out from under him. He rested his arms above him and fell forward to rest his forehead against the Plexiglas.

And then a voice.

"*It's got you now.*"

Andy's head shot up. He came face-to-face with Edward Carter staring at him through the small window. Edward's face was streaked with horrible bulges of open herpes sores.

Andy screamed and stumbled away from the door, falling backwards.

"*Facini entfaste blackened side,*" Edward spoke through the glass.

Andy lay on the floor staring upward. He could only see a faint outline where the window would be. A dark shape blocked the glass.

"Help!" he screamed as he pushed backwards along the floor. He came to rest on the opposite wall as far from the door as possible. His ears strained for the sound of a bolt clicking, unlocking the door, allowing Edward entrance.

"Help!" he screamed again.

And then the black shadow dissolved from the window.

Andy felt tears fill his eyes. His body shook from exhaustion and the cold sweat that covered him. He gagged and coughed. His choking scratched the back of his throat and he suddenly felt nauseous. He rolled onto his side and his stomach twisted and retched, forcing bile up into the back of his mouth. He tried to swallow but didn't have the strength and he leaned further to his side and opened his mouth.

He gagged as the vomit spilled out of him. Only it wasn't vomit. Something cold, wet, and black dropped out of his mouth. It was so black that it took shape against the rest of the room. It spun and twisted as piece after piece of blackness dropped out of him. Some of it collected on the floor beside him but most of it floated out of his mouth and drifted up past his head, violently spasming through the air.

The sight made him choke and his eyes opened wide in disgust but he couldn't stop. The black vomit continued to force itself out of him and fill the air around him. The smell of sulfur or something rotting assaulted him.

With every turn of his stomach he felt more of his strength leave him, until he was near to losing consciousness. He welcomed the opportunity to escape these events, but just as he was sure he would pass out the vomiting stopped.

He swallowed with difficulty and stared at the space around him. The last remnants of the black things were twisting away. He let his head fall to the side and rest on the floor. The smell of something rotten was still strong.

His breath came in ragged bursts as he tried to regain his composure.

After a moment he thought the worst was over. The smell was lifting slightly and he could no longer see twisting black shapes in the air around him.

He finally collapsed completely onto the floor. He lay facing the ceiling and praying for release from this room.

But as soon as he relaxed his whole body shook with such violence that it lifted off the floor. He felt waves travel from the tips of his toes up through every inch of his body to the top of his head. Something inside him rippled back and forth, up and down, through him, shoving his internal organs to the side, bruising him at every turn. He gritted his teeth against the onslaught and held his breath in an attempt to remain motionless. With each ripple through him the thing became more powerful and his body spasmed and rocked under the assault.

Andy knew he would die. He knew he couldn't survive being ripped apart from the inside. There was something inside him, something dark and horrible that was slamming back and forth trying to kill him. He gritted his teeth so hard that he was sure he felt the enamel turning to powder.

The force of the intruder continued to increase until Andy could feel blood seeping out of every joint, every orifice on his body. He felt the warm trickle of blood running out of his eyes, down his cheeks. His ears burned with the blood being pressed out of his eardrums. Blood seeped out of his nipples, his fingers, his penis and rectum, and blood pooled around the nails on his toes. He was about to die.

He screamed his last scream as he felt the cold, black thing burst out of him at every point on his skin. His body exploded in one all-encompassing symphony of pain and Andy shot bolt upright in his bed. He continued to scream in terror and pain as his body settled to the floor around him.

"Honey?" Donna called from his side. "Are you okay?"

From his seated position he turned to see his wife struggling up beside him. He blinked and stared, barely able to recognize her and not fully aware of where he was.

"What's going on? You screamed."

He didn't know how to answer. He looked around the room, his bedroom, and didn't understand.

"Honey," she said in a more relaxed voice, "you're soaked in sweat. You must've just had a bad dream. Are you okay now?"

He turned to look at her again but still couldn't answer.

Donna sniffed the air and straightened a little more. She pulled the covers back and looked down at the bed.

"Oh my gosh," she cried out. "You had a little accident." She threw the covers down to the end of the bed. "Let's get you out of here."

She slid off her side and came around to Andy. He let her help him stand. As she led him to the bathroom he looked back at the soiled bed. In the dark wet patch he saw something that was blacker than the rest. A small shape that twisted and flipped on the urine-stained sheet. He closed his eyes and began to cry.

thirty-one

116th day (monday)

"How was your weekend, Andy?" Dorothy asked as she took a seat at the table. It was Monday morning and rounds were about to begin. Diego, Dorothy, Andy, and Rhonda sat at the table in the conference room next to the nursing station. Brian Claric and Georgia O'Connors were standing to one side talking.

"Fine," Andy said tersely, without making eye contact.

"You feeling all right?" Dorothy asked. "You look a little pale."

"I'm fine."

"I guess we can begin," Rhonda announced to the table. Dr. Claric and Dr. O'Connors moved to their seats.

Rhonda waited for them to settle and began. "We need to review Edward Carter. Given the status of the case, he's on for brief updates during each round. Dr. O'Connors, do you want to begin?"

"Well Andy and I met with Dr. Leonard Darious last week. That's Edward's psychiatrist from the community. He swore up and down that Edward isn't the perpetrator but he had little else to say. He's very concerned about him being here. We tried to get some idea about possible social support in the community but Dr. Darious seemed to think there was nothing." She turned to Andy. "Is that about right?"

Andy nodded.

Dr. O'Connors frowned. She'd expected Andy to take over at this point and provide a summary of his work.

"Andy, were you able to glean anything from Edward himself? You told me that you'd try to speak with him last Friday."

Andy looked around the table slowly. His face was pale and beads of sweat glistened on his forehead even though the room was slightly cool. "I didn't find anything."

"Did you get a chance to see him last week?" Dr. O'Connors asked.

"Not really," Andy said in a distracted manner.

Dr. O'Connors frowned again.

Rhonda jumped in. "According to the chart you and Milton saw Edward last Friday afternoon. Milton sat in with you for a bit but had to go because there was some ruckus on the unit."

"Yeah," Andy said flatly.

"I saw Milton's brief note on the chart but there wasn't any note from you," Rhonda said.

"Must not have had a chance," Andy responded. A bead of sweat broke free from his forehead, trickled down over his nose, and hung precariously on the tip.

"Is everything okay?" Dr. Claric asked with a concerned expression.

"It's...Yeah."

"Is there something you want to say, Andy?" Dr. O'Connors asked.

Andy didn't respond. He looked as though he wanted to speak but couldn't find the words. The team members watched him, waiting for him to say something.

"I'm not a fag," he whispered. "I love my wife."

"What?" Dr. Claric said in surprise.

"I'm not a fucking faggot," Andy said. "It was just something stupid. That doesn't make me a queer!"

"What are you talking about?" Diego asked in genuine confusion.

Dorothy reached out and put a hand over Andy's on the table. The unexpected tension had virtually paralyzed the staff and everyone was silent.

Finally, Dr. O'Connors decided to take the direct route. "What's going on? Andy, are you ill?"

Andy turned his head sideways to look across the table at her. His pale, sweaty face broke and a grin spread across it. "I can't fight it anymore. It's inside me."

"What the hell are you doing, Andy?" Diego asked. "That's not funny."

"I know."

Dorothy pulled her hand away quickly and leaned back from him.

Then, without warning, Andy jumped up from his seat. His chair toppled behind him and the other team members started at the sudden movement.

A moment passed when everyone was frozen in shock and then Andy was the first to move. He snarled and leapt across the table, reaching for Dr. O'Connors. She backed away just enough that his hands slipped past her neck. Still on the table, Andy leapt onto his hands and knees and tried to scurry ahead to reach for Dr. O'Connors again. By this time the other team members were able to react. Diego reached out with his large, muscular arms and grabbed Andy around the waist. The older man was unable to break free and he was restrained firmly.

Dr. O'Connors now stood away from the table. "Call security. Let's get Andy into a quiet room."

Rhonda quickly left the room to use the intercom in the nursing station.

Andy went limp in Diego's grasp. Diego pulled Andy off the table into a standing position and held him steady with a hand on each shoulder. The rest of the team stared as if some unbelievable performance had just ended.

Dr. Claric stepped closer to Andy. "Are you okay? What's happened?"

Andy's eyes were closed and his head dropped to his chest in defeat. He mumbled something and Dr. Claric looked to Diego to see if he'd heard. Diego shook his head and Dr. Claric moved closer.

"What's going on, Andy?"

There was another mumble, but the words were unintelligible.

Dr. Claric placed one hand on the table, leaning forward to get a better position from which to hear. The security team had just arrived in the doorway.

"What's happened to you, Andy?"

Andy suddenly raised his head and stared into Dr. Claric's eyes. "I'm controlled by evil," he spat out and raised his arm with a pencil he'd taken from the table. He brought the pencil down onto the back of Dr. Claric's hand and stabbed it through.

Dr. Claric howled in pain and the security guards, who'd only been watching the strange situation, leapt into action. The guards grabbed Andy, one on each arm. They spun him around, out of Diego's grasp, and bent him over into a practiced hold.

"You're all gonna die!" Andy screamed as they restrained him. "He's in every one of you!"

"Get him out of here," Dr. O'Connors yelled as she moved to Dr. Claric's side.

The security guards roughly pulled Andy from the room while Dr. Claric held his hand up to his chest, covering both the pencil and wound with his good hand. Dr. O'Connors placed an arm around him and watched as Dr. Claric gripped the end of the pencil and pulled in one sharp movement. The pencil came out with a shower of blood. Dorothy suddenly felt faint and dropped back into a chair to avoid complete collapse. Dr. O'Connors carefully guided Dr. Claric into a chair as Rhonda ran into the room with an emergency medical kit.

Soon, Diego was escorting Dr. Claric to the emergency room. Andy was locked in the therapeutic quiet room. The rest of the staff huddled in the back of the nursing station trying desperately to understand what was happening.

Dorothy, Rhonda, and Dr. O'Connors stayed in the conference room. Papers were strewn over the table and floor. Housekeeping had not been in to wipe up the blood and the table was still shiny in the spot where Dr. Claric's hand had been pierced.

"What's going on?" Dorothy asked, still shaken by what she'd seen.

"I don't know, Dorothy. I just don't know," Dr. O'Connors said, shaking her head.

"That's the second one," Rhonda said quietly.

Dr. O'Connors turned and looked at her. "What do you mean?"

"You heard that Rebecca Ly had an accident, right?"

"Yes."

Dorothy's lip trembled as she listened. She could barely hold back her tears and was still partially in shock.

"Well, we just got word over the weekend. Rebecca didn't have an accident. She went home after her night shift and tried to kill herself with a butcher knife."

"What?" Dorothy blurted out and tears began to fall.

"That's right," Rhonda continued. "And she did it right in front of Marcus. She just flipped out and tried to cut her wrist."

Dorothy buried her face in her hands and sobbed.

Dr. O'Connors looked at Rhonda in disbelief. "So what are you saying?"

"People are flipping out around here. People are flipping out and it's after they've had contact with that Edward Carter bastard. He's driving people insane—us included!"

thirty-two

117th day (tuesday)

Dr. Michael Wenton sat in his office with a prospective graduate student, Brent Bytasky. Brent was finishing his honour's undergraduate degree in psychology and had applied to the clinical psychology master's program. He needed to find a research supervisor who would support his application. He was a good student in his mid-twenties, with dark hair and dark eyes. Over the last five years he'd taken every course Dr. Michael Wenton had offered and had always done well. He was now nervously answering questions in order to win Wenton over. It was not an easy job.

Wenton sighed. "What are your career goals?"

"I'd like to combine a clinical and an academic practice somehow," Brent answered. "I was thinking of something like a job at a forensic hospital with a connection to a university."

"So your plan would be to go right through to your doctorate?"

"Yessir."

"What is it about my research that makes you want to work with me?"

"Well, I'm very interested in specializing in forensics and you're the only professor with that interest." He paused after the words came out. He didn't like the way it sounded and he tried to correct it. "But more than that, I really am interested in studying psychopaths and serial killers."

Wenton frowned. It wasn't an answer that impressed him. An interest in psychopaths and serial killers reeked of sensationalism.

Brent read Wenton's not-so-subtle, non-verbal cues and continued quickly. "I think I'd like to get involved in a project that picks apart some of the core personality characteristics of these offender groups. I was thinking about a project that somehow correlated personality variables to the maladaptive coping mechanisms that are common among them."

Wenton nodded. That answer made more sense.

Just then the phone rang. The volume was set very high and made Brent jump. It elicited no reaction from Wenton.

Wenton let the phone ring a second time before he lifted the receiver to his ear. "Yeah?"

Georgia O'Connors was surprised by the abrupt greeting. "Dr. Wenton?"

"Yeah."

"This is Dr. Georgia O'Connors. I'm the clinical leader on North Bay at the Maximum Security Psychiatric Centre. I believe we've met a few times before."

"I think so," Wenton said without inflection.

Dr. O'Connors expected him to say more but the line was silent. She decided to continue. "Listen Dr. Wenton, we have a bit of a problem out here and we were wondering if you'd mind coming out."

"What kind of problem?"

"Well we have an urgent assessment that's taken some rather bizarre twists and I think we really need your expertise."

"Where's Brian?"

"Oh," Dr. O'Connors said, not anticipating answering that question on the phone. "He's, ah, he's temporarily absent. He's had an accident."

Wenton didn't like her evasiveness.

"Did Brian tell you to call me?"

"As a matter of fact he did recommend that."

"When?"

"I'm sorry?"

"When do you want to meet?"

"Well, I guess, as soon as possible."

"My time is $250 an hour and starts when I set foot in the Centre."

Brent raised an eyebrow as he listened.

Dr. O'Connors continued to be surprised by Wenton's tone. She knew he had a reputation for being abrupt, almost rude, but she'd never directly encountered it. She also knew that no one was considered more of an expert at the psychology of violence and the assessment of risk than Dr. Wenton.

"That's fine," she said reluctantly.

"Tomorrow morning, nine o'clock."

"Yes, that's good."

Wenton hung up the phone without waiting for any more discussion. He felt that the inconvenience of a phone call to his university office should have warranted a more thorough report of the details of the case. He let his hand rest on the receiver for a moment as he thought about what could have happened to Brian Claric. He knew the Centre's psychologist from overlap on cases they'd worked. It was Wenton's opinion that he was a competent psychologist who'd be able to handle any case that ended up at the MSPC.

"Dr. Wenton," Brent said tentatively, "should I go?"

Wenton looked up and for a moment saw a different graduate student in his office. It was a face that struck a chord of anger and regret as he remembered the lives that had been lost at the hands of Dennis Choler. He felt an instant surge of adrenaline and his hand gripped the phone reflexively before he realized that it was just Brent Bytasky sitting across from him.

"Yeah," Wenton finally said. "As far as I'm concerned we're done."

Brent's faced drained as he stood. He knew he'd missed his chance to work with Dr. Wenton. He turned to leave.

Wenton let his chair turn and he looked out the window behind him. He heard the door close as the student left and he closed his eyes.

thirty-three

118th day (wednesday)

Michael Wenton brought his black Dodge Durango to a stop in the parking lot of the MSPC. He was slightly early for his nine o'clock appointment with Dr. O'Connors. Wenton never arrived late for a meeting. Moreover, he expected promptness from the people with whom he worked. It was not uncommon to witness him leave a meeting before it began because it was late starting.

He leaned across to the passenger side and opened his glove compartment. Inside were the manual to his vehicle, a flashlight, and a number of security badges. Given his renown in the field of forensics, he had acquired clearance at most of the institutions in the city and surrounding area. He took the badge for the MSPC and clipped it to his sport coat.

"Thank you for coming Dr. Wenton," Dr. O'Connors greeted him as he entered the facility. Being aware of his attention to detail and punctuality, she felt it prudent to meet him personally.

"Good morning, Doctor," he replied, taking her hand.

"Let's go to my office." She turned and nodded at the security guard behind her. The guard pressed a button to release the door to Dark Alley.

"No security scan?" Wenton asked, nodding at the electronic wand on the desk.

She looked back at him, surprised. "No. Your clearance is up to date and you're wearing your badge, so technically you're an employee."

They walked quickly and silently back to Dr. O'Connors' office. She'd been tempted to make small talk but found her own comfort level didn't permit it. Once they were seated in her office she began.

"So, thank you again for coming today. As I mentioned to you on the phone we have kind of a strange situation and we'd like to use your expertise."

Wenton didn't show any signs of interest and continued to watch Dr. O'Connors, impassively. He had questions, but thought he'd hold them until she'd had her chance to fill in more of the details.

She waited, briefly, for a reply and continued, "So there are two different, but related, issues here. One, we need a thorough psychological, psychosexual, and risk assessment on the individual in question as part of his court-ordered evaluation. But secondly, there's a bit of an hysteria following this guy around." She paused, making a face, as she tried to figure out how to convey the issue. "The staff here are quite concerned, scared even, about working with this guy, but not for any reason we've ever confronted before. People are really scared that he has the power to make you, well, to make you go insane."

"We're talking about Edward Carter, I presume."

"Yes, how'd you know that?"

"His name and picture were in the paper a few weeks ago in association with those rapes. I'd heard that some of the victims were suffering serious psychiatric problems afterwards, but I didn't know much else."

"Not some, Dr. Wenton. All. All of the rape victims developed psychotic symptoms during their recovery and none of the symptoms have remitted yet. The first victim was approximately four months ago. She's now diagnosed with schizophrenia."

Wenton grunted an acknowledgment.

"Of course people were thinking some kind of severe PTSD reaction but there's real psychosis present. Hallucinations. Delusions of control by evil."

He nodded.

Dr. O'Connors waited for the impact of that information to sink in before she continued. "That in itself wouldn't be enough to put the staff here on edge. As you know, we've had all manner of disturbed offenders in here, and we've dealt with the entire spectrum of grisly crimes. The fact that Edward Carter's sexual assault makes his victim susceptible to a psychotic break only made it a bit of mystery for us."

"Until staff here started showing psychotic symptoms," Wenton interjected.

Dr. O'Connors' mouth dropped, "Ye-yes. How'd you know that?"

"That was the implication," he said matter-of-factly. "And is Brian Claric one of the recent individuals to be affected?"

"No," Dr. O'Connors said quickly. "There have been two staff members who've had contact with Edward Carter. One was a staff nurse, and the other is our social worker. We know that Rebecca, the nurse, had some problem in Edward's room during a night check. There was another nurse outside the door, but she didn't accompany Rebecca into the room during the check. However she did report that Rebecca couldn't have been in the room for more then a second or two. It was a close obs night check. Very routine."

"What were her symptoms?"

"Um," Dr. O'Connors began, somewhat uncomfortable with sharing too much information about a staff member's difficulties. "She finished her shift—it was a night shift—and went home. There were no other reports of anything out of the ordinary from other staff that night. When Rebecca got home she was a little disoriented and eventually made a suicide attempt. Her boyfriend was there and brought her to the hospital."

"What were the psychotic symptoms?"

"I'm not really sure. I guess she was saying something about being evil or that she was unfaithful to her boyfriend. I don't know everything about it."

Wenton nodded.

"The other case involves our veteran social worker, Andy Thomas. He was working on a social history with Edward. Again, he was only alone with Edward for a few minutes. The nurse who was sitting in on the interview had to leave because of an incident on the unit. When the nurse returned, the interview had ended and Andy seemed, like Rebecca, somewhat disoriented. No one knew about Rebecca yet, and so no one thought anything of Andy's reaction. It was Friday and when he returned to work on Monday there was an incident and—"

"Dr. O'Connors," Wenton interrupted, "if I have clearance and will be consulting on this case, I'd appreciate more candour than 'there was an incident.' Please stop being vague."

Dr. O'Connors looked at him with surprise and then softened. "You're absolutely right. I'm very uncomfortable with the whole situation. I'm not used to talking about my own staff this way and I feel as though I'm betraying a confidence." She looked to Wenton for an acknowledgment but found none. She took a deep breath and continued. "Okay. Andy came into our weekly rounds meeting on Monday morning and just lost it. He said something about not being a faggot and then leapt across that table at me. He had to be physically subdued and during the struggle Brian got hurt. He actually had a pencil jammed right through his hand." She looked at Wenton for a reaction but couldn't read his expression. "So Brian's out of commission. He's okay but his hand is pretty messed up. Andy, on the other hand, is on the psychiatric unit at Atlantic. Brian didn't want to press charges."

Wenton grunted again to acknowledge his appreciation of the situation. Without thinking, he lifted his left hand and slowly flexed it, watching the deformed joint on his ring finger. "Is his hand going to be okay?"

Dr. O'Connors watched him curiously. She nodded. "He'll be okay. The pencil missed bone and tendons so it was just a matter of cleaning it up and..." She paused, contemplating a personal question. "Dr. Wenton, did you hurt your hand?"

His eyes shot up and he let his hand drop to his lap. "It's not important, never mind," he said coolly. He didn't want to go through the story again. He didn't want to talk about a house where the police were facing off with Dennis Choler. He didn't want to talk about Choler breaking two fingers on Wenton's left hand before Wenton managed to subdue him. Most people considered Wenton to be a kind of hero. He may have saved the lives of two people being held hostage, but Wenton didn't feel like a hero. He was angry about the third hostage who was killed. He was angry about the women who died before Choler was caught. He was angry that Choler had been a graduate student in the psychology department for the duration of the killings, yet Wenton hadn't noticed anything. But he wasn't going to share any of that with Dr. O'Connors.

She waited to see if he would say anything else. When Wenton didn't speak she continued. "Anyway, as I'm sure you can imagine, people are pretty nervous about Edward Carter. He continues to be on close obs and there's a mandatory two-person contact rule. Access to Edward is restricted until we get a better handle on this. It wasn't hard to convince staff to stay away from him, but for the safety of our other clients we extended the no-contact rule to them as well. That means that Edward has been confined to his room except for escorted trips to the bathroom. It's pretty restrictive, but we don't want to take any more chances with him. None of us is entirely sure what we're dealing with, especially after the effect he had on our own staff."

"You must have had contact with him."

"Me?" She nodded. "Yeah, I met with him a few times. He's a passive, quiet, deferential man. He's obviously ill. I didn't see anything unusual about him, but then I always met with him in the presence of another staff member."

"Are you saying that he's only dangerous when there's one-to-one contact?"

Dr. O'Connors smiled, slightly embarrassed by the lack of solid information she could offer. "I honestly don't know, Dr. Wenton. But it seems that people who've been most adversely affected have been alone when they interacted with him."

"Why would individual contact make a difference?"

"I'm hoping you can help us figure that out. There's not much about this case that makes sense at the moment."

"Do you have any hypotheses?"

"Well, the rape victims obviously suffered tremendous trauma and so we'd initially assumed that they were suffering from a variant of post-traumatic stress disorder. We're less convinced by that now that two of our staff are affected, but it may still have something to do with an individual's reaction to Edward."

"Are you talking about a self-fulfilling prophecy? If a person believes that Edward will make him insane, then Edward has more power to do just that?"

"It's one guess," she said without much enthusiasm.

"Fine," Wenton responded. "I imagine there's an extensive history on his chart."

"Yes. Everything since his arrival has been charted. We've got older charts from Atlantic and the nursing staff can get those for you. I could give you a verbal description of his history if that would help."

"No, it's better to get the information from a documented source. Thank you."

"Okay," she said with disappointment. It was obvious that she had intended on providing more information including a full history. "So how else can we help you get started?"

"I have classes to teach today. I'm going to book off all day tomorrow. It would be convenient to have an office here while I work."

"Oh yes," she answered. "Brian already offered his office. I have a spare key here." She picked it up from her desk and held it out. "I'll take you past there when we're done."

He nodded.

"And I'll make sure that the nursing staff know you'll be here tomorrow. Will you want to interview Edward tomorrow?"

"I'll likely spend the afternoon with him."

"Then I'll make sure that one of the staff is freed up to accompany you."

"That's not necessary," Wenton said without expression.

"I'm sorry?"

"I won't need someone to sit in with me."

She struggled to respond carefully. "Well, as I said, our rule is that no one sees him alone." She added quickly, "Until we know what's going on, anyway. I don't want to put people at risk."

"I appreciate that. I understand the reason for your concern but I don't think I'll be able to understand what's going on unless I see him alone."

"I'm not comfortable letting you take that risk," she said shaking her head.

Wenton sighed heavily. "It's not negotiable. I appreciate your concern but you must realize that I don't take chances lightly. There's something going on here and you've asked me to help figure it out. I will, but it will have to be alone."

Dr. O'Connors reluctantly nodded.

thirty-four

118th day (wednesday)

Wa sat limply on the sofa in his living room. He felt exhausted and knew he wasn't able to speak to anyone now, not even family.

"Dad!" Joshua, his youngest, screamed as he came running into the room.

Wa rolled his head to one side, but before he could respond, Gloria came hurrying down the hallway.

"Joshua," she said sternly, "your daddy's tired and you need to play downstairs with Lisa and Nick."

Joshua turned, frowning. "I'm sorry."

"That's okay, you little monster," Wa said. "I just need a little rest."

A smile returned to the child's face and he happily ran back down the stairs.

Gloria sat next to her husband on the sofa. "How're you doing?"

"Under the circumstances, okay, I suppose."

"Can I get you something? A drink?"

"No thanks."

"Do you want to talk about it?"

"I don't know. Not really. There's not much to say." He paused and turned his head to look at her. "I know it's not my fault. I also don't believe in omens or anything. It just makes me wonder about my line of work. That's the second partner I've lost. I just don't know."

"He never regained consciousness, did he?"

Wa shook his head. "No. There was too much blood loss. Too much brain damage. It would've been worse if he had pulled through."

"I'm sorry."

"It was just tough today. I mean his wife was there too. I was almost waiting for him to go, but now that he's gone..."

"I know. But there's nothing you could have done."

Wa let his head fall back against the sofa and closed his eyes.

"What happens to the asshole who did this?" she asked.

"The asshole...," he said. "The asshole who did this might just be a nut job."

"What do you mean?"

"At his arraignment he was more or less incoherent. Babbling about being evil or some shit. He's scheduled to go to the MSPC tomorrow. He was initially charged with attempted murder but that'll be upgraded to murder now."

"I know this is difficult for you, sweetie, but when you lost Tim last year, and now Roland...it just makes me worried."

"I'm worried too."

She looked at him as though she was going to say something else, but she bit her bottom lip and turned away.

"What?" Wa asked.

"Nothing. I just don't like all this stuff with you guys."

He frowned. "All what stuff?"

"Tim Dallons. Roland. It's just..." Her eyes filled with tears.

"Okay. Okay. I know what you mean."

"Just be careful," she whispered.

"You got it," he said leaning to embrace her.

thirty-five

120th day (friday morning)

"We got another high profile one in yesterday," Nicholas said as he sat down in the nursing station beside Samantha.

"What do you mean? That Henry Yargurl?"

"You haven't looked at the chart?"

"Not yet."

"He's the guy that stabbed the cop at the homeless shelter. The cop died a couple of days ago and now old Henry's charged with murder."

"He's the guy that freaked out at the shelter?" Samantha said.

"Yep. Fucking thing is that the cops were there investigating the whole Edward Carter mess. Mr. Carter'd been sleeping there after his last rape."

"No way," she said, enjoying the drama of the story.

Nicholas loved an audience and continued. "That's the story I heard. They'd already arrested Eddie-boy and were just back to collect when BAM! Henry goes psycho and starts whacking at one of the cops with a fucking kitchen knife."

"Son of a bitch!"

A voice caused both of them to turn: "Excuse me. I need Edward Carter's chart."

A large man stood in the doorway of the nursing station. He wore dark pants, and a dark blue sweater vest over a light coloured shirt. His expression was difficult for them to read but hovered somewhere between impatience and indifference.

Nicholas was the first to respond. "Dr. Wenton?"

"That's right."

"We were expecting you. Edward's chart is right here," he said as he pulled a green binder off a metal rack. He handed it to Wenton.

"It's nice to meet you, sir," Samantha said.

Wenton nodded at her and then addressed Nicholas. "I have access to Dr. Claric's office. I'm going to take the chart there. If you need it, call me."

"That's fine. We'll call you if we need something from it."

"Fine. When I return after lunch I'm going to see Mr. Carter. Make sure he's up and dressed."

"Dr. O'Connors said that you *didn't* want one of us to accompany you during your interview. Is that right?" Samantha asked.

"Exactly," Wenton said tersely, not wishing to explain himself twice. "I'll return the chart at noon." He turned and headed out of the nursing station.

Samantha and Nicholas stood in silence and watched him leave.

"What an asshole!" Samantha eventually said.

"Yep," Nicholas agreed. "But he's probably the best asshole in the biz."

"Whatever," she said casually and they both settled back into chairs.

thirty-six

120th day (friday afternoon)

Wenton sat next to a plastic table in an interview room. On the table was a pad of yellow paper, a pen, and a microcassette recorder. He carefully set the pen on top of the pad.

Nicholas poked his head into the room. "All set in here?"

Wenton nodded.

"I'll be right back," the nurse said and disappeared. Wenton had requested that Edward be brought to the interview room. He preferred to wait for the client rather than go to the client's room.

In a few moments the door opened and Nicholas stepped into the room. A thin, sad looking man with dishevelled hair and rumpled hospital clothes stood immediately behind. Wenton noted that a second nurse was standing behind Edward. Even on a short trip to escort Edward to the interview room the staff travelled in pairs.

"Edward, this is Dr. Wenton," Nicholas said. "He's going to speak to you for a while."

Wenton stood and reached out to Edward who looked at his hand as though he was unsure of what to do. After the brief hesitation he took Wenton's hand and shook it.

"Please have a seat, Mr. Carter," Wenton said gesturing to a plastic chair.

Edward looked at the chair, then back to Wenton. He slowly eased himself down.

Nicholas caught Wenton's attention and mouthed the words, "Are you okay?"

Wenton nodded once and watched as Nicholas retreated out of the room, letting the door shut. He then sat back in his chair and looked across the table at Edward.

"So, Mr. Carter, as the nurse said, I'm Dr. Wenton. I'm a forensic psychologist and I'll be completing a fairly extensive assessment of you. To ensure the accuracy of the assessment I would like to audio tape the interview. That's what this is for." He held up the small cassette recorder. "Is it okay with you if I record this interview?"

Edward nodded passively, avoiding eye contact.

Wenton took the recorder and pressed a button then set it back on the table. Wenton thanked Edward for his consent and then provided an introduction for the tape, stating the date, time, Edward's name, and the location of the interview. Once he'd finished with the preamble, he addressed Edward.

"All right, let's begin. The main focus of the assessment will be on personality functioning, psychosexual issues, and risk for offending. Do you understand what I mean by that?"

Edward looked blankly at Wenton for a moment and then nodded slowly.

Wenton rubbed his chin roughly as he watched Edward. "Okay, tell me what I just said, then."

"You're checking me for personality, sexual issues, and risk." His voice was slow and deliberate.

Wenton raised an eyebrow but nodded. "Good. Okay. Well, today I'm going to spend most of our time talking to you. I want to run through your history from birth to present, focusing on a few important things. I may ask you some questions you've already answered, but I need to get my information directly from you. I've read through your hospital chart so I have an idea about your past, but please try to be as complete and honest as you can. If I interrupt you at any time it's because there's some important information that I don't want to miss. Does that sound okay?"

Edward nodded.

Wenton reached for his pen and plucked it off the pad. He held it casually in his right hand. "Why are you here, Mr. Carter?"

Edward shrugged.

"How are you feeling right now?"

Another shrug.

"I'm going to need a little more than that," Wenton said patiently.

Edward looked up, making eye contact, and then dropped his head back.

"Do you hear any voices, other than mine, right now?"

Edward looked up again and then dropped his head. "Yes."

"What are they saying?"

"Don't know."

"What are they saying right now?"

"Nothing."

"Are they talking about me?"

"Kinda."

"What are they saying?"

He looked up again and his eyes were black. The dilation of his pupils virtually erased the whites of his eyes as he leaned forward. "*You're next.*"

Then Edward sunk back into his chair and lowered his eyes.

Wenton held the pen still. He watched Edward fall back and could still feel a strange resonance in the room, an almost palpable aftershock from Edward's voice. He turned his head slightly and the resonance dissipated. He reached for his chin again and roughly held it in his grip.

"Mr. Carter," he began, "what do the voices want you to do right now?"

Edward mumbled something.

"What do they want you to do?" Wenton asked again.

"They want me to talk to you," Edward said in a soft voice. He looked up again with the same blackness in his eyes. "*Motherfucker*."

The ringing waves of sound again battered Wenton. He stared at Edward's eyes, still unable to piece together what he was seeing. Edward's face seemed to shift and change, only his black eyes remaining solid. The face took on vaguely familiar female features. Someone from his past. *A patient?* Wenton's stomach twisted and he felt like he might be sick. It was the face of a patient who'd committed suicide early in Wenton's career.

"No," Wenton growled.

The shifting features suddenly resolved themselves into Edward's face again. He turned his head and looked away from Dr. Wenton.

A slight resonance continued to hum in the back of Wenton's mind. He shook his head slightly and felt the waves dissipate. He looked across the table where Edward sat with his head hung down.

"Edward," Wenton said sternly.

There was no response.

"What happens when you use that voice?"

Edward shook his head slightly.

"I want you to look at me," Wenton said in a flat, cold voice.

Edward again shook his head.

Wenton reached and picked up the tape recorder. He pushed a switch and the wheels stopped turning. He set the recorder back on the table. "I want you to fucking look at me," he said in a slow, deliberate voice.

Edward's head tilted up.

"I want you to pay attention and answer my questions. Is that understood?"

Edward nodded.

Wenton picked up the tape recorder and slid the pause button back. He checked to make sure the wheels were turning and set it on the table.

"Good. Now, sometimes the voice you use is not your own, right?"

A shrug.

"Tell me about that."

Edward drew in a deep breath. "I don't know what to tell. I don't want to hurt anybody. I don't want to be like this."

"Like what?"

Edward shook his head slowly.

"Like what?" Wenton repeated.

"Like a monster," Edward said quietly, and his eyes darted away from Wenton. Tears were welling up at the corners of Edward's eyes.

"What about the voice?"

"I don't know anything about a voice."

"A moment ago you called me 'motherfucker.'"

Edward's glance shot back to Wenton. He was genuinely surprised. "I...," he began but stopped.

"Do you remember saying that?"

"I wouldn't say that to you."

"Do you remember saying that to me?"

Edward's head dropped down again. "Yes."

"Why did you call me a motherfucker?"

Edward took another deep breath. "I didn't. It's just that..." His voice faded away again.

"Tell me, Edward."

Tears exploded from Edward's eyes and he threw his head down onto his arms. He sobbed in heavy gasps.

Wenton didn't move. He watched patiently as Edward's body heaved with each sob.

After a few moments, Edward pulled his head up. His face was damp and streaked with red. As he spoke, a line of saliva escaped the corner of his mouth and clung to his chin.

"It's just that my head is so full of shit. I can't even think anymore. There's nothing but these thoughts. These horrible, horrible, thoughts. I can't do anything. It's all around me. I'm so full of this that it just comes out. I don't have any control over it. I don't want to be like this. I don't want to be evil. It just is. I can't do anything."

Wenton recognized that Edward was nearly hysterical but didn't want to interrupt the catharsis.

"Every day I want to be dead. Every time I think it's over, it isn't. I can't be okay. I can't do it. There's no place I can run. The only thing to do is kill myself, but I can't do that either. I just don't want to be this thing anymore. Please help me. Please help me be okay?" He reached across the table with his hands open. "Please help me get this out of me."

Wenton nodded. Edward dropped his head back to the table and continued to sob.

Consolation was not part of Wenton's approach with clients. He let Edward cry until he gained enough composure to continue with the interview.

"I need to ask you an important question. When you called me that name you used a different voice. Do you remember?"

Edward looked at him with a curious expression. "I don't think I know what you mean."

"Your voice changed when you called me a motherfucker."

Edward shook his head in genuine ignorance.

Wenton decided to continue. "Okay. Tell me why you think you're evil."

"I just am. Look at what's happened," he said in disgust.

"But why you?"

"You must know where I came from. Who my parents were."

"I've read the chart."

Edward shrugged.

"No one has control over their parents. You're not responsible for them," Wenton said.

Edward sighed. "That's not it. I know I didn't kill them. I know. But I'm a bastard. I'm the reason they all died. It was me. I came out of it. Everything bad in them is in me."

"So what makes you evil?"

"It's all the little stuff. It's all the big stuff."

"I'm not following you."

"You sin," Edward said with conviction. "You do bad and how does that make you feel?"

Wenton looked at Edward with cold eyes. "I'm not being interviewed."

Edward nodded and continued. "Everyone does bad things. Everyone has a bad secret. Something they regret. For some it's small and for others it's big. But whatever it is, it will get you. It will hurt you."

"What's your point?" Wenton interrupted.

Edward smiled. "My point is we all have the bad thing. It pushes us, makes us who we are. The bad makes us hate and do bad. It is bad. The only question is: Do you let the bad use you? Do you let it take over?"

Wenton thought Edward was still psychotic and decided not to waste any more time on him.

"What do you do to the women you rape? Why do they go insane?"

Edward's eyes blazed at the question. He spoke slowly through clenched teeth. "Who do you think you are to ask me that?"

Wenton shrugged. "You aren't answering my questions. You're just spouting bullshit about evil and having evil in your body. That's all just bullshit, so I want to cut to the meat of the issue. Why did those women go insane? What did you say to Mr. Thomas, the social worker?"

Edward's face contorted with anger. His upper lip curled up and his eyes became narrow slits of fire. The tears burned away before they had a chance to escape his eyelids.

"Don't test me."

"This is just an interview. I'll conduct the psychological testing at a later session," Wenton responded caustically.

Edward's face continued to contort and his eyes burned with black. "*Facini entfaste blackened side*," he said rapidly.

"I don't speak Italian," Wenton hissed back, "so don't play fucking games, Edward."

"*Facini entfaste blackened side.*"

"Edward!" Wenton barked.

Edward's voice was deep and low and it physically rumbled through Wenton. "*Fuck you. You don't understand evil. You can never understand the evil. You're a fucking doctor with no idea. No idea about desire and loss of control. No fucking idea whatsoever.*"

Wenton's head hummed with the intrusive voice but he remained calm and watched the bizarre transformation in front of him. Edward's eyes occupied nearly half of his face now. The rest of his face buckled around the enormous black shapes. The appearance was almost buglike.

"*I can't talk to something like you,*" Edward continued in a throaty growl. "*You are beneath me. Face me.*" He leaned forward and reached out with both hands.

Wenton watched Edward lean toward him and saw the hands extending to either side of his head. Edward's words continued to bounce and rattle though his mind making it difficult to concentrate. Difficult but not impossible.

Wenton dropped his pad of paper onto the table and used both arms to swat Edward's hands away. "Get the fuck away from me." As he spoke he saw Edward's features swirl back into place.

The resistance took Edward by surprise. He fell back into his chair and let his arms drop to the table.

The man Wenton was looking at now was without distortion. It was the weak, frail Edward Carter who had entered the room. As Wenton studied him he noticed his own heartbeat slowing. He realized his anger had somehow disconnected him from whatever process was taking place.

The room was eerily silent as both men sat motionless, staring across the table at one another.

"How are you feeling now, Mr. Carter?" Wenton finally asked.

Edward shook his head slowly. "I don't know."

Wenton nodded but waited for more.

"Why?" Edward asked.

"Why what?"

"Why doesn't the evil bother you?"

"What do you mean?"

"I can't control what's in me. It just happens. But it doesn't do anything to you. Why?"

Wenton shrugged, unwilling to offer any hypothesis to Edward.

Edward looked at him with a strange expression before he spoke again. "I'm you," he finally said.

"What?" Wenton asked in genuine confusion.

"I am you. You are me. I'm in you already," Edward said softly and looked away.

thirty-seven

122nd day (sunday)

Henry Yargurl didn't know why he was at the psychiatric hospital. Everything seemed unreal. He'd been drifting around from place to place for a while now. And people were so angry at him. He didn't understand that. So angry. Everywhere he went people were so angry. And they said horrible things. Horrible things.

Henry took a seat in the common area of North Bay. He quickly scanned the other people in the room. There was a large, overweight man in one chair. He stared straight ahead and never said a word to anyone. The other patients stayed away from him. In the corner there were two men playing cards. All the other clients were in their rooms. Henry didn't know how many people were here. Most stayed in their rooms. Henry didn't care about any of them. They didn't mean anything to him.

Except for one person.

Henry tried to watch TV. The set was fixed high in the corner of the room in a Plexiglas box. The protective plastic was slightly murky and streaked, which distorted the picture. Being Sunday afternoon there were few choices for programs—sports, infomercials, or religious shows. Right now Henry was watching a man in a long blue robe striding back and forth across a stage. It was almost comical how intense the man was as he reached the end of the stage, spun, and started back.

The volume on the TV was set quite low but Henry could just make it out.

"...and without first reaching inside yourself how can you expect to let GOD reach inside you! For it is GOD who can cleanse you. It is GOD who can set you free. But it is you who must take that first step! Take that step! Take that step! Let our GOD, our GOD of mercy, our GOD of LOVE, our GOD of..."

Henry smiled. He'd never been a very religious person. He thought that religion was silly. The only time he'd ever prayed, his prayer wasn't answered. That had been enough. The only time he'd ever needed a God was when he and his wife were struggling. He remembered what it was like when he fought with her all the time and his smile faded away. The kids would scream and cry because they didn't understand. He wanted to tell the kids that Daddy was sorry and he would be better, but Mommy was so mad. Henry shook his head. It felt like his life ended when she left and took the kids. He lost everything. He lost his family, his house, his job...everything. He kept struggling to make it back. He needed to make it back, if only for his kids. He wanted to see them, to help support them but he just didn't have the strength. He kept ending up on the streets, ending up at halfway houses or homeless shelters.

"Henry!"

A voice called to him, interrupting his thoughts. He looked around but saw no one. The big man was still staring. The two other patients were still playing cards. There was no one in the doorway of the nursing station. The two nurses sitting behind the desk weren't looking at him.

"Henry, you useless incestuous motherfucker!"

He jumped to his feet.

"You better believe in God, Henry, because your soul belongs to Satan."

The voice was coming from the TV. He stared up at the set and saw the man still striding back and forth with his blue robe billowing. He looked at the other men in the room to see if they'd reacted to the preacher's words. They hadn't.

"What's your problem, Henry? You know that you belong to evil and you'll do whatever you're told. You obeyed me when I asked you to touch your children."

Henry sank back into his chair. He couldn't believe what was happening. He stared at the television.

The evangelist swept across the stage again, more quickly this time.

"Don't," Henry said quietly.

"Don't fucking talk back to me you worthless slave. Everyone hates you, despises you for what you've done. You're a child-fucker."

He couldn't believe no one else was reacting to what was happening. He looked at the other patients again but they were undisturbed. He turned back to the TV and the preacher was becoming a blur of motion as he swept back and forth. Henry wondered if there was something wrong with the set. He looked over his shoulder, thinking he might call out to the nursing staff to have them check.

"Pay attention, child-fucker!"

His head snapped back.

"You need to go and see Edward. Help him. Everything is for him."

Henry felt cold all over. Beads of sweat collected across his forehead and dripped down his back. The figure on the TV was a blur now. There were only long, looping waves of static running across the screen.

"Your life doesn't mean anything. Do it. Do everything for him."

"I can't," Henry weakly protested.

"Look at your arms."

He let his eyes fall to his arms and sucked in his breath. The skin bubbled and twisted. He could feel something beneath his skin, crawling and digging. Then the outline of something pushed through his skin. It was his oldest daughter's face and she was crying. He opened his mouth to scream but his stomach retched and silenced him.

"*Do you see now?*" the TV asked.

"Stop it," he said unable to tear his eyes away from his burning arms.

"*Do what is needed.*"

"No." His arms bulged under the pressure of the invasion and the pain swelled into his mind.

"Do what I want."

"No. I can't," he said so softly he didn't know if the words had left his mouth. He wanted to cry out in pain but he knew he needed to be perfectly still. If he moved, if he tried to scream, he knew that his arms would explode.

"You will."

A sharper pain burned through his left elbow. His rippling skin seemed to be converging on this one spot and he watched his elbow swelling. There was the faint outline of another face. His baby girl. He twisted his arm on the chair and tried to flatten the bunching skin. It didn't help; the writhing, burning thing inside him kept pushing out toward his elbow. He lifted his arm and brought it down hard on the chair. His elbow exploded with pain and his skin burst. He let his arm fall limply down and watched something dark push through the seeping blood of his wound. Soon his arm was alive with black shapes pushing out through his torn skin. The black things twisted and flipped in the air as they tore out of him. His stomach retched again and he only barely choked back the rising bile.

"Get out of me," he said through clenched teeth.

"*Do what you must,*" the TV answered.

"Get out. Get out. GET OUT!" he finally screamed. He banged his arm against the chair. The black things spilled out of him in even greater numbers.

"Hey! What's going on in there?" a voice called from the nursing station.

Henry stopped and looked over his shoulder. A nurse was standing in the doorway watching him.

"Nothing," he called back, rising.

"Take it easy on the furniture, pal," the nurse said before turning back into the station.

Henry nodded and waited until the nurse was no longer watching before he sat back in the chair. As he did so, he noticed that the large man was staring at him. The two others had also stopped their card game and were watching him.

"Your arm's bleeding," the big man said passively.

Henry looked down at his elbow. The skin was broken and blood was collecting in the wound. He didn't see any evidence of the black shapes and his arms no longer rippled.

"Yeah," he said.

The big man turned away and continued to stare into space. The other two resumed their game.

Henry stared at his arm. He couldn't understand where the dark things had gone. Then he remembered the TV. His head shot up and he saw only static, like the station had gone off the air.

He stood and looked quickly around the room. No one was paying attention to him anymore. He left the common room and headed down one of the hallways. He knew what he had to do now.

He looked quickly behind him. This wasn't the hallway where his room was. This hallway had single rooms—Henry was sharing a room with two other patients. He hurried to the end of the corridor and stopped at the last door. He stepped to the small window in the door and looked through.

"Hello?" he called quietly and glanced down the hallway toward the nursing station to see if he'd drawn any attention.

Edward's face appeared in the window, startling him.

"I'm ready to serve you," Henry whispered urgently through the glass.

Edward stared back at him. "What do you mean?"

"You command me and I will do what must be done."

Edward shook his head and turned back to his bed.

"Satan!" Henry shouted.

"Hey!" a voice called from down the hall. "Get away from there!"

"Satan! I am here!" Henry yelled through the window.

Edward spun back toward the door. His eyes were dark pools that shone in the dimly lit room. "Serve me, whore!" he spat out.

The words echoed through Henry. He barely registered the pounding footsteps of the nursing staff running toward him.

"I will serve you!" Henry said and pressed his face against the plastic window.

Edward leapt at the door and brought his body crashing against it, pressing his face against the window's other side. "*Kill them all!*" he hissed. "*Kill them all so that I might live*."

"I will. I will."

"Okay, let's go," Carl said as he placed a hand on Henry's shoulder. "You know you aren't supposed to be down here."

"I'm sorry," Henry said compliantly and turned with the nurse.

"That's the second time we've warned you today," Milton said. "And I know they told you the same thing yesterday. You aren't supposed to be down here. Stay out of this hallway."

"I'm sorry. I guess I just got confused."

"Don't let it happen again or we'll have to isolate you," Carl said as the three began walking back up the hallway.

"It won't," he assured them.

"It better not... Hey! Is your arm bleeding?" Milton said, looking down at Henry.

Carl stopped as Milton took hold of Henry's wrist and lifted the arm. "It is bleeding. You banged up your elbow."

Milton looked at Carl who just rolled his eyes. "We better have a look at that. Clean it up and put a bandage on it."

"Everything okay?" Samantha called from the doorway of the nursing station.

Carl and Milton looked down the hallway at her. "Yeah," Carl called. "He's just banged up his arm somehow. We need to clean it up."

Samantha nodded and retreated into the nursing station.

The Treatment Room, located in the middle of the corridor, was the general examination room that held all the unit's surplus medical equipment, including bandages.

"You go ahead," Milton said as he turned to a doorway immediately behind him. "I'll do this quickly."

"Okay," Carl said and waited until the Treatment Room door was opened. Henry and Milton stepped inside and Carl continued down the corridor.

"What was going on down there?" Samantha asked when Carl sat down beside her.

"Nothing. Henry's just being weird."

"Was he actually talking to Edward?"

"Don't know. Doubt it. I think he's just really ill. I'm not sure Henry knows what's going on. His elbow was all cut up."

She looked at him with a puzzled expression. "His arm?"

"Yeah, his left elbow was kinda banged up and bleeding. I think he probably hurt it when he was smacking around in the chair." He nodded towards the common room.

They were quiet for a moment before Carl spoke again. "Shelley's still on her break, eh?"

"She'll be back soon. She just needed to pick something up. It's her husband's birthday tomorrow."

Suddenly a voice screamed from the common area. "You fuckin' cheat!"

Samantha and Carl jumped to their feet. The two guys playing cards were standing face-to-face and the cards were scattered around the floor.

"Great," Carl said and stepped out of the nursing station with Samantha following.

"So what'd you do here, Henry?" Milton asked as he sat the other man down in a chair next to a small medical table on wheels. "Lay your arm up here, please."

Henry was silent as he laid his arm on the table.

"Looks like you banged this up pretty good. You feeling okay?"

Henry nodded and looked away.

"Well, I'm just going clean this up a bit and make sure you don't need further medical attention. If you don't, we'll just put a bandage on it and that'll be it."

Henry was silent.

Milton pulled a sterile swab out of a container behind him and took a bottle off the counter. The room was packed with medical equipment. Bandages, tape, and swabs were lined up carefully on shelves on one side of the room. Under the shelves was a countertop complete with a sink. Cupboards beneath the counter held more medical equipment and supplies. The other side of the room had a full-length gurney for treating or transporting patients. There were also seats and wheeled tables used for giving needles, taking blood, and other minor medical procedures.

"Okay," Milton said as he leaned over Henry's arm with a cotton swab. "This might sting a bit but it'll only take a second." He began dabbing at the wound to clean away some of the blood.

A voice sounded from down the hall. "You fuckin' cheat!"

Milton froze.

"What was that?" he said and turned away from Henry. He listened for a moment but didn't hear anything else. He stepped toward the door and looked down the hallway. He saw Carl and Samantha hurrying out of the nursing station.

"Everything okay?" he called to them.

Samantha waved him back, then she and Carl disappeared into the common area, out of his view.

He shrugged and stepped back into the treatment room. As he turned, something hard stung him in the nose and sent waves of pain crashing through his head. Before he could recover something snapped against the side of his head and his eardrum sang in a high-pitched squeal. He dropped to the floor on his knees and, through eyes filling with tears, he saw Henry standing over him holding the plastic tray from the table.

"Let's break this up, guys. Have a seat," Carl said forcefully as he stood in the centre of the common area, a safe distance away from the two men who were facing off.

"This fuckin' guy's cheating," one of them said.

"Blow me," the other answered.

Samantha came and stood next to Carl, watching the men carefully. She hoped Mark, the security guard, was wide awake in the control room.

"That's enough. Let's go back to our rooms then. If we can't play nice then we won't play at all," Carl said.

The two men looked at Carl. Both their faces were distorted with anger. Samantha always felt uneasy about this part of the job. She hoped that Milton finished up with Henry soon and got out here.

The men looked like they were contemplating their choices as they stared back at Carl.

"Come on," Samantha said. "Let's just relax. We'll sort this one out."

She was surprised to see their expressions change and soften noticeably. She wondered if it would be that easy. The men looked surprised and kind of humbled. But she realized they weren't looking at her, and they weren't looking at Carl either. They were staring at something behind them.

Out of the corner of her eye, she detected a flash of motion and turned. The other patient in the room, the large quiet one, had stood and moved into position behind her. She felt a hand grab the back of her head and strong fingers grip her tightly. She instinctively reached up but her head was already being swung toward Carl. She barely noticed that the man held Carl's head in his other hand as her head met his with a dull thud. Blackness dropped over her.

"Holy shit!" Mark yelled as he watched Carl and Samantha crumple to the floor. Blood had burst forth as their heads were slammed together.

Mark leapt to his feet, unsure of what to do. He'd only worked at the MSPC for two months and had never seen anything like this happen before. He'd seen patients yelling and carrying on, but it never amounted to anything. These guys always seemed to back down and do what they're told. The other security guards told him nothing ever happened around here. *Well something was fucking happening now!*

He jumped from one side of the security station to the other, trying to figure out what to do. He went to grab his phone but knew he didn't have time to call anyone. Then he remembered the distress button. He tried to scan his console for the red button. He found it, flipped the protective plastic cover back, and pounded his fist down. Red lights began to spin outside the station an alarm sounded throughout the unit.

He glanced up on his monitor and saw the large patient standing over the two nurses. "Fuck!" he screamed. "Fuck! Fuck! Fuck!"

He looked around the small station for something to grab, a weapon, anything. There was nothing there. A clipboard. Pens, pencils. A flashlight! He grabbed it and threw open the door.

The control room was directly across from the nursing station and adjacent to the common area. Mark came to a halt in the doorway and stared across at the large man who continued to stand, motionless, over the fallen nurses.

"Hey!" he screamed. "Back the fuck off!"

And then a sharp pain doubled him over. He screamed and the flashlight dropped out of his hands, rolling across the floor. The pain in his stomach was tremendous and he fell to his knees, grasping at something that protruded from his midsection.

There was someone standing over him and he looked up to see Henry's face.

Henry looked down at him without expression. He pushed the security guard aside and stepped into the control room.

As Henry passed, Mark looked down at his stomach. A pair of surgical scissors was buried to the handle. Blood was soaking through his uniform and making a dark ring around the entry point. Mark's head began to swim and he looked away from the gruesome sight. He couldn't regain his balance and fell to one side, against the wall. He closed his eyes and prayed that this was all just a dream. He slid down the wall until he was lying flat on the floor.

Henry dragged the body into the command station and then took a seat at the controls. Edward Carter soon joined him. The rest of North Bay became chaotic. The other remand patients began to riot, destroying the unit. Henry calmly picked up the security phone, which was equipped with a direct line to the main security desk.

"Security," a voice answered on the other end. "What the hell's going on down there? Did you hit the alarm?"

"We got a riot going on in North Bay," Henry said. "Send in the Emergency Response Unit."

"Son of a bitch. Are you serious?"

"Get them in here, now!" Henry screamed, then hung up the phone. He turned to Edward who had donned a riot helmet and was pulling the riot helmet visor down to obscure his face. Fully dressed in the security uniform he was indistinguishable from any other guard—especially in the middle of an actual riot.

thirty-eight

123rd day (monday morning)

Mitchell Wa walked into the operations room of the police station and found himself in the midst of a flurry of activity. The operations room was a series of desks with computers and phones. Bulletin boards and chalkboards lined the walls. Wa's office bordered the room, along with some others.

"Mitchell!" a voice called to him. "Where have you been?"

Detective Margaret Meredith hurried up to him. "We've been trying to page you all morning."

"I left my pager in my office," Wa said. "What's going on?"

"There was an incident at the MSPC."

"What do you mean?"

"Let's go into your office," Margaret answered and turned to scan the room. She saw her partner, Laurie Abrahms, and waved her over. The three detectives quickly moved into Wa's office and closed the door.

"So don't you watch the news?" Margaret asked.

"We had the kids out at the park all day yesterday. I didn't watch the news this morning."

"Doesn't matter," she said. "All hell broke loose at the MSPC yesterday. We had units respond to a riot call on the remand unit."

"The remand unit!"

"Yep. It was an ugly scene. Two staff were killed. Three more went to the hospital, two with serious injuries. The tactical team swarmed the place to get them out. It looked bad in there."

"What's that got to do with us?" Wa asked. "Did Edward get killed?"

Both Margaret and Laurie shook their heads.

"It took a while to get things settled," Margaret said. "The place was a real mess but it looked like none of the remands were hurt. It also looked like everyone was accounted for. Everyone, including Henry Yargurl."

"Henry?" Wa said. "You mean the guy that attacked Roland?"

"Yeah. He was there for a psychiatric evaluation because he's been babbling about Satan ever since he attacked you guys, and it looks like he was one of the guys involved in the riot. He may even have attacked a couple of the staff there."

"Fuck," Wa breathed.

"That's not all," Margaret said. "They locked the place down, including throwing that Henry guy in solitary, and then they did a head count." She stopped and looked at Laurie before she continued. "And they couldn't find Edward."

"What?"

"They did a sweep around the hospital and found a security guard's uniform and a tactical helmet. He must've slipped out when everything was going crazy."

"Son of a bitch," Wa growled and began to rub his temples. He could feel a headache starting as he contemplated how difficult his life had just become. Finally, he snapped his head back. "I'm going over there."

"Thank you for meeting with me on such short notice, Dr. O'Connors," Wa said as he sat in a chair in the psychiatrist's office.

"I'm happy to help," she said as she took her seat at the desk.

"You'll pardon me if I just jump right in and skip the pleasantries," Wa said. "Could you tell me how something like this happens?"

"I'll be honest with you, Detective. I'm at a loss to explain this one. This is not a normal case. There's something else going on here. Something I've not seen before."

"What does that mean?"

She drew in a deep breath. "Well, since Edward Carter got here we've had problems. Two of my staff—both competent, respected professionals—have been hospitalized."

"We're not talking about the staff from yesterday's riot?"

"No. The staff members I'm speaking of went to the psychiatric unit at Atlantic."

Wa waited for an explanation.

"One was a nurse, Rebecca Ly, who reportedly had some contact with Edward during a night shift. The next morning she nearly hacked off her left hand in an attempt to kill herself. She was convinced that the devil was in her.

"A few days later our veteran social worker, Andy Thomas, had an interview with Edward. Some staff thought he was acting a little strange at the end of the interview. A few days later he had a psychotic break and attacked me and another psychologist during a team meeting. He was speaking about not being a faggot. Naturally, we became concerned about what was happening and quarantined Edward Carter in his room with strict rules that no staff should be alone with him."

Wa was becoming frustrated. "What does this have to do with him *walking* out of here yesterday?"

"I think it has everything to do with it," she replied. "You see Henry

Yargurl was one of the instigators of the incident yesterday. Over the last few days he'd repeatedly been warned to stay away from Edward's room. He kept going to that end of the hall and looking in—possibly speaking to Edward."

"So you're saying that Henry was the accomplice?"

"Not exactly."

"I don't have time for riddles, Doctor."

"We learned that Henry and Edward were at the homeless shelter at the same time, and so they may have—"

"I know all that. Roland Makum—the detective that Henry murdered—was my partner. I was with him when Henry stabbed him. I arrested that son of a bitch."

Dr. O'Connors sat back in her chair. She hadn't made the connection. Suddenly she realized she'd seen Wa's name in the Yargurl file.

"Oh," she said. "I'm sorry. I didn't realize."

"Whatever," he said. "What does that have to do with anything?"

"I was going to say that I think Edward had contact with Henry while at the homeless shelter and—"

"Their cots were side by side."

She stared at Wa. "They were? How do you know?"

"One of the workers at Second Chance mentioned it because it seemed like such a coincidence."

"Well, Detective, I don't know how to say this, but I think that Edward Carter has the power to make people psychotic."

"What?"

"All of his victims. Two of my staff. Henry Yargurl. I don't know how many others are all certifiably insane after having contact with Edward Carter."

Wa didn't know how to respond.

"I know it doesn't make any sense," she continued, "but the facts are stacking up. And Henry Yargurl is heavily sedated right now because after the incident yesterday he became completely incoherent. His psychosis has become unmanageable. I know it sounds crazy, but anyone who has one-to-one contact with Edward Carter goes insane."

Wa struggled to make sense of what he was being told. "But...but you're his doctor. You must have had contact with him. You're not insane, are you?"

"I think a person has to be alone with him. I never saw Edward without being accompanied by nursing staff."

Wa shook his head. The whole case was getting out of control. At first it was nearly impossible to track Edward down because they couldn't get a description. Then they got lucky and things finally came together. But just as quickly things had come apart again. Roland was dead, Edward had escaped, and now his psychiatrist was saying that Edward Carter could make people insane just by being in their presence.

"You know," Dr. O'Connors said, "we should probably talk to Dr. Wenton. He was the last person who had contact with Edward. He might have some—"

"Michael Wenton?" Wa asked with surprise.

"Yes, Michael Wenton. Do you know him?"

"Of course. He's worked with the police before."

"I should have known," she said. "Dr. Wenton was here last Friday to review the file and interview Edward. He was going to give us his impression of the situation and conduct a personality and risk assessment. He might have some more insight for us. Shall I call him?"

"I know how to get hold of him," Wa said.

The idea of calling in Dr. Wenton didn't sit well with Wa. He knew it would be a struggle since Wenton didn't like working with the police. In addition, the last time Wa saw Wenton was during the hostage standoff that ended Tim Dallons' career. Unfortunately, Wa also knew that he needed Wenton's kind of help on this case.

thirty-nine

124th day (tuesday)

Mitchell Wa, Margaret Meredith, Laurie Abrahms, and Bill Lawrence sat around the conference room table at the police station. The investigating team had assembled for an emergency meeting with Michael Wenton.

"Thank you for coming on such short notice, Dr. Wenton," Wa said to begin the proceedings. "I know you can appreciate the urgency of this matter and the timeline we're working against."

Wenton was seated at the head of the table and had already briefly acknowledged each of the team members. Only Bill was unfamiliar to him.

"Well, by my calculations, you only have a couple of days before this guy commits another assault," Wenton said.

"That's right," Wa responded. He looked around the table to make sure the other team members understood the importance of their timeline. The grave faces assured him that they did. "I called you in today because I spoke with Dr. Georgia O'Connors at MSPC and she mentioned that you were involved with this case. I guess you were consulted to conduct an assessment of personality and risk?"

Wenton sighed. He expected that details like that could have been dispensed with before he arrived. "That's right. I met with Edward Carter for the first time last Friday. Do you want me to get on with what I know?"

Margaret was so focused on learning about Edward Carter that she missed the edge in Wenton's tone.

"What *can* you tell us?" she asked earnestly. "Is there any light you can shed on who this guy really is?"

Wenton turned slowly to face her before he responded. The motion made Margaret feel distinctly uncomfortable.

"I'm concerned," he said. "Very concerned about this individual. I think we're seeing something different. A new type of mental illness combined with some physical abnormality or defect." Wenton carefully watched the expressions of the individuals in the room.

Bill shifted in his seat. Margaret stared at Wenton with an expression that resembled someone in pain. Laurie could not maintain eye contact with anyone.

Finally, Wa spoke. "We're just cops, Doctor, so you'd better spell everything out in detail. Don't assume we know what you're talking about."

Wenton sighed heavily. "Okay. Edward Carter is psychotic. He's very ill and likely quite dangerous. But that's not what's most troubling. I think that he can create psychosis in other people. I think there's something unique about his illness and his biological make-up that allows him to project his insanity onto others under certain circumstances."

"Dr. O'Connors said something about that," Wa said. "He can drive another person insane?"

"Holy shit," Bill whistled.

"I'm not entirely sure," Wenton continued. "But the evidence points to it. People who've had direct contact with him have become psychotic."

"But what does that mean?" Wa asked. "How can this guy drive other people insane?"

Wenton looked carefully at everyone in the room. He studied each face separately until he stopped at Bill Lawrence.

"Bill," he said so suddenly that the constable jumped in his chair. "What are you feeling right now?"

Bill looked around at his colleagues for support before he answered. "I don't know. I guess I'm feeling a little nervous. I mean, I don't know, this guy can make people insane?"

Wenton turned to the person on Bill's right. "And you Detective Abrahms?"

"This is crazy," Laurie said. "I don't know what to think."

Wenton looked at Wa. "What about you?"

"I'm really lost on this one, Dr. Wenton. I don't know either. This is really getting fucked up."

Wenton turned to the last detective and nodded.

"I can't believe it," Margaret said. "But I've seen what he did to those poor women. They've all been affected in such dramatic ways. I can't believe someone can do that to another person's mind, but I know it's happened."

Wenton nodded and looked around the room again. "There's a lot of emotion in this room right now. I'm sure that you can all feel it. Pretty tense in here." He looked at each of the team members again. "Some of you are ready to burst. It's getting pretty difficult to keep perspective on this case, eh?"

"What's your point?" Wa barked.

Wenton stopped and stared at him. The detective knew he'd made a tactical mistake. There was always a fairly clear division of power in dealings with Dr. Wenton. He'd made it clear to the police that he didn't want to work with them, and when he deigned to do so, the relationship was always tenuous.

"Detective Wa," Wenton said, "the point is that there's a lot of power in emotion. In fact research has provided ample evidence of emotionally primed learning. That means certain things are learned in a very powerful way during certain powerful emotional states. Our brains can be primed by emotion. In the same way, our brains can be primed for mental illness by emotion."

"So if we're feeling a certain way, we're more likely to learn something, right?" Laurie said slowly.

"Or," added Margaret, "if we're feeling a certain way we're more vulnerable to getting a mental illness—like going insane? Is that right?"

"Basically," Wenton nodded. "In fact, the current psychiatric classification system includes entire sections of disorders that are primarily based on emotional states—mood disorders or anxiety disorders, for instance. Moreover, there's one mental disorder that's actually created by emotional priming. I'm sure you've all heard of post-traumatic stress disorder? The classic example is the soldier returning from battle irrevocably traumatized. The fear and terror of war traumatizes the individual so badly that he or she develops a mental illness. In essence, the intensity of the fear creates the illness."

A few members of the group nodded.

"So these women are so freaked out by the sexual assault that they go insane?" Margaret asked.

"I don't think so," Wenton answered. "Not exactly, anyway. Fear is a part of it, but fear is just the emotional prime—it gets the person's brain ready for the next attack." He paused again, not wanting to overwhelm them.

"Which is what?" Wa said impatiently.

"There's something about what Edward Carter says and how he says it."

The table was silent as they waited for more details.

"I believe there's a particular resonance in Edward's voice at certain times that has an effect at a neurological level. In addition, the things that Edward says influence the direction of that neurological disruption. Thus, fear primes the victim, and then the combination of Edward's peculiar tone of voice with his religious delusions and hallucinations creates psychosis."

"That's ridiculous," Wa said flatly.

"Well why are all those women insane then?" Margaret asked angrily.

"Just because Edward is a fucking wacko doesn't mean that he can use a spooky voice to make other people insane," Wa responded.

"Then *you* explain what the hell's going on." Margaret yelled.

"Come on," Laurie said, holding her hands up. "Let's cool it. We're all feeling the stress on this one."

The table fell silent for a moment before Bill spoke tentatively. "Excuse me, but if his power is in the way he talks, why aren't more people insane? I mean, he's had contact with a lot of people. What about the rest of the staff at the psychiatric centre? What about..."

"Yeah," Wa said, his expression brightening. "What about his boss at the barbershop? And what about you, for fuck's sake? You met with him last Friday!"

"It's partially as a result of that meeting that I'm suggesting this theory. I experienced the peculiar resonance first hand."

"And you're okay?" Margaret asked. "How?"

"I'm okay because not all of the elements were present in order to make me go insane."

"Like what?" Wa said throwing his arms in the air.

"Fear," Wenton said flatly.

The table was silent again.

After a moment Laurie spoke quietly. "Why not?"

"Why not what?" Wenton said addressing his question directly to her.

"Why weren't you afraid if everybody else has been?"

"First of all, not everybody has been afraid, obviously, because not everybody who has come into contact with Edward has developed a mental disorder. Second, there are individual differences in people's ranges of emotion."

"But...," Wa began, struggling to put everything into perspective, "why hasn't anyone noticed this before?"

"It may have only begun recently—the particular vocal resonance, anyway. But the resonance doesn't occur all the time. It may be related to his illness. When his hallucinations or delusions are stronger, the voice is more likely. Possibly the resonance effect is stronger too."

"You mean if his mental illness is worse, then his ability to make others insane is stronger?" Bill asked incredulously.

"Perhaps."

"Well he's probably not on meds right now. Would that affect this thing?" Wa asked.

"If the medication that helped to control his mental illness is removed..." Wenton shrugged his shoulders.

"Oh fuck," Laurie said softly.

"Well what should we do?" Wa asked. "How are we supposed to catch this guy under conditions like this? We'd have to fuckin' shoot him on sight so he doesn't make us go nuts!"

"No," Wenton said. "I already said that there was a pre-condition: the fear. I think that a powerful emotional state needs to prime the recipient's brain for the resonance and message of Edward's voice to have its full effect. I experienced the resonance but it had little effect on me. I could tell what was happening, but it was nothing for me to shake it off—to dismiss him."

"Well then you'll just have to catch him," Laurie said flippantly.

He purposely ignored her and stood. "Are there any other questions?"

"No, hold on," Wa said quickly. "What do you suggest we do? Is there any way to protect ourselves?"

"It's all just a theory," Wenton said casually. "I don't even know if you need to worry. You just asked for my opinion."

"Come on," Wa pleaded. "You know what I mean. I'm sorry if we're a bit out of sorts over this but..."

Wenton took a deep breath and leaned on the table. "You have something working in your favour right now. I don't believe the media has picked up on the insanity thing yet. It's been pretty well hidden. That means that you have beat cops and officers who won't, necessarily, be afraid to take Edward Carter down. At least they wouldn't be afraid that they'd lose their minds in the bargain."

"It's a little late for that. I've heard rumours in the department already," Laurie said. "Word's gotten out."

"The only other option is to keep your distance, wear ear plugs, or find people who aren't afraid."

"Does wearing ear plugs prevent it?" Bill asked hopefully.

"Probably not," Wenton said as he began walking towards the door.

"But other than you, who wouldn't be afraid of losing their mind?" Margaret asked.

Wenton turned back. "Look for people who have nothing to lose." And then he opened the door and left.

"Un-fuckin'-believable!" Bill said, lifting both arms and putting his hands behind his head.

"What are we going to do now?" Margaret asked.

"This is crap," Wa said.

"I'm not so sure," Laurie said.

"Why?" Wa said.

"I had an aunt with epilepsy."

"So?"

"So, one of the things that sometimes set her off was the TV. Certain flashes of light triggered a reaction in her brain—made her go into a seizure."

"But it didn't make her go insane," Wa said.

"No it didn't make her insane, but it shows that stuff we see, or hear, might have an effect on our brains. It's plausible that Edward can make people insane, especially given the state of his victims."

Wa had to agree with her.

"So," Margaret said, "what now?"

The group was silent until Laurie noticed a strange expression on Wa's face.

"What are you thinking?" she asked.

"I'm going to go," he said. "If this bullshit story is really what we're going to go with, there's someone I should talk to."

"Who?" Laurie asked.

"I think I know someone who can help."

forty

123rd day (monday evening)

Wa stepped through the front door and looked up the stairs. Gloria was standing with her arms wrapped around her chest and a nervous expression on her face.

"Is it true?" she asked.

"Is what true?"

"What they're saying on the news about Edward Carter?"

"Now what?"

"It's all over the news tonight. That rapist has some strange mental disorder that's contagious. Staff at the psychiatric hospital went insane after just talking to him. Is it true?"

"Oh shit," he said.

"People are freaking out. People are being told not to answer the door, the phone, not to talk to anyone they don't know."

"What?"

"Yeah, the news said there's never been anything like this and that no one knows exactly who's at risk. They talked to some cop down at the station who told them..."

Wa held his hand up as he walked up the stairs towards her. "Where are the kids?"

"Downstairs. Lisa wanted to go to her friend's house but I didn't want them out of my sight."

Wa passed his wife and entered the living room. He dropped onto the couch with his legs straight out in front.

"So," Gloria said as she came to stand nervously beside him. "Is it true?"

"I guess so."

"What do you mean '*I guess so*'?"

"Dr. Wenton briefed the team today. He thinks that Edward can make people insane. He thinks it's something about his voice but the victim has to be primed for it."

"Primed? How?"

"Fear. That's what Wenton thinks. If the person Edward is talking to is afraid then it can do something to their head."

"Well the whole city's afraid now!"

"I know. We were hoping that this wouldn't get out. It doesn't exactly help us. If I find out who the cop with the big mouth is, I'll—"

"And people are even more afraid because they're saying that he'll strike again this Thursday."

Wa nodded. "I'm going to catch him before that."

Gloria sat down on the couch beside him and held his arm. "I don't want you doing it."

He turned his head to look at her. "What do you mean? Doing what?"

"I'm scared. I don't want anything happening to you. I need you. The kids need you."

"Don't be silly," he said looking away.

"I'm not," she said. "I just don't want you going after him and—"

"It's my job!" he interrupted harshly.

"Your job isn't to go crazy so that you can't even recognize your family anymore," she said, tears welling in her eyes.

He wrapped his arm around her shoulders, pulling her into him. "I know. I'll be careful."

"You promise?"

"Yes," he smiled at her.

forty-one

124th day (tuesday)

Edward shivered in the corner of an empty closet. *No more*, he thought. *I won't be like that anymore. Please*.

He couldn't remember how he'd gotten here. He couldn't remember leaving the forensic hospital. He vaguely remembered a large man looking through the door into his room and then he heard the nursing staff yelling. He closed his eyes tightly. *No, no, no.* He could feel, more than remember, that something bad had happened.

He opened his eyes again and looked around the cramped room. From his position crouched in the unfinished closet he had a view of the entire bedroom. The bare walls, tarps over the windows, and absence of furniture suggested a house that was still under construction.

"*What are we doing here?*" a voice hissed from somewhere nearby.

Edward spun his head to see who was speaking.

"You worthless fuck. Find someone quickly."

"No," he said weakly. He felt so tired. His stomach rumbled and twisted. The sweat that soaked his clothes left them damp and he shivered continuously. He'd discarded the security outfit, leaving him with just the light hospital-issued clothes. He'd spent an entire evening running through the forest. His bare feet were cover in small cuts, and bruises decorated his ankles.

"You've always been ours."

"Why?"

"Because you were born of evil when I took my daughter to bed."

"Don't say that," Edward cried holding his hands over his ears.

"Why not? Don't you love your mommy—my daughter? She loved you. Until she hanged herself."

"Please stop."

"Go find someone for us and I'll stop."

"I can't."

And then the voices disappeared. His hands fell to either side and he stared straight up. "I'll be okay," he told himself.

On the unfinished ceiling he saw a dark spot on one of the rough boards directly above his face. His attention was drawn to this spot and he watched it. It was an imperfection on the wood, a knothole, easily visible even in the dim light of the room. He wanted to let his head fall to one side and close his eyes but he couldn't. He continued to watch the black spot.

As he watched the spot bulged slightly. It was as if an air bubble drifted through the wood and found a weakness. The bulge disappeared as quickly as it had appeared.

He frowned but continued to watch.

A small bulge pulsed through the knot again, this time forcing the imperfection further out. It sunk back and was still.

A few minutes passed.

Then the black mark pushed out once more. The round bulge stretched out and formed into a small point on the end. The pointed end disconnected from the rest of the bulging protrusion and fell. Edward clenched his teeth as the spot splattered against his forehead. He'd expected pain, but the soft substance slapped against him and oozed out in all directions. Trails of the substance ran down into his hair and some of it dripped down into his eyes. His nostrils were filled with the pungent smell of freshly cut grass. Even as the black mess seeped into his eyes, he watched the dark spot above. It pulsed again, preparing to jettison more of the black liquid. His eyes suddenly stung and he blinked rapidly. The dark, thick liquid coated his eyes as he blinked and the pain intensified. Another projectile dropped onto his forehead. The sensation startled him and he jerked.

He freed an arm and brought a hand to his face. He wiped his face from one side to the other and the substance smeared like oil. The smell of grass was stronger now and he wiped his face harder. Another drip fell on the back of his hand as he was trying to clean himself. He couldn't wipe the substance away. It smeared and left a heavy trail. He wanted to use his other hand, to sit up or move, but he couldn't. His eyes still burned.

Then the thick, black liquid began to ripple. He felt the skin on his face caressed by each wave of the substance and soon it was travelling down his neck. He continued to wipe at it with his free hand but it was useless. More of the thick liquid dripped from the ceiling to coat his face. It travelled down over his neck and under his shirt. Wherever it touched it left him feeling cold and slippery. Soon it had moved down over his stomach and filled his belly button. It continued downwards and slid under the elastic of the hospital pants to twist around his genitals. The cold, rubbery liquid coated him, pulsed against him. Edward shivered as his penis was steadily stroked and rapidly grew hard. The thick black liquid began to pour out of the dark spot on the ceiling and smother him. He gasped for breath as it flowed over his face. His eyes burned and the thick black fluid gripped his penis more firmly and stroked.

"Stop!" he cried out.

"Serve us."

"No!"

"Find someone."

"Why?"

"You want it."

He shivered and felt the reflexive wrenching of his orgasm sweep over him. The black fluid swirled away from his penis and flowed up and down the length of his body in a frenzy. His whole body shook and spasmed from the sensation of having every inch of his skin massaged by the substance. His eyes continued to burn and he was still unable to resist the assault.

"Okay," he said softly.

And the blackness was gone, replaced by beads of sweat across his body. He felt a dampness below his stomach, near his genitals. He lifted his head to look down the length of his body and saw his hospital pants were pulled down. His semi-erect penis was laying to one side and a string of semen dripped down to his thigh. He pulled his pants closed and sat up as if in a daze. He stood and walked to a window, pulling the tarp back.

He was on the top floor of the three-storey house, in what would eventually be the master bedroom. He pushed the tarp out far enough to see into the large front yard. It was difficult to see through the thick trees on the lot but he knew the street was empty. It was empty now, but he knew someone would come. Someone would have to come so he could finish.

forty-two

124th day (tuesday)

Wa pulled up alongside the curb on a quiet residential street. He looked out the passenger window at the square, two-storey saltbox. The house looked weathered and old. The lawn was neglected. The bushes that bordered the house on all sides were overgrown and uneven. He sighed and stepped out of his unmarked police sedan.

He walked quickly up the steps and stood at the door. He looked for the doorbell and hesitated before pressing it. He wondered whether he was doing the right thing. He felt trapped. Since the news had broken about Edward spreading psychosis, the police station was in turmoil. The controversy had forced the police commissioner to issue a directive that any officer's involvement in the pursuit and apprehension of Edward Carter was voluntary. It was becoming a publicity nightmare for the department. Under the conditions, the commissioner was happy to provide full authorization for what Wa was doing now.

He rang the bell, holding it for a second or two longer than most would. He wanted to be sure that the door was answered.

Silence. Wa strained to listen for footsteps or the sound of movement but heard nothing.

He rang the bell again and listened to ensure that the buzzer sounded inside the home. It did.

Still nothing.

He stepped to one side and looked through the frosted glass that bordered the door. He could only make out the vague shapes of furniture inside the home. He headed back down the steps and moved to the front window. Peering over the bushes he looked into the living room. He couldn't see much, but he thought he saw a display case leaning precariously against a wall. He jumped once to get a better view and saw that the room had been ransacked. He jumped a second time and saw something else. Someone was sitting on the couch.

He headed back up the stairs and knocked loudly on the door. "Dallons!" he yelled. "It's me, Mitchell."

No answer.

He banged on the door again. "Come on. I need to talk to you. Open the door or I'll kick it in. I know you're in there."

Suddenly the door swung open and Wa stepped back.

"What do you want?" Detective Tim Dallons asked angrily.

"Tim!" Wa cried, more from surprise than anything.

Dallons leaned heavily against the door jamb and squinted at his ex-partner.

"Um, I went to the hospital but they said you'd discharged yourself."

"They fuckin' kicked me out. They said I didn't need to be there. I told them to fuck themselves and here I am."

He turned away and headed back to the living room with unsteady steps. Wa followed. Dallons dropped back onto the couch. Cushions were unevenly spaced on the sofa and the room had obviously been ransacked.

"What the hell happened?" Wa asked.

"Nothing," Dallons muttered and reached for a glass on an end table. "I didn't like the way things looked in here so I remodelled." He drank heavily from the small glass and then rested it on his leg.

Wa noticed an empty rye bottle on the floor near Dallons' feet. He decided not to mention it.

"How are you doing?"

"Fucking awesome."

"Why'd the hospital kick you out?"

"I guess they're overfull with nuts. They needed my fuckin' bed and they said I'm *fine*. They gave me a clean bill of health just to get my fuckin' bed." He paused, taking another drink. "That's fine, anyway. I don't need that shit. Especially with those rape victims all over and everyone whispering about shit." His words slurred slightly.

"What shit?"

"The shit about the rapist making everyone insane."

"What have you heard?" Wa asked sitting carefully on the arm of an oversized chair.

"I heard the hospital staff talking from the start. They thought it was fuckin' fascinating how the rapist made those girls psychotic."

Wa nodded.

"I guess those bastards never thought they'd be vulnerable too. They started shitting their pants when they heard that Edward Carter made staff at the forensic facility crazy too." He laughed a cold laugh that turned into a dry cough. He sat up and looked around the room, and pushed a hand into the cushion next to him. He pulled a bottle out and poured another healthy glass of rye. He swallowed, then shook violently and let his arms drop down, resting the glass on his leg and holding the bottle loosely in the other hand.

"Tim," Wa said in a stern, official-sounding voice. "Edward Carter is the reason I'm here. I really need to talk to you about this case."

Dallons didn't respond but stared straight ahead, lost in a stupor.

"We need your help," Wa continued. "You might be the only one who can catch this guy."

Dallons' face distorted and he looked at Wa. "What are you talking about? I'm not even a fuckin' cop anymore. I'm on permanent suspension or long term disability or some shit. I'm off the fuckin' force."

"Not anymore. Not if you want back. I've been authorized to invite you back on a probationary period to help with this case. If you help out then the probation's done and you're back."

"What the fuck are you talking about?" Dallons mumbled angrily as he took another drink.

"I'm going to tell you straight out, Tim. This Edward Carter guy is causing a real stink. He's dangerous, he's psychotic, and he's poised to strike again in two days. It's turned into a public relations nightmare. The police commissioner's upset. One of the beat cops told me that none of the officers want to touch this case. The whole city's in a panic about where this guy's going to end up."

Dallons took another drink. "What's this got to do with me?"

"Well, Dr. Wenton suggested that—"

"Wenton!"

Wa shut his eyes and gritted his teeth. He hadn't planned on mentioning Michael Wenton's involvement. "Yes. He'd assessed Edward Carter."

"Michael fuckin' Wenton," Dallons breathed slowly.

"Anyway, the theory is that Edward Carter may be able to make people go crazy, but only if they're already frightened. Being frightened somehow primes a person and makes them more susceptible to whatever Edward does."

"This is the brilliant Dr. Wenton's theory, is it?"

"Well, yes, but other professionals have suggested it too."

"Did Wenton tell you to come talk to me?"

"No. That was my idea."

"Why me?"

"You might be one of the only people in the city who can bring this guy in."

"Why's that?"

"Because you've established yourself as someone without any fear. You've gone into all kinds of situations in the past, faced down all sorts of psychos and—"

"Because I have nothing to lose, right?"

Wa nodded his head.

Dallons took a drink. "When my wife killed herself I didn't give a fuck about anything. I started being reckless. I kicked in some doors that only a suicidal jerk would kick in. I tackled a guy twice my size and beat the living shit out of him. I faced down a few psychopathic criminals at gunpoint without blinking an eye. And for all that shit they gave me medals. They gave me praise and said how fuckin' brave I was. Is that why you want me now?"

Wa simply looked at his ex-partner without speaking.

"I don't care whether I live or die and that makes me immune to Edward Carter, does it?"

Wa nodded slowly. "I think so." The two men looked at each other without speaking. Dallons drained the glass.

"And without your help this guy might slip through our fingers and put more women at risk," Wa concluded.

Dallons looked at the empty glass in his hand. After a moment he looked up and casually examined the damage in the room. Finally he looked back at Wa.

"I'll take this guy, but I don't care about getting back on the force. This is a one-time thing because Edward Carter is a sick son of a bitch. I'm not a cop anymore."

Wa breathed out in relief and stood. "We just need your help. If that's all then that's all."

"That's all," Dallons answered and wedged the bottle of rye back into the cushion beside him.

forty-three

126th day (thursday morning)

"Today is the day," Edward said quietly as he stood behind a tree near the entrance to the dirt driveway of the house where he was staying.

It was early morning and the sun was beginning to show through the trees, slowly melting the frost from the night before. Although the air was still cool, sweat covered Edward's forehead. He shivered and held tightly to the rough bark of the tree. He was exhausted from lack of sleep and food.

"One more and that's all. Satan will leave after one more," he whispered urgently.

"Find someone."

He blinked rapidly, attempting to clear the mist that had formed over his eyes. His heart raced and he gripped the tree more tightly.

"Find someone. Do it now."

He nodded.

He strained to watch the road nearby. He was sure that someone would come. This was how it worked. He waited and someone came.

The road was no more than thirty feet in front of him. The thick trees hid Edward from view, but he could see the clearing created by the paved road.

"You want to help us fuck."

He shivered violently and closed his eyes. His stomach twisted slightly and he would have vomited if there'd been anything to expel.

"It is powerful, isn't it?"

A smooth, cold sensation rippled over his chest and down toward the waist of his hospital pants.

"You'll be ready."

The blackness travelled beneath his pants and circled slowly around his penis. He shivered again at this new sensation and stumbled backwards before clutching the tree again.

"You'll have to be ready."

His penis slowly responded to the cool touch and he let his head fall forward to rest against the bark.

"I don't want to...," he began.

"FUCK, YOU SLAVE!"

He moaned as he felt his balls twisted and pinched. His legs shook and he knew he was about to collapse. Pain resonated from his genitals and pressed through him in all directions. His stomach retched again but he couldn't find strength to vomit. He blinked and the tears that filled his eyes dropped away.

"Just do what you need to."

"I will," he said weakly.

A faint sound made him freeze. He pulled his hand out of his pants and held onto the tree with both hands, leaning forward to look at the road. His vision was still clouded but he could make out the shape of someone walking slowly along.

"*It's her*," the voices hissed.

He shivered again and stumbled away from the tree.

"Just give me another second," Chris Farrell called downstairs.

Tammy stood at the bottom of the spiral staircase and called back. "Don't worry about it. I'm going to get a ride with Lewis."

"You sure?"

"Yep. But I gotta go or I'll miss him."

"All right, I'll see you later."

She stepped through a corridor and leaned into the kitchen. "See you, Mom."

Tammy's mother was sitting at the kitchen table with her coffee and the newspaper. "Have a good day honey."

Tammy turned away, swung her backpack over her shoulder, and slid out the front door.

The Farrells had moved into their new house four months ago. They'd designed the house themselves and so far it had been a dream come true. The three-storey, five bedroom home was large for a family of three, but they wanted room enough for guests and family.

There were only five other finished homes on their block and the rest of the large lots were either still for sale or at various stages of construction. Tammy had quickly made new friends in the new community. After starting at the high school, she'd learned there was only one other classmate on her block, Lewis. He lived four lots down from her and he was a really nice guy. They soon became friends and with some frequency Tammy got rides to the high school, which was a twenty-minute drive away.

As she stepped onto the front porch and closed the door, she breathed a sigh of relief. Being an only child meant undivided attention from her parents and she was beginning to feel smothered. She knew she had lots of time to get to Lewis' place but at that moment she just wanted to get out of the house.

She strolled down their driveway making foggy little puffs of breath as she went. It was cool out this morning.

She walked casually down the road. She was pleased not to hear the banging of construction or the rumble of large trucks, which was a part of everyday life in this neighbourhood. She was desperate for the other houses to be finished because the noise made being outside almost annoying at times. Plus she wanted to meet the rest of the neighbourhood and find some more friends like Lewis.

Tammy readjusted her backpack and continued to stroll. As she walked, she looked from one side of the street to the other. She liked keeping track of what stage the construction was at so that she'd know when it was time for the moving trucks to arrive. She believed you could tell a lot about a family by their furniture.

One house intrigued her more than the others. It was a large house right between hers and Lewis'. It was at least as big as her family's home, but the front of this house looked as if it might be something special. She could tell that the builder was leaving brickwork on the front because the rough plywood boards had not been finished with shingles or siding yet. She slowed as she passed and peered through the thick trees to the massive house at the back of the lot. There still hadn't been any work on the front and she assumed the crew had moved inside to finish before they came back out.

She strained to see through the trees and suddenly she saw something else. There was something in the woods near the road. She sucked her breath in and stopped walking as movement behind the large trees caught her attention. *Was it an animal? Were there bears up here?*

Then something bolted and ran toward her. She screamed and fell backwards, barely staying on her feet. The thing continued to rush straight at her with its arms held high over its head.

Tammy froze. This couldn't be happening. The thing had the slim body of a man. The dirty, ill-fitting clothes that hung off it were barely recognizable as such because they were torn and covered with dark stains. She couldn't pull her eyes away from the thing's face.

What she was staring at was a wild-eyed monster. Its hair was a mass of twisted tangles that stood out in all places. Its eyes were sunken into its sallow, hollow face. Bone was obvious beneath its features, pressing hard against skin that had stretched to the limits of its endurance. The mouth hung open and bits of saliva clung to the sides of its lips and slid over its unshaven chin. Its beard grew in uneven clumps and coalesced with the dirt that decorated its face.

Tammy screamed again and found the strength to turn. She took a step but glanced back at the thing, and noticed that it held a large rock in an outstretched hand. She lifted her arms to protect herself, but it was no use. A sharp bolt of pain and bright light creased her consciousness before the world went black.

forty-four

126th day (thursday afternoon)

His office was not intended to accommodate the number of people who now occupied it. An exhausted Mitchell Wa sat behind his desk and listened to the team's reports. Detective Laurie Abrahms and Constable Bill Lawrence stood immediately in front of Wa's desk, and a reasonably sober Tim Dallons sat in a chair off to one side, observing the scene with little obvious interest.

"Are you sure you should be here?" Laurie asked with concern. "You've been up all night and we still haven't got anything. We could just call you as soon as—"

"Don't worry about that," Wa cut her off. He turned his attention to Constable Lawrence. "Where are the troops at?"

"We're still knocking on doors in the areas closest to the forensic facility, but given the length of time since the escape we're starting to think there's no point. He could be anywhere by now."

Wa nodded.

"I've got guys downtown too. Just keeping an eye on some of the halfway houses and drop-in shelters. I mean, we got lucky last time."

"What about the line?" Wa asked, referring to the hotline they'd set up for the public to call in tips. "Unless this guy's lying dead in the woods someone's got to have seen him."

"I just checked with Norma and there's nothing," Laurie answered. "Margaret's still going through some of the calls and calling a few people back, but most of it's just people freaking out about what to do *if* they see him."

Wa shook his head. He knew they were running out of time. Because of the publicity they were having trouble getting cooperation both outside and inside the department. No officers were eager to corner Edward.

"Excuse me, Detective?" a voice called from the doorway.

Everyone turned to find an officer standing there nervously.

"What?" Wa said.

"I know you were asking all departments to report anything new to your team, especially if it involves a missing person or anything related to this guy's—"

"I know what the memo said," Wa interrupted. "I wrote it."

From the corner of the room Dallons smiled at his old partner. He enjoyed seeing Wa in a new role and with a new attitude.

"Right," the officer continued. "I just wanted to tell you that we got a call from a frantic parent, Mr. Chris Farrell, who said his daughter's disappeared."

"I'm listening," Wa said sitting up in his chair and leaning on the desk.

"His daughter is sixteen years old and left early this morning to go to school. She was going to get a ride with a neighbour boy but apparently never made it to his house. The parents didn't find out until the school called about her being absent."

"It was just this morning?" Wa said.

"Right," he answered. "And the Farrell's live in that new development outside of town, Cedar Mews."

Laurie raised an eyebrow and looked to Wa.

"What?" Bill asked, noticing the eye contact between the detectives.

Wa sank back in his chair again. "Cedar Mews is about ten kilometres away from the forensic hospital."

Just then Margaret Meredith pushed into the room past the officer. "I think we found him," she almost shouted in between gasps of breath.

"Oh thank God!" Laurie said. "We were just talking about some poor sixteen-year-old girl going missing..." She shook her head sadly.

"Well, I don't know anything about a girl, but we got a call from a contractor. He was checking out a house he's working on where they'd temporarily stopped construction. He said he tried to get into the place and was confronted by some madman who fits Edward's description. We have patrol cars heading out there now to secure the building until we decide what the next move is. No one wants to go in and confront Edward if they don't have to."

"Let's get out there," Wa said turning to look at Dallons who shrugged nonchalantly. "Where is this place?"

"Cedar Mews," Margaret said flatly and the room froze.

forty-five

126th day (thursday, early evening)

"This is ridiculous," Wa said.

Chief of Police Louise Parker nodded.

The two were standing outside a mobile command centre. The police had surrounded a house in the Cedar Mews subdivision and the best guess was that Edward Carter and his teenage hostage, Tammy Farrell, were inside. The problem was that everyone was just guessing at this point. Repeated attempts to establish contact with the occupants had gone unanswered. Tammy's backpack had been found in the woods near the road which helped confirm the theory that she'd been abducted by whoever was in the house now. Police surveillance verified movement in the master bedroom; at least they weren't surrounding an empty building.

"We haven't had visual confirmation. We don't even fuckin' know if it's actually Edward Carter in there!" Wa said with frustration.

"We'll have to do something soon," Chief Parker answered. "Do we even have an idea about whether this guy is armed?"

"Best guess is no. If it is Edward, he escaped from the MSPC and likely ran here on foot. Not much chance to pick up a weapon along the way unless he found an old rifle in the woods."

"So we aren't even sure we have Edward Carter in there?" Chief Parker asked.

"The contractor's fairly confident it's Edward. He looked at the photos and positively identified Edward as the person at the house earlier today," replied Wa.

"Has anyone suggested we send in the tactical team?"

Wa breathed heavily. "It's not an entry situation yet. Besides, the team is pretty nervous about all the hype about Edward being able to make people insane."

"This is a nightmare," Chief Parker announced as she turned to walk away. Suddenly, she turned back. "Haven't I heard Dr. Wenton's name mentioned in connection with this case?"

"Yeah. He was working on an assessment of Edward before he escaped."

"Let's get Wenton down here."

Wa turned to look at Tim Dallons who was standing near the woods watching the house. He looked back at Parker. "What for?"

"Dr. Wenton might be able to assist us in getting this guy out of the house peacefully. If Wenton already knows him then he might know what to do to establish contact. Get him down here."

Wa nodded reluctantly. Having Dallons and Wenton together might just make the situation go from bad to worse.

forty-six

126th day (thursday, mid-evening)

A slight dusk had settled across the house. The half-built home looked eerily deserted except for the circle of tactical police officers spaced around the perimeter. No light shone behind the tarps over the numerous windows. There was no motion evident within the house. Most members of the police team and negotiating squad were beginning to suspect there might not be anyone left to rescue. As police, they expected the worst even though they hoped for the best.

"Thank you for coming, Dr. Wenton," Chief Parker said. A small group stood in the mobile command centre van. Wa stood with the chief negotiator, Lincoln Whitley. Normally, Whitley served as the site commander in hostage situations, but under the unusual circumstances he was going to fill a different role. Dallons refused to enter the Emergency Response Team van and maintained his vigil on the edge of the clearing near the house.

"Is there anything you can tell us to help us deal with Edward Carter?" Parker continued.

"I'm not going to tell you anything you'll want to hear," Wenton answered. "For example, if there was a sixteen-year-old girl in there, then she's dead or insane by now."

"Oh fuck," Whitley said in frustration and turned away.

"You're right. That's not the kind of information we want to hear, Doctor," Chief Parker answered.

"Edward Carter has the ability to create serious psychiatric disorders in people with whom he's had much less contact than he has with the hostage in that house. If she's been in there with him all day then she's probably better off dead." Wenton paused before adding, "In my opinion."

"So is that supposed to be helpful?" Wa asked throwing his hands out.

"Could be."

"Could be how?" Wa demanded.

"Because the odds are that the girl is either fucked up or dead. Either way, you can send the troops into that house without worrying too much about the hostage."

"Oh for fuck's sake," Whitley said.

"You're saying we should go in?" Wa asked.

"Edward isn't going to be armed." Wenton said. "He's mentally ill and unpredictable, but overall there's been little evidence of overt aggression. The illness appears to direct him specifically to sexual offending. I don't think it would take much to go in and arrest Edward. He won't put up a fight."

"I don't want to put my people at unnecessary risk," Chief Parker stated.

"I can't guarantee there's no risk. I'm just saying that Edward is probably not armed nor is he planning on physically attacking the police."

"But...," Wa said. He knew there was a punch linc that wouldn't be good.

"But if I'm correct about his ability to make people insane, and if I'm correct about that ability being stronger when Edward's off medication..."

"Then Edward Carter might drive every police officer who sets foot in that house insane," Wa finished.

"Youcan't be serious," Chief Parker said.

"All I'm saying is that your entry team better be ready for anything and better not go in there if they're too anxious about the outcome."

"Because fear will make them even more vulnerable," Wa said.

"I think so."

"Well I don't know if the pep talk exists that can help get my tactical team into that house without being nervous about it," Chief Parker said.

"No kidding," Whitley said.

"I'll go in," a voice announced from the entrance to the van.

They turned to see Tim Dallons watching them.

"I'll go in and get this freak. I don't give a flying fuck about this 'he'll make you go insane' bullshit."

The group was silent for a moment.

Wa spoke first. "Are you sure, Tim?"

"I'm straight on sure," he said gruffly. "But I'm not going in there alone."

The group looked at him with surprise, waiting for him to continue.

"There's only one other person who isn't bothered by this insanity stuff. There's only one person who sat one-on-one with this guy without going bonkers." He paused and looked directly at Dr. Wenton. "You're coming with me."

Given the huge breach in protocol, it took some time before proper clearances could be obtained. In the end, the team realized there was no way they could authorize this unorthodox entry strategy, but there were no other options. Both men were fitted with standard ERT gear including Kevlar vests and black fatigues. Dallons was not a stranger to the routine, having served on ERT before. Wenton, too, was familiar with most of the ERT rules of engagement. He was frequently on site for psychological consultation and also ran classes on negotiation and mental status assessment for ERT trainees.

By now, night had fallen and the house was dark. Massive spotlights were brought in and set up around the house. The harsh glare ricocheted off tarped windows and cast numerous shadows.

The negotiation team, Louise Parker, and Mitchell Wa took up position inside the communications van. From there they could monitor the entry through mics and video relays. More than seventy nervous police officers watched silently as Tim Dallons and Michael Wenton approached the front entrance of the house.

forty-seven

126th day (thursday evening)

Tim Dallons and Michael Wenton stood on the doorstep facing each other. Light shone around them from the ERT spotlights. The house itself was dark inside. The door was unfinished steel without even a knob.

"I feel an obligation to be honest with you," Dallons whispered.

Wenton nodded, "I'd appreciate that."

"Your safety is not going to be my number one priority once we're inside."

Wenton snorted. "I would've thought you'd owe me one after I saved your life."

"Not exactly," Dallons replied. "So stay behind me when we get in there."

Wenton shrugged.

"What the fuck are you ladies gabbing about?" a voice crackled through their earpieces.

Dallons scowled at Wenton before he spoke into his mouth piece. "Nothing. We're going in now. How's the audio and video?"

There was a brief pause before Whitley spoke again. "We're set. Everything's good in here. Just remember to maintain an audio stream."

"Yep." Dallons held his police-issue firearm in both hands and raised it to one side with his elbows bent. He used his shoulder to press against the door and swing it open.

"We're going through the front door," he said, stepping into the house.

Dallons quickly put his back against a wall and scanned the floor. "I can't see shit in here," he said. "There's light reflecting in all directions and shadows everywhere. The plastic tarps over the windows are screwing up the lighting."

"I can see that," Whitley answered from the communications van. "The video feed's poor. What do you want us to do?"

"Hold on."

Dallons crouched and scanned the floor quickly. He took one hand off his gun and pulled a flashlight from his belt. He waved the beam around the room. The main entrance of the house led to a massive living room on the left and another room on the right. Further back there was an elaborate staircase and behind that another doorway. There were wooden crates, ladders, and other equipment scattered around the rough wood floor. The light reflecting through the tarps spread out in uneven waves and left flickering shadows around the equipment. Dallons attempted to uncover each dark spot with his flashlight.

"It's tough to see in here," he announced again.

"Do you want the spotlights off? Would that help?" Whitley asked.

"No," he said and then turned to Wenton, who was in the corner near the doorway, leaning against the door jamb. He looked as if he might've been waiting for a bus.

"Doctor," Dallons said sarcastically, "if you aren't too busy, do you want to turn your flashlight on?"

Wenton pulled a flashlight off his belt and switched it on. He shone the beam across the room as he came to Dallons' side.

"You*ordered* me to stay behind you," he whispered.

"Fuck you," Dallons shot back. He spoke into his mic again. "This room looks clear. There're a lot of crates and equipment around but I don't see anything else. We're going further back." He crept forward and Wenton followed closely behind.

"There's another room back here. Looks like a big kitchen and dining room. Light's even worse back here. Lots of empty spots around, I guess where the appliances are going to go. Can't see shit."

The two men slowly made their way through the kitchen, letting their flashlights drift back and forth, up and down.

"There's another door here. I'm guessing it leads to the basement."

Dallons and Wenton came to the end of the dining room.

"That's it for the first floor. We're heading upstairs."

Static crackled back through their earpieces.

"Control, you're breaking up on audio," Dallons said as he stopped moving and held a hand over his ear.

More static.

He looked at Wenton. "How's your signal?"

The doctor shook his head.

"Whitley!" Dallons said loudly. "What the fuck's going on out there?"

"We...so...but the...ing. Please...," Whitley's voice broke in between electronic noise.

"What would we do without their fucking little toys, eh?" Dallons said angrily. "Let's go upstairs."

Wenton smiled and followed him to the staircase.

They paused at the bottom and shone their beams up. The staircase went up to a landing, then turned ninety degrees and continued to the second floor.

"I don't know if you can hear me anymore, but we're going upstairs now," Dallons announced.

Their earpieces were silent. There was no longer even static.

Dallons crept up the stairs, keeping his light fixed in front. The staircase was located toward the middle of the house and the light from the spots didn't make it this far. Although the stairs themselves seemed finished, the construction crew hadn't installed the banister and both men were being cautious with their footing.

"How you doing, Doctor?" Dallons asked with mock concern.

"I'm getting a little sleepy, but otherwise, fine."

"Smartass," Dallons mumbled and stopped on the small landing. He spun around to look at the second floor. From his position he could see a hallway above with open doorways. His light didn't reach into the rooms from this angle and he continued up the staircase.

Dallons looked down to find his footing and stepped carefully onto the next step. He kept close to the wall to avoid the drop where the railing should be. He brought the beam up over the stairs to gauge how much farther they had to go. As his beam reached the last step, he stopped suddenly. He shone the light up and saw the face of a girl standing above them.

The girl stood motionless at the top of the stairs. She stood with her eyes closed and her hands at her sides. Her clothes were rumpled, stained, and dirty. She wore only a light shirt that hung off one shoulder. Her jeans were undone and hung loosely on her hips. A patch of pubic hair was visible just at the point where her jeans opened. She wasn't wearing any shoes.

"Tammy?" Dallons called.

She didn't move.

Dallons looked back at Wenton and then turned to the girl again.

"Tammy, this is the police. We're here to help you. Are you okay?"

No answer.

Dallons slid his gun back into its holster and tentatively moved up the stairs, stopping a few steps below her. "Hey, are you okay? Can you hear me?"

Wenton watched Dallons approach the girl. He shone his flashlight over her. She looked bruised and beaten. Her dirty clothes might have been torn in places. Wenton's light shone briefly on the small patch of pubic hair protruding from her jeans, and his mind instantly filled with thoughts of naked skin. He wanted to move the flashlight's beam from the girl's mid-section but found he couldn't.

What the fuck are you doing? he asked himself but held the light steadily on the young girl's exposed pubic hair. *Stop it before Dallons notices!* he warned himself. Finally, he tore the beam away.

The girl remained motionless with her eyes shut and head tilted slightly back. Her arms were flat against her sides. From this distance,

Dallons thought that some of the dark stains on her clothes might be blood. He shone his flashlight across her head and saw a patch of hair that was plastered down. A trail of dried blood ran down her cheek. She needed medical help.

He looked up and shone the light down the hallway in both directions. He wanted to be sure that Edward wasn't waiting for them. The hall was empty and he took another step up toward the girl.

"Tammy, sweetheart, you're going to need some help. I'm Detective Tim Dallons and I want to take you outside, to where your parents are waiting."

Silence.

He took one more step and came up next to her. A strange smell caught his attention. It smelled like something rotten. He didn't know why, but he thought it smelled like death.

Wenton shook his head to erase the sexual images that danced in his mind. He had difficulty keeping himself from focusing his flashlight on the girl's crotch, or shining it over her breasts to look for the hint of a nipple. *Fuck this!* he said to himself. He moved up behind Dallons. He stopped and noticed that Dallons was looking at him with a questioning face. Wenton knew Dallons was waiting for him to say something.

He drew in a breath to refocus his thoughts before he spoke.

"Tammy," he said calmly, "you're safe now. We'll take you away. Would you please come with us?"

The smell was becoming stronger and Dallons felt himself gag. He wondered if Wenton could smell it. He knew he needed to get this girl out of here.

"I don't know if you're getting this but I'm bringing the girl out," Dallons said into his mic. "Have EMS waiting." He put his arm around Tammy and spoke softly, "Okay, let's go."

As his hand touched her she spasmed and her eyes shot open. Her arms flung out to the sides and she screamed a horrible, high-pitched scream.

Dallons stumbled backwards as her hand swiped past his face. He felt something sharp pull against his cheek and then a strange sensation of warmth.

"Watch out!" Wenton called and reached out for Dallons. The detective was standing near the edge of the stairs and almost stepped out into thin air. Wenton reached out to steady the detective.

"Son of a bitch!" Dallons yelled, holding a hand to his face.

"Are you okay?" Wenton asked.

Dallons looked at the blood on his hand. His head shot up and he scanned the hallway. It was empty. "Where'd she go?"

Wenton waved his flashlight back and forth along the hallway. "She must've run when I grabbed you."

Dallons pulled a cloth from his pocket and held it to his face. "Any professional opinion on the mental status of our hostage?" he asked sarcastically.

"I'd already predicted she'd be in bad shape."

The detective turned away from him and stepped into the hallway, shining his flashlight down its length.

"Command," he spoke into his mic. "I still don't know if you're receiving us but we located the girl. She's fled into one of the rooms. We're going to try and find her."

The hallway stretched along the length of the home with one side overlooking the downstairs and the other showing numerous doorways. At the end of the hallway there was another staircase that led to the master bedroom.

The light was exceptionally bad in this area. The doorways didn't permit light from under the bedroom window tarps to sneak in. Dallons retrieved his gun and pointed the barrel up as he moved slowly down the hall, carefully scanning each direction. He stopped at the first door.

"We're going into the first room."

He motioned for Wenton to stay behind him and then crouched down next to the door. He darted his head around to take a quick look into the room. He completed this exercise a few more times until he was sure the room was clear. He stood and cautiously stepped into the entrance, keeping his flashlight in front of him.

The room was empty. A plastic tarp covered the extra-large window at the back. A slight wind made the plastic vibrate and twist. Occasionally, one end of the plastic snapped as the breeze caught it at just the right angle. Dallons shone the light across each corner of the room until he was satisfied and then turned back to the doorway.

"First room's clear," he said into his mic.

He stepped into the hall and moved to the second room, crouching next to the frame. He quickly looked into the room, using his flashlight to partially shield his face. This room was an unfinished bathroom. The tub, sink, and linen closet were only roughed in and provided numerous obscure areas for someone to hide in. He was about to take a second look when Wenton spoke.

"Um, Detective, I think I know where she is."

Dallons turned and looked back at him. Wenton was pointing down the hallway. Dallons turned and looked down the hall. As he brought his flashlight around he saw the outline of a figure. Tammy stood at the bottom of the staircase leading up to the third floor.

He trained his light on her. She was standing with her eyes closed and her hands at her sides. Her head was tilted slightly backwards.

"Tammy?" Dallons called out. "Can you hear me?"

No answer.

"We found her again," he said softly into his mic, and he took a step toward her. Then he remembered the rooms next to him. He stopped and kept the light fixed on Tammy. "Wenton, keep your eyes on that girl. If she moves you tell me. I need to make sure these rooms are clear."

"Got it."

Dallons took another step and scanned his light across the unfinished bathroom. He took a step inside and shone the light into the recessed areas for the tub and linen closet. Nothing. The room was clear. He stepped out and checked down the hall again. Tammy continued to stand at the bottom of the stairs to the third floor. He looked back at Wenton who also stood motionless with his light trained on the girl. There was one more room to check. Dallons crept along the wall toward it.

Wenton kept his flashlight on the girl. He felt a strange hum in the back of his mind but tried to ignore it. Her pants still hung low on her body and he let the beam drop until he found the outline of her dark patch of hair. He strained to see the coarse hair but the girl stepped back. He frowned. He wanted to see her skin. He felt an urgency that he hadn't felt in a long time. An urgency that he'd consciously shut off years ago.

He glanced to his side to make sure that Dallons was still occupied with the room search. He was, so Wenton leaned forward to try and get a better view of the girl. He could almost taste the salt on her skin. The sweat. The filth. He moaned softly. He flicked the light back to her face and suddenly it wasn't Tammy anymore. It was Sandra Evans, a patient from his distant past. As he tried to understand how that could be, the girl's features instantly changed, and he was again looking at Tammy. He shook his head. "What the fuck?" he whispered to himself.

"What?" Dallons voice slapped him sharply.

Wenton spun to face him. "Hunh?"

"Did you say something?" Dallons whispered through gritted teeth.

"Um," Wenton stumbled. "Nothing."

Dallons turned to look down the hall. "Did she move?"

"Yeah, she took one step back. I think if we move toward her, she'll move back up the stairs."

"So she's watching us, then?" he asked.

"Nope. Her eyes haven't opened."

"So what now?" Dallons whispered without taking his eyes off Tammy.

"*Facini entfaste.*"

Dallons turned sharply to Wenton. "What?"

"I didn't say anything," Wenton responded calmly.

"Don't start fucking with me," he warned and turned away. "You keep an eye on her because I need to check this last room."

Dallons kept his flashlight trained on Tammy and stepped toward the next bedroom. As he moved she leaned backwards and stepped up one stair before she became motionless again.

"Fuck," Dallons muttered. He broke his light away from her as he reached the doorway. "Don't lose sight of her," he said to Wenton, then crouched beside the next entrance.

He held his gun to one side and poked his head quickly around the door frame. He shone the flashlight across the room and darted back. He took another look, this time letting the light linger a little longer. There was nothing there. It was a large empty bedroom. A closet in the corner had no doors and he could see that it, too, was empty. He stood and stepped into the doorway, shining his flashlight over every inch of the room in a more methodical fashion. His beam crossed over the floor and the walls in a long sweeping pattern. As he moved the beam across the far wall, it encountered a strange distortion. Dallons choked because the image his flashlight illuminated was a young girl's face screaming in terror. He quickly brought the beam back but couldn't find the spot where he'd seen the face. As he searched frantically for the image, the light flickered. He kept waving the light, but the beam flickered a few more times and died.

"Fuck," he said and put his gun back into its holster. He slapped the head of the flashlight with his open palm a few times with no result. He vigorously flipped the light on and off without any effect. "Fuck," he said again and clipped the flashlight back onto his belt.

"What's going on?" Wenton asked.

"Light's dead."

"Do you need this one?"

Dallons peered through the dark at the wall where he'd seen the distortion and shook his head. "Nah, just keep that light on the girl. This room's clear anyway."

"Got her." Wenton moved the beam up and down the girl's body and waved it slowly over her chest. The hum in the back of his mind continued. It seemed to originate with the girl, but he wasn't sure. He quickly trained the beam on her face when Dallons came to stand next to him.

Tammy was still standing on the second step. The wind was picking up outside and the tarps on the windows shook with an increased intensity that caused a strange flapping noise inside the house. The moving tarps made the light from the exterior spots flick and shift. Light coursed through the hall in waves.

"Has she opened her eyes?"

"Nothing," Wenton answered. "Except, I'm sure she's saying something over and over. I can't really hear because of the wind, but I think there's a sound coming from her."

"So maybe we can talk her out of here?" Dallons whispered.

"I don't think so. I think, if anything, she's just babbling to try and soothe herself. She's been traumatized and she's likely quite ill right now. You won't be able to reason with her."

"So she needs medical attention," Dallons said.

"Yeah."

"I'm just going to grab her then."

Dallons took a step toward her and she moved away from him, up one stair. He looked back at Wenton with a questioning expression. Wenton shrugged and kept the light trained on her. The detective again took a slow step toward her and she again stepped backwards, up the stairs.

The wind outside shifted and the tarps in the bedrooms snapped at the strain. At the same time a strong smell swept over Dallons. He froze and turned his head away from the odour. He looked back at Wenton who cringed as the smell hit him.

"What the fuck was that?" Dallons whispered.

Wenton shook his head.

"*Facini.*"

"Did you say something, Wenton?"

"No."

The detective turned back to the girl. She was standing on the fourth step, close to a small landing where the stairs turned and went up to the master bedroom. As Dallons watched the light from Wenton's flashlight began to fade. The glow from the bulb went from white to yellow to brown before it went dark.

"What the fuck?" Dallons said.

Wenton held the light in both hands to examine it. He shook it and banged it into his open palm but it was dead.

"For fuck's sake," Dallons whispered. "Both our flashlights have given out," he said into his mic. "If you guys can hear me, someone's going to get his ass kicked over this bullshit." He looked at Wenton. "We're just going to have to grab her and get her out of here. I'm going to rush her but I might need you to grab an arm or a leg if she starts flailing around. Got it?"

"Yeah."

Dallons spoke into his mic again. "We're going to bring her out. If you're reading me get EMS ready."

He looked back at the staircase. Without the flashlight he could barely see Tammy. He could only see the faint outline of a figure in the shadows. He took a step toward her and she backed up into the corner of the stairwell, moving even further into the shadows. As she backed away the outline of her body shifted slightly. It was enough to cause both Wenton and Dallons to stop.

"*Facini entfaste.*"

Dallons looked over at Wenton. He heard something. The soft voice was like a cool breath against his ear. Wenton wasn't even looking at him, so he knew it didn't come from him. He looked back at Tammy.

As both men watched, Tammy's body sunk into the dark shadows of the staircase. The wind blew with an increased force that caused the tarps to shake violently. The overpowering stench continued to sink down and flow over them until their eyes watered.

"*Blackened side.*"

Wenton felt a cold, twisting sensation in his stomach and strained to focus on Tammy. He could barely discern her outline; what he was seeing wasn't consistent with a human form. It was as if her body was losing its cohesiveness and was slowly dissipating into the shadows. The borders were breaking away, melting into the darkness that surrounded her.

Things were happening so quickly that neither Dallons nor Wenton could react. They watched in amazement as Tammy's body spread out into the air around her, swirling away into the shadows. The hallway shook from the wind, the plastic tarps cracked under the assault, the stench of rot and decay stung their nostrils.

Amidst the noise, a voice resounded through the hall.

"And face the black inside."

Both men heard it clearly and turned to look at each other.

"What's going on?" Dallons yelled.

The dark shape on the stairs, pulsed and grew. The shadows couldn't contain the writhing black mass. Dallons and Wenton were unable to pull their attention away from the shifting shape.

"Black inside, black inside."

And then the shape took form. A massive head lifted out of the amorphous black mass. Two eyes spun through the blackness and centred on the face.

"Face me and face the black inside."

Dallons stumbled to one side and leaned heavily on the wall.

"Inside."

The black mass continued to pulse and the newly formed head shifted with it, but the eyes continued to focus on Dallons and Wenton. The wind howled through the house, shaking even the floor beneath their feet. The stench of something dead and rotting filled their nostrils.

Dallons felt something grip his arm.

"Wenton!" he yelled, but Wenton was gone.

Dallons felt like he was going to be sick. His head spun and his stomach was a mass of knots. The noise pounded his head and the smell continued to assault him. He turned to find Wenton staring into his eyes.

"Fight it!" Wenton yelled. "None of this is real!"

"What?"

"It's not real," Wenton screamed above the howling wind.

"What do you mean?"

"We need to get her out of here, now!"

Dallons didn't understand what was happening, but he knew he needed to get the girl out. Without thinking he turned and rushed down the hall toward the black shape, toward Tammy.

"Hey!" Wenton screamed after him.

Dallons took the stairs two at a time, reaching out to grab for Tammy. The black spot where her outline had been swallowed him as he moved through it. A cold chill gripped him and he crashed into the wall, twisting his wrist badly. He screamed in pain and collapsed. There was no Tammy. The black air around him swirled and faded away leaving only the darkness of the night.

Wenton came up behind Dallons and crouched awkwardly next to him on the stairs. "Where the fuck did she go?"

"I don't know."

Again the powerful smell wafted through the air to surround them. Dallons turned to look into the master bedroom. He shouted in alarm and stood quickly.

"She's there!" he yelled pointing to the top of the staircase.

Enough light was filtering in from the windows in the master bedroom to show the shape of a body lying at the top of the stairs. It was Tammy.

Dallons helped Wenton to stand and they stepped up to get a better look at her. Her eyes were wide open and she lay with her neck at an awkward angle. Standing close to her it was obvious that the stench was originating from her. Wounds showed across her face and on the exposed parts of her body. The blood they could see had been dry for some time. Dallons knelt beside her and placed two fingers on her neck.

"She's completely cold," he said quietly.

Wenton stood silently above them.

"There's no pulse," Dallons continued. He turned to Wenton who looked down without expression.

Dallons pulled his hand away from Tammy and looked around the room. "Hey," he said suddenly, "the wind's gone."

Wenton listened. It was completely calm and still. The constant hum of the wind and cracking of the tarps was gone. Sound seemed to be swallowed and the resulting quiet was almost painful. Before either man could comment, a muffled blast sounded from outside.

The noise made Dallons jerk away from Tammy and stand. "What the fuck was that?"

"It came from outside," Wenton responded as he looked back down the stairs.

"It sounded like a gun...," Dallons began but his words were cut short by a blast of static as his earpiece suddenly came alive and crackled with noise. Reflexively, he reached for his ear and held the receiver. "Are you guys there? What's going on out there?"

More static.

"Are you guys there?" Dallons asked angrily.

More static.

"Just turn it off," he said in frustration as he reached for the pack connected to his belt.

As his hand reached the switch a voice broke through the static, "Help...made...van..."

"What?" Dallons yelled back.

More static and then Lincoln Whitley's panicked voice came through. "Edward made it out of the house. He was in the van." He paused and they heard him breathing heavily before he continued. "I think Mitchell Wa's dead."

forty-eight

127th day (early friday morning)

Within seconds Dallons and Wenton burst out the front door. They knew as soon as they exited the house that there was trouble. Some of the tactical officers had given up their positions around the house and taken up new positions around the van with weapons trained, waiting for movement.

"Status!" Dallons barked as he approached the tactical perimeter.

An officer's head snapped back. "Um, there was a gunshot from inside the van. We've heard nothing else."

Dallons pressed his lips together and looked at the silent vehicle. An officer approached from behind.

"Excuse me, sir?" Constable Bill Lawrence said.

Dallons turned slowly.

Bill's expression changed to one of surprise as Dallons faced him. He stumbled over his words. "The house was, ah, secure. None of my, I mean, the men never saw anyone exit the building at any time."

"I'd already assumed that, Constable."

"We'll move on, I mean, we'll take—"

"What's the problem, Constable?" Dallons asked impatiently.

"Are you okay, sir?"

"Why?"

"You've got blood on your face," Bill said, pointing to Dallons' cheek.

Dallons brought the back of his hand up and wiped it across his cheek. "Forget it. I want an entry team ready now. We're going in."

The noise of a latch opening drew their attention to the van. The tactical team adjusted, training their weapons on the back door as it swung open. Dallons, Wenton, and Lawrence watched as Lincoln Whitley stepped into the doorway.

He stood precariously in the back of the van and looked around at the officers. His eyes were wide with curiosity, much like a child seeing something interesting for the first time.

Dallons stepped through the police line. "Whitley! Are you okay?"

Whitley's eyes drifted lazily back to focus on Dallons. "Hi," he said awkwardly.

Dallons looked back at Wenton and frowned before continuing in a slow, steady voice, emphasizing every word. "Lincoln, are you okay? Is Edward still in the van?"

He nodded slowly.

"He *is* still in the van?" Dallons yelled.

Lincoln looked concerned and then shook his head vigorously. He stopped suddenly and looked directly at Dallons. "What do you mean?"

"Who's in the van, Lincoln?"

He screwed up his face as he considered the question. "I guess it's just me and Louise and Mitchell." He paused before he added, "But I think Mitchell's dead."

Dallons looked around at the tactical officers to get their attention. He held up four fingers and motioned toward the van. "Let's go."

Four officers stepped out of the perimeter and moved quickly toward the van. They pulled Lincoln out and two more officers took him by the arms, leading him away. The remaining officers set up for entry at the back doors. Quickly and with obvious precision, two of the officers entered. The other two kept their weapons down and watched from behind.

Dallons didn't move. He watched and waited for a report from the entry team. It wasn't long before one the officers stepped back into the rear doorway and jumped out. The second officer appeared and looked around for Dallons, who waved him over with two fingers.

"What do we have?" Dallons asked.

"It's fucked up," he said quietly. "You better see." The officer looked past Dallons. "Get EMS ready," he yelled.

Dallons jumped into the back of the van. The first thing he saw was Mitchell Wa's body. His head lay in a pool of blood and a massive wound was evident on the side. As Dallons scanned the area, he quickly noticed Louise Parker sitting huddled in the front of the van near the driver's area. He peered at her through the dim light.

"Chief?"

She didn't answer but shifted further back into the corner.

"Are you okay, Louise?"

Still no answer.

"Let's go. We need to get you help. We need to get Mitchell some help."

There was a slight giggle from her direction.

"Louise?" he said with confusion.

He stepped over Wa's body, being careful to avoid the blood, and reached a hand toward Chief Parker. "Let's go."

She shook her head violently and hugged her legs to her chest more tightly.

"Come on," he said. "We need to get you out of here. Get someone in here for Mitchell!" he shouted over his shoulder.

There was a small giggle again and then in a soft voice Louise said, "I killed him."

Dallons leaned toward her. "What?"

She laughed out loud, but the laugh barely escaped her mouth before turning into a choking sob. "I killed him. I shot him." She reached down and picked up a gun, holding it in the palm of her hand.

Dallons reacted instantly. He bent and swatted the gun out of her hand. In the same motion he grabbed her wrist and pulled her to her feet, wrapping his other arm around her waist. He half-dragged, half-carried her out of the van and called for EMS as he stepped out.

Wenton and Dallons watched the flashing lights of two ambulances disappear down the street. Chief Louise Parker lay inside one and the body of Mitchell Wa was in the other. Constable Bill Lawrence had escorted Lincoln Whitley from the scene, presumably to the hospital. Although Whitley wasn't physically injured, he was incoherent and needed to be checked out. All of them suspected that Whitley had succumbed to Edward's strange power, but none of them wanted to say it out loud. A forensics team, including more EMS, was inside the house attending to Tammy's body.

The two men were silent even though they were surrounded by activity. Finally, Dallons spoke. "You might as well go."

Wenton looked at him and noticed that at some point one of the EMS people had bandaged the gash on his face.

"We're going to have to call in some more men and start another search pattern," Dallons said. He shook his head slowly. "I can't fucking believe this mess."

Wenton nodded but didn't respond.

Dallons turned to him. "What the hell happened in that house, anyway? What was all that shit we saw?"

Wenton shrugged. "I honestly don't know. If it's true that Edward wasn't even in the house, then I don't know what happened."

The detective scowled. "I don't want you to say shit about what went on in there. As far as I'm concerned we entered the house, moved upstairs, and found the dead girl. That's all. I don't want to hear word one about us seeing that girl walking around. Got it? Our story is that she was dead before we got there."

Wenton nodded.

"You can go," Dallons said as he turned away. "We'll call you if I think we need you again. The police department would appreciate it if you stayed near a phone." He scanned the area and saw a group of officers collecting. He moved toward them, leaving Wenton behind.

Wenton swung into the driver's seat of his black Dodge Durango. He took a deep breath as he inserted his key in the ignition. It had been a long, strange evening and nothing had been accomplished. The frustration was pressing through his fatigue, and he felt anger close behind. He knew he needed to stay in control if he was going to be effective.

He put the truck in gear and pulled away from the curb, making a sharp U-turn away from the flashing lights in front of him. Soon he arrived at the exit to the Cedar Mews subdivision that would take him back to the highway. A checkpoint was already established and he pulled to a stop beside an officer.

Wenton rolled his window down and looked at the man without expression.

"Oh, I'm sorry Dr. Wenton," the constable said as his demeanour quickly changed. "I didn't realize it was you."

Wenton didn't respond.

"Go ahead, sir," the constable said as he stepped back from the truck and motioned Wenton ahead.

He drove slowly between two parked police cars and was soon on the highway.

I saw Edward Carter just last Friday, he thought. *Just one week ago. There's another girl dead. Was dead. It's unbelievable. I should have seen this coming. I should've fuckin' known or I shouldn't have gotten involved.*

He blinked heavily and took an exit that led back to his condo.

And what the fuck was happening in that house? How could that girl be dead if Dallons and I saw her on the staircase? For fuck's sake Dallons even got a cut on his face when she hit him!

He felt the truck drifting and looked quickly at the road. He had moved off to the right and was in danger of hitting the curb. He pulled the truck sharply back into his lane.

It's a good thing it's three in the morning, he thought and quickly glanced in the rear-view mirror to see if there was any traffic behind him. A man sat in the centre of the back seat staring straight ahead. Wenton let his foot off the gas.

"Hello Edward," Wenton said calmly.

Edward didn't answer.

forty-nine

127th day (early friday morning)

"How did you know which car was mine?" Wenton asked as he pulled into an empty parking lot.

"Where are we?" Edward asked looking out one window and then the other.

Wenton watched him in his rear-view mirror. "I took us to a department store. It's early. There won't be anybody else here for a few hours. It's a nice private location for us to talk."

Edward sunk back into the seat and closed his eyes.

Wenton turned to look at him. There was a palpable odour of filth. Edward's clothes were dirty, stained, and ripped. His hair was a mess of tangles pressing out in all directions and shiny with oil. His face was bruised and dirty with rough patches of hair across his chin and over his lip. He was thin, almost emaciated, and his body slumped in the back seat with little energy to hold himself up. He breathed heavily through his mouth and a thin line of saliva dripped out the corner and stretched to his hospital gown.

"Edward?" Wenton asked. "Are you still alive?"

Edward's eyes fluttered and opened. He found Wenton's face and focused on it without saying a word.

"How are you feeling?"

Edward just stared back.

"Been better, eh?" Wenton said. "So what do you want from me?"

Edward closed his eyes again before he answered. "Help."

"With what?"

"I don't want to be evil."

"What do you mean?"

"I don't have any control over this. It just happens. I'm not insane."

"What makes you think I can help you?" Wenton asked.

"Because I know about you and what you are. Face me and face you."

"What?"

"Facinientfaste."

"What?" Wenton repeated.

"Evil is in you, Dr. Wenton."

"What the fuck does that mean?"

Edward's eyelids opened again. His eyes were gone, replaced by black liquid that dripped down his face like tears. "*Dr. Wenton,*" a voice projected from Edward. "*Why did you specialize in forensic work?*"

The voice penetrated Wenton. It travelled deep inside and resonated through his mind in waves that bordered on pain.

"I don't know what you mean," Wenton said.

"*Come on, Doctor,*" Edward said with a smirk. "*Am I really so different?*"

"What the fuck are you talking about?"

"*You and I,*" Edward said and leaned forward to stare into Wenton's face. "*Are we really so different?*"

From this distance Wenton could see more clearly the shifting liquid blackness in Edward's eyes. It moved independently and continued to send streams down his face.

Wenton felt like his head might cave in from all sides. There was enormous pressure burning through him. He wanted to scream, to run, to fight, but he couldn't find the strength or willpower.

"Get away from me," Wenton whispered and shifted slightly to turn away from Edward.

Edward's cold hands shot out and gripped the sides of Wenton's head. The grip was surprisingly strong for someone who looked so emaciated. Edward's hands reeked of filth—sweat, urine, excrement, and every manner of rotted fluid and dirt stung Wenton's nose. Edward roughly turned Wenton's head to face him and spoke deliberately and slowly.

"Dr. Wenton, do you know what sublimation is?"

He could not answer.

"Sublimation is a defensive reaction against an unacceptable unconscious impulse. When an angry, violent criminal type puts all that energy into playing football, that's sublimation. It's considered a healthy defense of one's ego."

Edward stopped talking and leaned forward. He pressed his lips tightly against Wenton's. The Doctor arched his back and bucked in protest but couldn't escape.

Edward pulled away from Wenton and continued to hiss. "*So why did you become a forensic specialist?*"

Wenton squinted back at Edward. The gut-twisting smell, the black, bubbling eyes, and the lingering sensation of cold lips on his own robbed his mind of reason. He couldn't fully understand Edward's words. He struggled just to stay conscious.

"I don't know what you mean," Wenton said quietly.

Edward's eyes blazed and the black liquid bulged forth. "*Well, let me jog your memory.*" He leaned forward again and pressed his lips onto Wenton's. At the same time he dropped one hand down and placed it between Wenton's legs, finding and squeezing the crotch of his pants.

Wenton reflexively resisted this intrusion and found the strength to break free of Edward's touch. He fell back against the dashboard and badly bruised his shoulder blade.

"*So. Have you figured it out yet?*" Edward sneered.

Wenton's body hung awkwardly over the edge of the passenger seat as he furiously rubbed his mouth with the back of his hand. He couldn't remove the taste and smell of filth from his lips.

"*Sandra Evans*," Edward said.

Wenton stopped rubbing his mouth and looked up at Edward who was perched between the two front seats watching him.

"*Does that name ring a bell?*" Edward asked innocently. The voice continued to move in rhythmic waves and penetrated Wenton's mind.

Wenton nodded weakly.

"You were fresh out of university. You had just finished your Ph.D. in clinical psychology and were all set to start helping people. Your training was adult clinical psychology with a specialization in anxiety and depression. Do you remember?"

Wenton nodded again.

"And you got a job at a local hospital. You worked as a fresh-faced, eager young psychologist. You ran groups for people with anxiety problems. You saw clients individually. You were really working hard and making a difference. Do you remember?"

Wenton nodded.

"But there was something that a lot of people didn't know, wasn't there? Something about how you spent your spare time?"

Wenton looked away from the monster and slumped further down onto the floor of the Durango.

"The personable, dedicated, young doctor was also a sexual addict. You spent every spare second watching hardcore pornography, masturbating, visiting prostitutes, convincing casual girlfriends to try anal sex, visiting strip clubs, buying sex toys, organizing clandestine orgies."

Wenton closed his eyes against the memories.

"Sex was everything to you. There was no one and nothing that you didn't want to fuck. Nothing was taboo for you—not if it meant another sexual high, another orgasm."

Tears found their way into Wenton's eyes as he listened. His mind vibrated with every word but he made no effort to escape.

"You thought you had it under control. You even convinced yourself you had limits, boundaries, a clear division between work and pleasure. Lines you wouldn't cross. That was funny, eh?"

Wenton was silent.

"Shortly into your career at the hospital you started working with a pretty young client, Sandra Evans. Poor Sandra was really messed up. Multiple suicide attempts. Failed relationships. A little histrionic. She also reported multiple elaborate symptoms from depression to psychosis. A classic borderline personality disorder. Right, Dr. Wenton?"

He briefly opened his eyes to look at Edward. He closed his eyes and nodded.

"*Right! A classic borderline. Unstable in thought, mood, behaviour, and most importantly: relationships. A truly messed-up individual—so much so that even her own family had given up on her. But not Dr. Wenton. He took the case on and worked hard to establish a therapeutic relationship with the young woman. Very professional. Very dedicated. Very noble.*" Edward smiled a large grin of stained teeth.

"*But Sandra Evans was also fantastically good-looking, wasn't she Doctor? Wow, this girl was unbelievable. Luckily you had your rigid professional boundaries to protect her from your cock. Otherwise it would have been hard for you to resist her, to sexualize her, and try and use her for your own pleasure. Right Doctor? Your rigid, professional boundaries protected this girl.*"

Wenton covered his face with his hands. "Fuck you," he whispered.

"*Nooooo,*" Edward screamed in mock frustration. "*Not fuck me. Fuck her! Remember? You fucked that poor, unstable woman right in your office! You fucked her right there on the floor of your office with the rest of the staff walking around outside the door. It must have been so exciting! Wondering if you might get caught. Knowing full well how naughty you were being. Oh my gosh, you bad, bad psychologist!*"

Edward stopped and leaned forward into the front seat. "*Dr. Wenton, seriously,*" he said with a slow, solemn tone, "*how was she?*"

"Fuck you," Wenton said softly.

Edward ignored him and continued. "*Well I guess Sandra wasn't a very good fuck because you sure panicked after it was over. You knew you'd messed up and it could cost you your job. You just wanted to tidy the whole mess up. Get Sandra dressed and out of your office but that dumb bitch was too unstable, wasn't she doctor? The dumb bitch was going to mess everything up simply because you'd had a moment of weakness. Well, that wasn't fair. You shouldn't have to waste ten years of university because of a simple mistake with an unstable, horny, dumb bitch. Right, Doctor? No sir! You needed to take control of that dumb bitch any way you could. You needed to make that dumb bitch understand that there was nothing wrong. But how? How, Doctor? How do you get that dumb bitch on your side as you rush her to get dressed and out of your office?*"

"Stop calling her a dumb bitch," Wenton growled.

"*Ooooooo,*" Edward moaned, slapping his hands against his face. "*Did I strike a nerve in the great Dr. Wenton? Is it possible the stoic Dr. Wenton, the badass, heartless, son of a bitch actually has feelings!*"

Wenton didn't respond.

"*Anyway,*" Edward continued, "*do you remember how you gained control over poor, unstable, little Sandra? Her biggest issue was trust and relationships. She'd been trying for her entire life to sort out how to fit into a world she felt reject -*

ed by. Do you remember what you told her to gain her trust after your sexual misadventure? No? Let me remind you. You told her that you loved her. Do you remember now?"

Wenton was motionless.

"Do you know what that would do to an unstable person like Sandra? The double messages, the double bind? Her psychologist fucking her and telling her he loves her just to send her packing out of his office? Wow! What do you think it would do to a person? Maybe drive her over the deep-end? Maybe make her stop the suicidal gestures and get down to the real thing, eh? Exactly. Sandra went home that night and killed herself. Do you remember now?"

Tears escaped Wenton's eyes and rolled down his cheeks.

"It's a little late to get all misty," Edward said caustically. He watched Wenton for a moment before he continued. *"So back to my original question: Do you know what sublimation is?"*

Wenton looked up at Edward through eyes fogged by tears.

"You quit your job at the hospital. You went into hiding, more or less, and emerged as a specialist in forensic psychology. More importantly, you appeared to be an expert in sexual violence, psychopathy, serial killers and all manner of horrible, unspeakable crimes that most people would want nothing to do with. But you live and breathe the most disgusting, horrendous aspects of humanity. And your contribution in this area is undeniably the most influential body of research in the entire field. You are the king of violent sexual perversion. Long live the king!"

Edward paused and lowered his voice. *"But what happened to that little problem with sexual addiction?"* He sat back in the Durango and folded his arms across his chest. *"Hmm, that's a curious question. What happened to Dr. Wenton's insatiable thirst for deviant sex? Is it possible he's just been suppressing it, using the subconscious energy from his addiction to fuel his passion for his forensic work? Hmm, that is an interesting question. A sexual monster doing research on, and helping the police catch, other sexual monsters."*

Edward stopped and leaned between the front seats again. With an intense expression of concern he asked, *"How does that work? Hmm, Dr. Wenton? How does that work, Dr. Wenton? Dr. Wenton?"*

The voice continued to pierce him. Wenton couldn't answer. He slumped further onto the floor of the Durango and waited to drop into unconsciousness.

"*Dr. Wenton?*" the voice called.

"Dr. Wenton?"

"Dr. Wenton?" A sharp rap against the passenger window broke through his consciousness. He shifted slightly and his eyes fluttered, but didn't open.

"Dr. Wenton, are you okay?" the voice called again.

The voice was strangely muffled. It took a moment but Wenton finally realized that it originated outside the Durango. He struggled and pushed himself up on one arm. He looked out the driver's side window and saw nothing. He turned to the passenger window and saw a man peering in, shrouded on all sides by the morning sun.

"Dr. Wenton?" the man called. "Are you okay?"

Wenton quickly looked into the back seat. There was no one there. The back seat was empty. No Edward.

There was a tap at the glass and he again looked out the passenger window. He now recognized the man as a uniformed police officer. He reached for his keys and turned the auxiliary power on to roll down the passenger window.

The officer leaned into the vehicle. "Dr. Wenton. We've been looking for you all morning. You left the scene last night before we could debrief you. Detective Wa and the Chief want to talk to you about what happened in the house."

Wenton shook his head slightly, hoping that his mind would suddenly clear and he'd understand.

"I'm sorry," he finally responded. "Did you say Mitchell Wa wants to talk to me?"

"Well, the whole team really. Detective Wa, the site commander, Whitley, Chief Parker, Detective Dallons. You can't just leave the scene like that—"

Wenton interrupted sharply. "Wa? What do you mean, Wa?"

The officer looked surprised. "Um, Mitchell Wa was the detective who helped track—"

"I know who he is," Wenton interrupted angrily. "He's alive?"

The officer laughed slightly. "I guess so. He was swearing a blue streak up and down about you leaving the scene."

Wenton shook his head again and lifted his hands to his face.

"Is there something wrong, Doctor?"

He pulled his hands away and looked at the constable. "Edward Carter?" he said. "Did they catch Edward Carter yet?"

The officer again looked surprised. "*Catch him?*" he asked in surprise. "You and Dallons found him inside the house. He was dead."

fifty

130th day (monday)

"So what happened inside the house, Dallons?" Mitchell Wa asked as the group took their seats around the conference room table.

In addition to Dallons and Wa, Chief Louise Parker, Detectives Margaret Meredith and Laurie Abrahms, Lincoln Whitley, and Constable William Lawrence were all present.

"I don't know," Dallons said gruffly.

"We've had our people working on the audio and video all weekend and couldn't get anything off the tapes," Whitley said. "I don't know why we lost the feed during the entry, but since we did, we're all in the dark about the specifics, Detective."

"The quality of the equipment wasn't my responsibility," Dallons replied. "I was just going into that house so that the pretty boys on the ERT wouldn't have to risk going insane."

"I wasn't implying that the equipment failure was your fault, Detective," Whitley continued patiently. "In fact it wasn't an equipment failure. There was something interfering with our signal. It was like there was interference in the area. We're still working on it."

"I think what Lincoln means," interrupted Chief Parker, "is that you're our only source of knowledge for what actually happened in that house last Thursday night. We've all read your report and Dr. Wenton has agreed with it, but we feel there might be something else you want to tell us. All you've told us so far is that you entered the house, conducted a room-by-room search, and located the bodies of Tammy Farrell and Edward Carter. The coroner determined that Edward died first. He was dead for probably a couple of hours before you guys even went in. The coroner thinks Tammy died after Edward, maybe by as much as an hour. But the way you two came bursting out of the house..." She paused. "What else happened in there, Tim?"

Dallons shrugged.

"Tim," Wa said, "come on. Help us out here. You guys come out of there and you've got a gash across your cheek. Wenton looks like he's seen a ghost. Before we know it, he takes off. To top it off when we eventually find him he's lying in his truck, virtually incoherent. The reports from the constable are that Wenton looked like he was sleeping in the vehicle. What was that about?"

"I don't know what to tell you. I can't speak for Wenton. You'll have to ask him yourself."

"Oh, we'll ask him," Wa said. "Don't worry about that. But that's not what I was asking you. I'm asking you point blank: did something happen to Dr. Wenton inside that house? Did you guys see or hear something that you haven't told us about?"

"I'm going to tell you one more time," Dallons said, "and then I'm leaving, because I don't work for the police department anymore. You guys sent Wenton and me into that house because everyone was afraid of what Edward Carter could do to a person's mind. We went into the house. We searched the house. I scraped my cheek on something—probably a nail—the house was under construction. Anyway, we conducted a room-by-room search—by the book—and eventually moved upstairs. We found Tammy dead in the stairwell and Edward Carter hanging from the ceiling in the bedroom. There wasn't much for us to do and we left. I don't know why Wenton took off. I don't know anything about what's going on with him. In fact, I don't care. I don't need to because that's not my job. Okay?"

The table was silent as the team considered Dallons' answer. It wasn't satisfying—not at all.

"That's it then," Wa said shaking his head in defeat.

Dallons nodded. "That's it."

fifty-one

130th day (monday evening)

Tim Dallons stared at the bottle. He knew it was the last one in his house and that was a problem. He didn't want to be sober. He wondered if he'd ever be sober again.

He gazed around the small living room. It was still in ruins. He'd wrecked it to try and erase some painful memories. It didn't work. He wasn't sure that burning this house to the ground would be enough to take away the memories of his dead wife.

He shook his head. *The whole world is a sick fucking mess,* he thought. *I don't understand why I ever bothered to try and make it a better place.*

He poured another drink. He'd given up on trying to make rye and cokes and was now drinking warm rye straight. He took a large mouthful and swallowed without flinching.

And that poor little girl in that house, he thought. *What the fuck happened in that house? I know Wa thinks I'm jerking him around but I can't tell him anything about it. I can't tell anyone. I don't know what happened in that damn house.*

He took another drink.

There's only one person who knows what happened in there and that's Wenton. That fucking psychologist. But he's never going to say anything. If what I saw is true he can't ever say anything.

We entered the house and everything was fine. He stayed out of my way and we searched the bottom. Just as we finished and were about to head upstairs, the two-way radios gave out. That was a nice stroke of luck. It meant that the rest of the events wouldn't have any record. Perfect, given how fucked up everything got.

So Wenton and I headed upstairs. This is where it gets fucked. I'm sure that girl was standing at the top of the stairs. I can't remember exactly what happened, but she was there, just standing there, watching us. I can't remember where Wenton was, but I think I approached her and she took off—ran back down the upstairs hallway.

So Wenton and I kept going. I was checking every room. I didn't find anything in those rooms. But it was so hard to concentrate, so hard to stay focused. Why was that? There was something going on. Something messing up my head—lights or something. I know the light was poor but what else? What else? Oh yeah, wind! There was a fuckin' gale outside shaking the tarps and making so much damn noise that I couldn't hear myself think.

So, I'm checking the rooms out with this wind shaking the hell out of everything and light reflecting off these damn tarps making shadows everywhere and of course what happened? My flashlight died. Now, I was in the dark. That was perfect.

Wenton gave me his light and we kept going. But not two seconds later, his flash -

light went out. Fine. We kept going. There's one more bedroom up the flight of stairs at the end of the hall. We headed there and that's where we found Edward. Dead as a fucking doorknob. He was still swinging from the beam on the ceiling. It was a horrible sight. And the smell! Oh yeah, the smell. There was a stench so incredible that my eyes watered. I guess it was Edward. After he'd hanged himself he'd shit and pissed his pants so there were huge puddles on the floor. It was fuckin' gross.

And that's all I remember...for sure. Wenton and I were standing there watching this rapist bastard swinging in the air. I remember thinking that the case was closed and I was pretty pleased. The wind was still howling outside. The room stunk so bad I thought I might puke and we didn't even have a flashlight. Our only light was a trickle sneaking in past the tarps rattling on the windows. And that's where my memory basically stops. The rest is just flashes of stuff that probably never happened.

In the flashes I see that girl over and over. I see her on the floor and Wenton's standing over her. I don't know what the hell to make of that.

I think the girl is struggling, fighting Wenton, so she must've still been alive but I can't be sure because my head is so screwed up about it.

I think Wenton took something out. Wenton handed something to the girl.

I don't know. Next thing the girl's dead. She's just lying there—dead.

Wenton's turned back to look at me only it wasn't Wenton at all. It wasn't human. It was something black. Something hideous. Fuck, it must be my imagination. The thing had pitch black eyes and hardly any facial features. It wasn't anything. It wasn't human.

Anyway, the next thing I knew we were both heading out the front door and Wenton disappeared. And there wasn't any wind when we got outside. It was calm as can be which makes my story even more full of shit so there's no way I'm going out on a limb with this garbage. No way.

He took another drink and finished the glass. He let it fall out of his hands onto the cushion beside him. He leaned over to look at the bottle on the floor. It was empty too. He fell back onto the couch and brought his hands to his face. He sobbed quietly. There was one other image from the house that burned in his memory. One other image that he couldn't erase. An image that he couldn't fit into the sequence anywhere.

Every time he closed his eyes he saw Tammy Farrell's frightened face. He clearly saw her frantic eyes, her open mouth locked in a silent scream. He could clearly see terror. But it wasn't her face exactly that sickened him. It was the angle from which he was looking at her. He was kneeling over her, pinning her to the floor and watching her face.

He threw his hands down and screamed in frustration at the memory.

"What the fuck happened in that house?" he cried out and let his hands fall to his sides.

His left hand fell against something hard. He turned and expected to see the discarded glass. It wasn't his glass. His hand was resting against his gun. Dallons stared at the weapon and then wrapped his fingers around the handle. He carefully examined it and checked to see if it was loaded. He knew it was, but he checked anyway.

He played with the gun, moving it back and forth between his hands. Tears filled his eyes. The image of Tammy Farrell's face flashed through his mind again and he became motionless, struggling to push the image out of his consciousness. He fought against the memory, desperate to replace it with something, anything. He finally found what he needed. He closed his eyes and pictured his wife. He smiled.

He lifted his gun. He rotated it until the barrel faced him. He lifted it further and brought it close to his mouth.

"I'm sorry, sweetheart," he said quietly, put the gun in his mouth and pulled the trigger.

fifty two

130th day (monday evening)

The meeting with Detective Dallons bothered Wa. No, the meeting didn't *bother* him, it pissed him off. He wanted answers. The whole case stunk right from the beginning and he was reluctant to just let it end with two bodies in a house.

He needed to know who killed Tammy. He needed to know why Dallons and Wenton were being so secretive. He needed to know what they were hiding. Something else had happened in that house. None of this made any sense.

He glanced at the road signs and sighed. He was close to defeat and he knew it. He banged on the steering wheel and stomped hard on the brake, turned sharply onto a ramp that took him up to the highway, looking over his shoulder as he merged into traffic.

Edward hanged himself, he thought. *That's fine. And maybe the girl killed herself too, but I doubt it. Edward's body was cold to the touch. The girl had only recently died. That doesn't make sense. Wenton's going to tell me what happened in that house. I deserve to know*.

He pulled the car across three lanes of traffic and down another ramp. The Saturn bounced wildly as he gunned the accelerator and did a U-turn across the rough grass and gravel and pulled into traffic going the other way.

After all the shit that I went though on this case I deserve some fucking answers.

"What?" Wenton's voice came through sharply on the intercom.

Wa stood in the lobby of Wenton's condominium. The intercom system operated over the phone lines and he'd almost given up on Wenton being home.

"Dr. Wenton, I'm sorry to bother you at home. This is Detective Mitchell Wa." He waited for an acknowledgment but the intercom was silent. "Could I speak to you for a moment?"

There was still no response but a sudden electronic buzz indicated that the door into the building was unlocked. Wa pulled it open and entered.

When he reached Wenton's door he was surprised to find it unlocked and ajar. He pushed it gently and stepped into the entranceway, calling out, "Dr. Wenton?"

"Come in," a voice responded from somewhere inside the apartment.

Wa entered cautiously and waited.

"All the way in," Wenton's voice called again. "And shut the door."

Wa closed the door and headed toward the living room. Wenton was seated on a sofa in the middle of the room.

"Is this official police business?" Wenton asked.

"Um," Wa stumbled, "I guess not."

"So I assume you'll pay me privately for the time?" Wenton asked.

Wa half-smiled in return. "Do you mind if I sit down?" he asked motioning to the only chair in the room.

Wenton waved a hand toward it and was silent.

"Dr. Wenton," Wa began, "I know something else happened in that house. I'm not going to close the book on this case until I know what the hell it was. I don't give a damn what Chief Parker says. When the autopsies come back I'm going..."

"Why are you here?" Wenton asked with obvious derision.

"I want to know what actually happened. I think I have a right to know. I think the parents of that young girl have a right to know."

"Why do *you* have a right?"

"Are you going to talk to me or not?"

"That's what we're doing."

"You're just mocking me."

"Go home to your wife," Wenton said, and slid forward onto the sofa in order to stand.

"Fuck you!" Wa's anger bubbled inside him and a strange buzz in the back of his head made him dizzy. He was having trouble focusing on Wenton.

"Temper, temper," Wenton said, wagging a finger at the detective. "You're letting this case get to you and that's a mistake."

Wa put a hand to his forehead to try and rub away the cobwebs. "Tell me what happened in that house!" He closed his eyes and a strong image flashed before him. It was Tammy's face. But she was smiling at him. His eyes burst open.

"You don't want to know," Wenton said quietly.

"The fuck I don't!" Wa screamed.

"It could kill you," Wenton said.

"What are you talking about?"

"Everything that's going on. Edward. The house. Dallons. Me," he smiled. "It could kill you. I saw it already. You died."

"What the fuck are you talking about?" Wa's head spun and he felt like he might be sick.

Wenton's expression was serious. He took a deep breath as if he was reluctant to continue. Finally, he spoke:

"I had a vision." He paused. "Well, more of an hallucination of sorts. I thought you were dead. I thought Edward had managed to get to you and kill you. Obviously, he didn't, but now I realize what that vision meant. When you showed up here tonight I finally realized."

"What?" Wa asked.

"That you're in danger. Everyone else was already tainted in some way. You could've pulled through this without so much as a scratch, but now you aren't going to. You won't let it go. You won't just go back to your little life. Your kids. Your wife."

"You're not making any sense!"

"You aren't listening. I'm trying to tell you that your search for answers is burying this thing too deeply in your head. You need to let it go before it takes you in."

"I have no idea what you're talking about."

Wenton sighed heavily. He looked at Wa with a curious expression. Finally, he spoke again. "I was wrong about the fear."

Wa felt like everything Wenton said was a riddle. He didn't know how to respond anymore. He didn't even know if they were still talking about the same thing. "Wrong about what?"

"The fear," Wenton said, and his features became darkly serious. He dropped back on the couch and leaned on his knees. "I was wrong about the fear. Well, not completely, but still..."

"You mean your theory that Edward made people crazy because of fear?"

He nodded. "It isn't just fear. There was something else going on. Edward was a little bit of everyone. He was a little bit of you. A little bit of me. Of Dallons. He borrowed from what he found in us."

"What?"

"The whole city reeks of it. There's not much left around us that's good. Most people have something dark inside them. Something they hide that they don't want other people to know about. Some dirty little secret. Something evil. Well, that's what Edward was. He couldn't help it. He just fed off all the shit around him. The sex was only one way to cope with it. He didn't want to hurt anybody. He just couldn't help it."

"So he wasn't crazy?" Wa asked with a frown.

"Oh no, he was crazy. His mind couldn't take all of the evil around him. He broke it off and made it pure. He took what little was left of the real Edward Carter and hid it somewhere. The rest was all the shit, all the evil. That was the force that did the damage. But Edward couldn't control it. It controlled him. The juxtaposition of those two forces made him crazy. It would happen to anyone confronted by their deepest, darkest, hidden parts—the things they don't want anyone to know. In Edward the whole process of uncovering his dark side was just more obvious than in most."

Wa shook his head. "But what's this got to do with people going crazy?" He closed his eyes and rubbed his face with his hands. The moment he did he saw Tammy. This time he saw her whole body. She was naked with her legs spread wide. He choked and opened his eyes to make the image disappear.

"Everything," Wenton said. "You can't directly confront evil without it affecting you. That's what Edward did. He affected people. But mainly when he was most potent—when the darkness was pure. When he was struggling, when he was trying to suppress it, the evil couldn't affect people."

"You're talking gibberish," Wa said.

"Maybe so."

Wa considered what Wenton had said. His head still spun and the image of Tammy continued to flicker whenever he even partially closed his eyes. He forced himself to keep his eyes open. With everything going on, it was difficult to completely digest the things he was hearing.

"Consider it this way, Detective," Wenton said. "Edward was like a key. He opened up parts of people that they didn't want opened. He helped find the little spots of fear, anger, desire, and madness that are normally suppressed. When this happens a person only has two choices. They can fight it. They can fight the recognition of the evil that's inside them and ultimately end up insane. Or, they can accept it. They can accept that they can be the authors of atrocity and suffer the consequences of their new personality."

"Suffer the consequences?"

"If someone's trying to hide the darkest parts of themselves and then those parts are opened, how can they stay sane? They can't unless they open themselves to it."

Wenton's words swung through the air and attacked Wa. He felt each word enter his ears and push through his eardrums. His stomach suddenly retched and he thought he was going to be sick. The room faded and returned. He wanted to stand, to leave, but he couldn't find the strength.

"That's bullshit," Wa said. He didn't want to believe, but something about what Wenton said rang true.

"I don't care if you believe me or not."

"Why those women? What did they do that was 'evil'?"

"I don't have a clue," Wenton said.

"Eight women were raped and left insane!" Wa screamed. "Not to mention that young girl..." An image of Tammy's young, lithe body splashed across his vision and he stopped speaking.

"I never said there was evil in them," Wenton corrected.

"But your theory—"

"Is just a theory," he finished and shrugged in a way that stabbed needles of frustration through Wa.

Wa was silent as he contemplated this new information. When he spoke it was in a quiet, conciliatory manner. "One of the victims I interviewed, Theresa McDouglas, told me she saw a child in the room when she was raped. She said it was the baby she'd aborted ten years earlier."

"There you go," Wenton said.

"There I go what?" Wa asked. "Why was there weird shit like that going on?"

"That *weird shit* is exactly the confrontation I was talking about. This woman's dark secret, the evil hidden inside her, was the abortion. She likely made the choice for the wrong reasons. She's felt guilty about her decision ever since. She feels responsible for murdering that unborn baby. That guilt confronted her when Edward attacked her. That was the child she saw in the room."

"Another victim reported that she saw her father as the attacker—a father who abused her and went to jail for the crime. The father had died in jail years before. How does that fit?"

"How was the sexual abuse by the father disclosed?"

"I guess she remembered during therapy as an adult. She had her father charged after she'd worked through the memories in therapy with a shrink like you."

"Thought so."

"What does that mean?"

"Recovered memories. There's a good chance the memories she recovered were bullshit. She put her dad through hell, had him thrown in prison where he died, and then found out that her *recovered memories* were crap. That's a pretty big boo-boo."

"So everybody had something in their past. A skeleton in the closet?"

"I'd say so."

"Does that include you?"

Wenton smiled. "Do you really want to ask that?"

Wa considered the challenge. He didn't know. He wasn't sure about anything right now.

Wenton stared across at him. "Do you think there's any evil in you?" he asked quietly.

Wa didn't answer.

"You're pushing awfully hard. What if some of this slips into you?"

"What the fuck are you talking about?" Wa asked, rubbing his temples and trying to clear his head of the thick cobwebs.

"Don't push for answers here. You've got all the answers there are to get. Just do your job. Catch the bad guys and move on. Keep moving on. Don't get caught in the bullshit."

An image of Tammy flashed in Wa's mind again. Her body was so tight, so young.

"Just tell me what happened in the house!"

"How far are you willing to go?" Wenton continued, ignoring his question. "Do you want to become a monster? Will you go that far?"

Wa put his hands on his knees to try and push himself to his feet. He wanted to face Wenton but he couldn't move. Something was horribly wrong. He couldn't move from the chair. "Just tell me who killed Tammy!"

Wenton shook his head in disgust. "You don't understand, do you? We all killed Tammy. Edward, Dallons, me...and even you."

"That's not an answer!"

"The fact that you care so much means that you're in too deeply. You're too wrapped up in all of this. That's what's killing you."

"You're full of shit," Wa said.

"Go home," Wenton answered in disgust and waved him away with his hand.

Wa pulled himself up onto shaky legs and stumbled to the door. He wanted to look back at Wenton, but he knew he needed to get out. He grabbed for the doorknob and swung it open so hard it banged against the doorstop and bounced back. He caught it just before it connected with his head. He staggered out the door before he lost the strength to escape.

Wa didn't know how he got home. He couldn't remember stumbling back to his car. He couldn't remember driving. He only knew that he was home, somehow. It was late and Gloria was already in bed.

He went straight to the bedroom and stood over his wife, watching her. He considered waking her but knew she might be angry that he hadn't called about being late. It was something he normally did.

"I'm not asleep," came a voice from the bed.

Wa sat on the side of the bed. "What are you doing then?"

"Waiting for you to get home."

"I'm sorry."

"What happened?" she asked.

"Just shit. Lots of shit. I think it's over now." He hoped.

"All because of Edward Carter?"

"Yeah."

"How's Tim?"

"I don't know. Fine, I guess. He just took off after our meeting. I'll give him a call tomorrow."

"And Wenton?"

He didn't know what to say. "He's...," he paused, "fine."

"Come to bed then," she said.

Wa stood and went to the bathroom. He closed the door behind him so the light wouldn't bother Gloria. He slipped out of his pants and shirt and stood in front of the mirror in his underwear.

Fuckin' Wenton, he thought. *What was he babbling about, anyway? The evil. What kind of shit is that? It won't change me. What a fucker. I oughta charge him with obstruction.*

He scanned the counter for his toothbrush. It wasn't there. He pulled the drawer open and rooted around, but still no toothbrush. He slammed it shut.

"For fuck's sake," he muttered and pulled the bathroom door open. "Gloria, where the fuck is my toothbrush?"

She partially sat up in the bed. "Hey. Hey. Take it easy. The toothbrushes were looking ratty so I tossed them. There's a new one in the bottom drawer."

Without a word, Wa shut the door roughly and bent to the bottom drawer. He pulled it open with such force that the contents slid forward and banged against the front. He found a new toothbrush and stood, kicking the drawer shut.

She couldn't fucking tell me that she went through the house throwing every - thing out? he thought. *Does everyone have to fucking piss me off?*

He pulled at the package but the hard plastic would only bend and not tear. He poked at the cardboard on the back but his finger was too thick to pierce it.

"Motherfucker," he whispered as he gripped the package in both hands and pulled with increased ferocity. Suddenly, the package split and the toothbrush soared through the air landing in the toilet.

He watched the toothbrush as if it were moving in slow motion. As it finally settled in the bottom of the toilet he clenched his teeth and fists and turned back to the sink. With all his power he resisted striking out, smashing the mirror, ripping the sink off the wall. After a moment of struggle, he finally relaxed his hands. He took a deep breath and reached for the toothpaste. He popped the cap and squeezed it directly into his mouth. He dropped the tube back onto the counter and swished the paste around his mouth. He bent to the tap and took a small mouthful of water.

He wiped his face with a towel and threw the towel onto the counter as he exited. He expected to be scolded in the morning for leaving a wet towel on the counter rather than carefully hanging it on the rack.

When he stepped back into the bedroom, he noticed that the bedside light was on and Gloria was sitting up in bed.

"Is everything okay?" she asked with concern.

He shrugged. "It's just been a difficult case."

"Is there anything I can do?"

He slid into bed beside her. "I don't think so." He reached under the covers and put his hand on her thigh and slowly massaged her leg.

"Hey!" she said in surprise.

"Come on," he urged and continued to stroke her.

She lay back in the bed and turned slightly toward him. His touch did feel nice. He continued to massage her thigh and slowly worked up until he reached the top of her pajama pants. He slipped his hand under the elastic and back down again. He ran his fingers through the small patch of pubic hair and onto the delicate skin beneath. She worked an arm underneath his shoulder and leaned to kiss him.

Their lips met only briefly and Wa pulled away. He tossed the covers back and knelt on the bed. He roughly pulled Gloria's pajama bottom off and then pushed his own underwear down. He grabbed her legs in each arm and lifted them as he entered her.

"Detective Wa!" she whispered in mock surprise at his aggressiveness.

He leaned low to her ear. "Don't call me that," he said sternly.

They moved together. Wa pushed in and drew out and Gloria arched against him. It felt good.

Then Gloria noticed a change. He was pushing harder and harder with each stroke. Their bodies banged together and she started to feel uncomfortable. She tried to see his face, but he'd buried it next to her. She gripped his shoulders and felt the tension in his body as he continued to press against her.

"That hurts a bit," she said very softly.

He ignored her and continued to pound against her with all his strength.

"Ow," she said more firmly.

Still no change from Wa.

"Go easy," she urged more strongly.

He stopped suddenly and she thought he mumbled something. She felt him pull out of her and kneel. He grabbed her hips and roughly flipped her over. She reluctantly cooperated. Once she was on her stomach he grabbed her waist and pulled her up onto her knees, entering her from behind.

"Mitchell?" she inquired softly and tried to look backwards at him. She felt slightly concerned now.

He started to press into her with the same ferocity.

Wa groaned and moved his hands down her back, underneath her pajama top. He dug his fingernails into her flesh.

Gloria closed her eyes and rested her head on the pillow. She wanted to say something, to tell him to stop, but she couldn't.

He groaned as he got closer to orgasm. His strokes came more quickly and he pressed his nails harder into her back. "Oh, yeah," he moaned softly, "take it in."

She reached back with one arm to try and knock his hands off her back. She could only manage to twist and bang at him with one elbow.

"Stop it," she whispered. "Mitchell, stop."

He moaned louder. "Oh fuck yes. You want it, don't you? You want to be fucked."

Gloria stopped struggling and buried her face in the pillow, hoping he'd be finished soon. He never spoke like this when they made love. She didn't understand. She used her arms to push the pillow around her ears to muffle his voice. She didn't want to hear him talk like that. She prayed that it didn't wake the kids.

"Yes, yes, yes," he continued to groan. "That's the way you want it, you fucking slut. Take it all the way in."

His words were only a faint murmur to her now. Tears began to form in her eyes.

"Do you like it? Hunh? Do you like it, Tammy?" he asked in a frenzy.

"Mitchell no!" Gloria shouted and launched herself away from him, rolling over the bed and standing.

He looked across at her, his eyes glazed over in an unnatural way.

"Mitchell?" she said, concerned. He didn't look right. He looked pale, sick.

He stared back at her, sweat dripping down over his eyes. He was staring at the young, naked body of Tammy Farrell.

"Mitchell?" Gloria tried again.

And then a scream sounded from one of the kid's rooms. It was Joshua. He was having a nightmare.

Suddenly, Wa's world came flooding back into focus. He jerked like he'd just been soaked in cold water. He stared around the room wildly. "What's that noise?" he yelled in a panic.

"It's Josh. He probably had a bad dream," Gloria answered in a daze. She still didn't understand what was happening.

"Josh?" he said as if he was just remembering the name.

"Mitchell?" she said, sitting back on the bed. "What happened to you? Are you okay?"

"I don't know," he whispered. His bottom lip began to shake as tears flooded his eyes. "I'm so sorry. I just don't know."

"It's okay," she said automatically. "It'll be okay." She reached over and put a hand on his shoulder.

He looked at her with wide eyes and tears streaming down his face. "I'm not sure it will be. I'm just not sure."

epilogue

130th day (monday evening)

Dr. Michael Wenton sat on the sofa in his living room. He hadn't bothered to check that the door was closed after Detective Wa had left. He didn't care.

He took a deep breath and tried to sort through his thoughts. His head was a mess. He understood most of what he'd told Wa, but the full implications of his explanation were unclear—even to him. He leaned forward to the coffee table, plucked a crystal tumbler up in one hand, and brought it to his lips. In two swallows he finished the rye and Coke and set it back on the table.

He considered speaking to Detective Dallons. He didn't know if that made sense, but he was curious about what Dallons thought had actually happened in the house. The images of the events that danced in Wenton's mind were distorted and unreal. He half suspected that he'd killed Tammy, but he wasn't sure. There were other horrible images that he could only vaguely capture. One was of Dallons on top of the girl, but he didn't know why, or what Dallons was doing. He might've been trying to save her. He might have been killing her. None of his memories connected properly. He knew it didn't matter, not really.

He sighed and lifted his legs onto the coffee table, stretching out and contemplating what to do next. He looked briefly at his bookcase and scanned the titles of his DVD collection. Nothing there interested him.

He looked at the remote control sitting next to his feet on the coffee table and then turned his attention to the big-screen TV. He realized he wasn't in the mood for TV and decided to get another drink instead. He stood, but his head started spinning, forcing him back down onto the couch. He knew he wasn't drunk. He'd only had one drink. He shook his head, trying to clear the cobwebs.

He leaned back on the couch and closed his eyes. Images immediately assaulted him. Images of Tammy's tight, young, teenage body. Images of her legs open wide, inviting him to be with her. He wanted her. He could almost smell her.

"Fuck!" he screamed bolting upright on the couch. He didn't want that in his head. He gritted his teeth, trying to force the image out of his consciousness. He couldn't. Every time he blinked he saw Tammy's face. He felt his penis getting hard.

"No fuckin' way," he growled. He refused to drift back to his days of sexual wantonness. He needed something to distract him. He needed another image to focus on.

He reached to the coffee table and took the remote control. He turned the TV on and watched the screen flicker to life. His breath was hard and heavy as he tried to concentrate on the screen. What he saw made him flinch.

Sandra Evans was on the screen. She smiled out at Wenton, leaning forward to give him a seductive view across the tops of her breasts.

"Motherfucker!" he screamed and threw the remote at the TV. "Get out of my head!"

The remote bounced off the screen, dropping to the floor. There was an obvious imperfection left on the screen where the remote had struck. Wenton stared at the spot and shook his head. Everything was going wrong. He felt rage boiling inside him.

And then something happened. As he stared at the mark on his screen, it shifted. He froze, unable to pull his eyes away as it swirled first one way and then the other. It pulled the rest of the glass with it as it spun and grew darker. Soon, it was a strong, black spot in the centre of the screen that bubbled and churned with life.

"What the fuck?" he whispered.

The motion on the screen stopped. There was a slight flicker as if the dark spot were a blinking eye and then it was still.

Wenton watched the screen for a moment longer, then slowly closed his eyes. He sighed heavily. Everything made sense now. He'd been running, hiding from the past, and now it was right here in front of him. It was just like he'd explained to Wa. You either fight what you find inside yourself, or you accept it. He figured he wasn't immune to that rule.

He chuckled. After everything that had happened it seemed almost too simple that he should return to his old self now. After all the years of being so cold, so lonely, so angry—to simply go back on his convictions and give up everything he'd accomplished made no sense. But he couldn't fight it anymore. Not if he wanted to keep his sanity.

He walked deliberately to the kitchen and opened a drawer. He pulled out the phone book and dropped it on the kitchen counter. He briefly flipped through the book before stopping and using his finger to scan down the numbers. He ignored the colourful pictures and stuck to the descriptions—he was looking for something in particular. Finally he found it. He reached to one side and plucked up his cordless phone. He punched in a number and held the receiver to his ear.

A voice answered after only two rings. "Sweet and Innocent Escorts."

"Can you send over a young-looking girl?" Wenton said in a voice heavy with anticipation.

Shortly, Wenton buzzed up a woman from the lobby. He wanted to go to the door and watch the young woman get off the elevator, but he didn't want to seem eager. He waited on his couch for the knock on his door.

Knock, knock.

He shot to his feet and moved quickly to the entrance. His head was perfectly clear now. No trace of the dizziness or confusion he'd felt earlier.

He pulled his door open and found himself face-to-face with a scrawny brunette. She wasn't attractive. She was a homely young girl hiding behind far too much make-up. Her dark complexion was marred by pockmarks that were barely covered in poorly applied foundation. He wanted to fuck her immediately.

"Come in," he said, waving with a hand. By this point he'd polished off another five rye and Cokes and he felt great.

The girl stepped tentatively through the doorway. She was obviously new to her profession. She had no confidence, no edge. She was vulnerable. Wenton loved that.

He moved to the side and let the girl walk in front of him toward the living room. He wanted to watch her ass move in her tight jeans. *Nice.*

Once they reached the living room the girl finally remembered her script. She turned to Wenton. "So, what do you want from me?" She tried to lick her lips afterward but it simply looked awkward.

Wenton stared at her. He was watching Tammy Farrell. She was young, bright, sexy. He wanted to explore every crevice of her body. He looked her up and down. *Fuck, she's hot!*

"Get your fuckin' clothes off, Tammy," he growled at her.

The girl shifted uncomfortably. "Um, money?" she said almost shyly. Obviously her rehearsed script included dealing with the money up front.

"You little bitch," Wenton mumbled. He was still staring at Tammy Farrell. "I'm going fuck you so hard."

Now the young girl was scared. She'd been warned about customers like this one. If you ever get a bad feeling about a client, get out of there! She knew she should leave, right now!

Her skin was so soft. He wanted to touch her. He moved closer but it wasn't Tammy anymore. Without warning, he was suddenly staring at Sandra Evans. "You fuckin' bitch," he yelled. "You ruined my life."

The young girl was stunned. Her head shot to the door. She wanted to run. This client was crazy.

"I've gotta go," she said and began walking to the door as quickly as she could.

"Wait!" Wenton cried out.

The young girl stopped.

A broad smile spread over his face as he looked at her.

"I'm sorry I scared you. I guess your incredible beauty just stole my breath away."

"My incredible beauty?" she repeated.

"You probably hear that all the time, I guess." Suddenly his thoughts were completely clear. He knew that a well-placed compliment would disarm the dumb little bitch.

"I...sure."

He smiled again. He knew he had her now. He knew she'd do whatever he wanted. Whatever he wanted. He could think of a lot of things for this young slut. He was going to teach her what it meant to be a whore. He laughed out loud and the young girl looked at him curiously for a second before she laughed too.

Wenton was still laughing when he grabbed the girl and threw her to the floor.